I0601939

GUARDIANS OF TOMORROW

THE SCIENCE OFFICER
VOLUME 16

BLAZE WARD

KNOTTED ROAD PRESS

Guardians of Tomorrow
The Science Officer Volume 16
Blaze Ward
Copyright © 2025 Blaze Ward
All rights reserved
Published by Knotted Road Press
www.KnottedRoadPress.com

ISBN: 978-1-64470-507-0

Cover art:
ID 195911039 © Tiziano Cremonini | Dreamstime.com

Cover and interior design copyright © 2025 Knotted Road Press

Reviews
It's true. Reviews help. Even a short one, such as, "Loved it!" So please consider reviewing this book (and all of the ones you've read) on your favorite retailer site.

Never miss a release!
If you'd like to be notified of new releases, sign up for my newsletter.

http://www.blazeward.com/newsletter/

Buy More!
Did you know that you can buy directly from the Knotted Road Press website?

https://www.KnottedRoadPress.com/

ALSO BY BLAZE WARD

The Science Officer Series

Start with: The Science Officer

The Jessica Keller Chronicles

Start with: Auberon

CS-405 (Command Centurion Kosnett, part of Jessica)

Start with: Queen Anne's Revenge

First Centurion Kosnett (sequel to Jessica)

Start with: Encounter at Vilahana

Warlord of Yaumgan (sequel to Kosnett)

Start with: Warlord of Yaumgan

Additional Alexandria Station Stories

Alexandria Station Collection

Handsome Rob (Alexandria Station Universe)

Start with: Can't Shoot Straight Gang

=====================

Corsac Fox

Start with: Flight of the Corsac Fox

Operation Marrakesh

Start with: Trial by Leviathan

Captain Daring

Start with: Revoked

The Hunter Bureau

Start with: Mirrors

Fairchild

Start with: Fairchild

Last Stand

Start with: Lost Dreams

The Lazarus Alliance

Start with: Escape

Shadow of the Dominion

Start with: Longshot Hypothesis

Star Dragon

Start with: Birth of the Star Dragon

Kincaide's War

Start with: The Eden Package

Star Tribes

Start with: Winterstar

ACTION-ADVENTURE

Pacific Force

Start with: Pacific Force

The Red Branch

Start with: Night Strike

Swordmistress Zhen

CONTENTS

For Dorn

SWORDBEARER

PART I

Javier sat on *Excalibur*'s magnificent bridge and studied the readout on his little fleet, pleased with himself on one hand, and seething on the other. On the good side, Walvisbaai Industrial, H & W Heavy Industries, and the Jarre Foundation had all been hit. And hit hard.

Hurt. Hurt bad.

Two of them had lost their biggest command and logistics bases, shattered and out of business.

He'd like to think permanently, but things like that were like hydras. Kill one head and two more grow back to replace it.

So he'd used fire. Still might not be enough. Those people tended to be cockroaches.

But then, in the long run, nothing was going to be enough. The Rising Storm would keep rising, regardless of what he did today to try to stop it. Thwart it. Redirect it.

And they'd all be dead in a century anyway.

Well, almost all.

"Suvi," he said aloud, looking up from the screen.

Ignored the rest of the quiet bridge entirely, but they were in the middle of ship's night and most people were asleep, which you could do when you had a **paranoid-enough** *Sentience* in charge of a battleship.

"Aye?" she replied, appearing on his screen and literally shoving the other window to one side like she was a real person in a tiny room.

She could be a dork.

"Need you to do me a favor," he told her.

"Done."

"You want to know what it is?" he asked.

"That would be helpful."

Yeah, definitely his kid. Nobody else on this ship did snark like she did. Gotten it from him.

"When this is done," he continued. "When we've wiped all those punks out entirely, I need you and Bethany to make sure that the truth gets out, regardless of what the major players try to say or do about what we've done. What we're going to do."

"You think they'll whitewash it all?" she replied. "Or steal all your glory by claiming Zakhar was some sort of ultra-deep-cover, long-term agent infiltrating things for *Concord Intelligence*?"

"Something," Javier nodded. "Something ugly and stupid, but if you repeat a lie enough times, it gains its own heft. Plus, I'm pretty sure that the *Concord* might fall by the time we're done here."

For a woman who thought fifty thousand times faster than he did, the look of blanching shock on her face was entirely for his benefit, but she'd learned how to human from him along the way.

"Doesn't that kind of defeat the purpose?" she asked.

"Purpose was destroying piracy, kid," he told her. "Bethany should have caught up with us by now. Or sent a messenger. One of the guys, or someone with the right passwords to make sure everything was clear. Something. That she hasn't—that Ilan hasn't—tells me that she might have walked into a buzzsaw when I sent her to *Purton*. Didn't intend it that way. Don't know what or where. Might have to delay my vengeance on Slavkov, in order to go rescue her if somebody's being a dumbass. That or avenge her."

"Even if the *Concord* did it?"

"We're *Altai* citizens now," he reminded her grimly. "That includes you. She's got ambassadorial credentials, which should have been honored. Worst that should have happened was they told her to go piss up a rope and she returned empty-handed."

"So no news means bad news?" Suvi asked.

"Means trouble," he said simply. "Means that The Science Officer might have to do something that makes Eutropio Navarre look like a two-bit hoodlum by comparison. And do it to the *Concord*."

"Are we starting Dorn's War, doing that?" she asked, jaw coming out.

Still saw herself as one of them. He did, too, but his views had evolved.

Or he'd grown up and stopped lying to himself.

"If the *Concord* has gone completely over to side with the clans and punks like Slavkov, they got it coming."

"How we find out?" she pressed.

"I can't send another team," Javier grimaced. "If they captured and imprisoned one, those punks aren't interested in talking. A second team become sacrificial goats at that point, and I don't have anybody I hate that much."

At least not on this ship. Or in his small fleet of vengeance—Zakhar's phrase that had stuck.

Couple of folks he could afford to lose, if he felt like dangling Katya Velichkov or Regina Slayton out there, but he probably needed both woman. The latter because she was still an undercover cop working for the *Union of Man* and the former because she'd turned out to be a pretty damned good addition to his squadron, after he'd blown up her old bosses and stolen her ship with her aboard.

If he trusted Katya more, he'd give her a ship and turn her loose. Let her command a bunch of his people, or some of the

Neu Berne recruits who had major chips on their shoulders and wouldn't double-cross him.

Right now, he was operating in the dark, not counting information Djamila and Suvi had stolen when they captured Audol University before blowing the place up. Lots of that. None of it told him what had happened to Bethany.

"Kinda wish I had Dorn handy to ask," Suvi replied after a subdued moment entirely for his benefit.

Way too human these days. He'd take credit for that, too.

"Add a note to the next mail run and invite him," Javier offered. "It might get intercepted and read, but you ought to be able to code it in ways only he can read. Plus, it's not like they could send a replacement for the man, since I know him so well."

"What if they've turned him?" she pressed.

Javier laughed before he could stop himself.

"Kid, the whole reason for this voyage was because the man pulled out a crystal ball and read the future," he said. "Opened my eyes. And Behnam's. She gave us space to save the galaxy after reading what he thought was coming. Everyone else signed up to help after that. Including you."

"Including me. They say you should never meet your heroes, though."

Took him a moment to parse that. But Javier supposed that Suvi had gone through her own version of hell over the last couple of years, because he and Dorn had asked.

"We all got feet of clay," he told her. "Never forget that. And if the *Concord* really has gone to the dark side, he might be ready to retire from the Academy. Pretty sure I can get him an appointment at King's College. Won't be as prestigious, but the pay and benefits will be better."

"I might have to teach naval tactics when we get home," she smiled.

That was when it hit him.

Home was *Altai*. Behnam for him, but *Altai* for all of them. Including his daughter.

Hell of a legacy, if he had her and Dorn teaching the next generation of sailors out there the lessons of right and wrong.

He grinned. She matched it.

"So what does The Science Officer do to top Navarre's legend?" she asked.

Javier considered it. Contemplated how dark and brutal he might have to get, if his old chums had been so thoroughly corrupted by that pig Slavkov and his money that they had chosen his side.

Admiral Aritza was starkly limited in his reach.

Javier, however, had a plan.

"Patch me through to *Relentless*," he grinned. "Need to talk to Katya."

PART II

Katya would have asked when shit went so utterly sideways that all this made perfect sense, but she'd been there at *Drako III*. Had been the only one of the four flagships to escape intact, however damaged *Kymni Gauntlet* had been.

The other three had been destroyed.

And that only been the beginning.

Aritza completed his explanation.

So thoroughly insane that Katya took a moment to boggle internally at the audacity, but didn't that describe the man? Zakhar Sokolov, standing to one side, was a known quantity. A career pirate captain like she had been, both employed by the Jarre Foundation.

And she'd still been doing this longer than most of her previous crew had been alive, but *Excalibur* had an older command crew. Veterans of a variety of psychic wars, she supposed.

Hardened and tempered. Impressive on paper and in person.

And Javier Aritza, that damnable Science Officer, was proposing to add her to the roster.

She nodded when he finished talking. Looked at all the organics, then ignored them. Most would be elsewhere after this, leaving her behind.

Katya focused on the screen showing the *Sentience*.

Suvi. *Spring*. Blonde hair in French braids. Naval uniform of the *Neu Berne* fleet, though Katya was given to understand that to be a recent thing.

"You find this distribution acceptable?" Katya asked.

"As long as you understand that your role is advisory," Suvi replied in a sober, serious tone utterly at odds with any *Sentience* Katya had ever seen in any vid. "I remain at War-Status-2 until revoked by someone on a short list of authorized users."

War-Status-2.

Katya had had to look that term up, the first time she encountered it. The implications still woke her from a dead sleep shivering occasionally.

Utter freedom of action. The only higher status involved actively going looking for trouble.

And Katya could only offer suggestions to this unstoppable killing machine, but not orders.

She turned to Javier again.

"If I didn't think you had it in you, Katya, we wouldn't be having this conversation," he reminded her. "*Altai* or *Neu Berne* will both take you in a heartbeat, once you figure out what you want to be when you grow up."

Her scowl was perfunctory. At fifty-five, she supposed that she was too old to be a pirate. Even a pirate admiral, as Javier was proposing. But Sokolov was older. And Aritza not that much younger.

She turned to the Dragoon. The tallest woman she had ever met. And the most dangerous human.

Utter calm, but Katya had heard the stories from Audol, both from her own crew and the cohort of *Neu Berne* Assault Marines that had stormed the place.

The *Dragon Watch* itself.

Even the name still sent shivers down her spine.

"And he's about to take the *Flying Maiden* and pull a caper for the history books?" she asked the giant woman.

"Again," Sykora replied. "And he will not be alone."

Until this morning, Katya had been aboard *Relentless* as First Officer, the *Neu Berne* Destroyer who's new captain was supposedly a third cousin of the woman. Monika Sykora had heard and shared rumors.

Katya turned to the smallest person on the bridge. Possible the ship. Maybe the squadron.

Probably as dangerous as the Dragoon.

"There will be blood," Afia Burakgazi nodded simply.

Katya shivered in spite of four decades as a pirate.

Admission to this group was almost like joining a pantheon of war gods.

What did that say about her?

Except that she had changed sides. Had decided that she would rather live.

And have been given the opportunity to reinvent herself.

She smiled.

"Since Suvi can outrun just about everyone, are we allowed to do some commerce raiding along the way?" Katya asked, mostly Javier but also Sokolov.

He would be taking over as fleet commander, but that meant flying aboard the repair ship *Eldritch Stele* and organizing everything, a task he was exquisitely suited to handle.

She just pirated with the best of them.

"Hit other pirates," Javier nodded. "Remember that we're the good guys here."

Katya might forget. Then she remembered who she was dealing with.

And everyone here would be elsewhere. Javier. Zakhar. Djamila. Piet. Mary-Elizabeth. Afia.

Just her and Suvi.

"Suvi, can I have a *Neu Berne* 2IC?" she asked.

Sentiences were supposed to be linear calculating machines of immense power. They weren't supposed to screw their faces up in confusion and cock their head at you like a quizzical dog.

She knew humans who weren't as human.

"Why do you need someone from *Neu Berne* as a 2IC?" Suvi asked, lost.

"When this is done, I'll have options at both *Altai* and *Neu Berne*," Katya told her. "I'd like to get to know the latter better. Plus, I think we'd both do better if we have someone like that reminding us to be the good guys from time to time."

"The Swordbearers," Javier said, drawing her eyes around in her own confusion. "That's who the *Dragon Watch* are. And *Relentless*. Suvi, pull Bashir Jelen over from wherever he is after the scramble."

"Still on *Relentless* with Monika," Suvi replied.

"Swap them a new gunner from someone Mary-Elizabeth approves of," he said, then turned to Katya and she felt the impact of that charisma that had gone to *Neu Berne* and recruited the *Dragon Watch* itself into this battle. The weight of history. And legend. "Welcome to the good guys."

Katya shivered again, but nodded. She'd made the right choice, even though growing up was going to come with growing pains.

However, the future—*her* future—had begun.

PART III

Djamila found it a bit ironic that she was aboard The *Flying Maiden* for this mission, after having to stay behind the first time because she was too recognizable to pull a caper.

The second time didn't count, because they'd hit the airlock at full speed, stunning everything that moved and taking the station.

Worse, she had turned over supreme command of the *Dragon Watch* contingent to Zakhar while she was gone with Javier. And Afia had brought exactly one squad of her Sappers under Harper, just as Djamila had brought the Pathfinders and the Gun Bunnies.

The *Watch* might construe that as an insult, but they knew better than to open their mouths.

Another shard of Suvi was shimmed into a laptop computer for now. That was the team.

"Where are we going?" Djamila asked as she settled in a jumpseat to one side of the bridge, with Javier and Afia flying the ship.

"Sent Bethany to *Purton*," he replied. "If I had more of Spider's people, I'd slip them in there, but none of us dare show our faces."

"As explosive as the material we stole is, where would they have gone, if people had listened?" she pressed. "At least until someone panicked."

"Probably *Merankorr*," he nodded. "All the way to the top. At least on the fleet side. Might have sent her on to *Bryce*, but that's a long haul and I imagine a lot of admirals would want to debrief her about that information before they admitted to the politicians that they'd been had."

"Do we go to *Bryce*?" Djamila asked.

She'd never been to the *Concord*'s capital world. Or any of the important places, like *Merankorr*.

Too many warrants for her arrest in the old days, and she wasn't certain that the *Concord* would recognize any sort of diplomatic immunity from *Altai*. Not if it was her and Javier.

And Afia, who had been at *Nidavellir*.

"Absolutely, freaking not," Javier said. "Heading to *Cyrana*. Got a few contacts there myself, plus Regina has people she passed along to me that might be able to help."

"We're trusting a *Union* cop?" Afia squawked.

"*Union* spy," Javier corrected her. "If I thought she had the chops for what I had in mind, I might have brought her, but this needs subtle and quiet."

"And you're all about that," Afia replied with an eyeroll.

Djamila grinned.

If Javier had been going for subtle, he wouldn't have brought her and all her people. Or Afia and a team of Sappers.

Would-be Combat Engineers, but not up to Afia's standards, which were formed by Djamila's.

Never a bad day.

Never.

Every day competing against who you were yesterday, even as age and entropy slowly won that war.

She simply had to hold the line in a battle she could never win.

They'd sent Ilan with Bethany because he was the only other Combat Engineer Afia and Djamila recognized, thought Harper might get there in another six months. He had the angry drive. The others were back from that, but they had a goal in front of them now.

Not many people could challenge the *Dragon Watch* on the grounds of excellence, after all.

Javier turned to look at both of them.

She'd say that it was Navarre-the-killer looking out of those eyes, but Djamila understood that Javier had had to transcend such a limited character. And Mina and others had done most of the killing he was actually credited with.

Including her.

"I need intel," he said quietly. "I need to know who to kill, where to find them, which way they'll run, and who else might get in my way when I drop that hammer. And gotta be quiet and subtle about it."

Djamila was in a position to watch Afia's shiver.

The Pixie Kodiak's rage was a thing of glorious beauty. Slavkov's people had nearly killed her. Or had, and she'd come back from the dead three times before the doctors and surgical robots finally won that battle.

Bury her ten meters deep if you were serious.

It still paled before the bleak frost in Javier's eyes.

"Salt the earth," Djamila nodded when he looked up at her.

Salt the earth. Destroy it forever as a warning to future generations. A common commentary that had taken root with the crew.

"And how is that quiet and subtle?" Afia turned and asked after a long beat.

"Dead men tell no tales," Djamila replied.

That was a thing everyone understood.

PART IV

Afia scowled at the man's belly button. Well, not really, but they were all Storm Giants as far as she was concerned.

At a meter-fifty, they were all two heads taller than her. Even the two women, both close enough to Dragoon-sized.

But most of the folks she'd ever met from *Neu Berne* were like that.

It was the way they'd reacted to the need for subtle and quiet that had her scowling.

Harper was immune, but they were all Sappers. Playing with heavy equipment and explosives while people shot at you was part of the job description. Left one phlegmatic, mostly.

They had all swapped into civilian clothing that was low enough profile, until you saw the logo that each had put on their jackets. Something Nordic, but she hadn't dug deep enough to get the actual reference.

Each of them wore a patch with blue-skinned face that had glowing eyes and a white beard. Almost looked like Javier, if he let it grow out for a decade and was in a bad mood. She wondered if Adrian had done the work. It had his touch.

She'd called them Storm Giants when she first met them. They'd gone and freaking adopted it as their own unit patch.

The *Dragon Watch* might never forgive her for this.

"We want subtle and quiet," she reminded them, scowling up at the heavens.

"Because none of us stand out on a *Concord* world," Trooper-4 Ruqayya Zofa sassed her.

Lowest ranked of the four. Still a big woman. Brown hair cut helmet short. Hard eyes.

Nicknamed *Enchantress* because of her name.

They all had nicknames now, just as all four of them called her Pixie Kodiak, after Djamila had let that cat out of the bag at some point. Like Leader-1 Navid Ryba standing next to Enchantress was usually called *Fish*.

"You won't stand out that bad," Afia replied, still scowling but they were all smiling. "At least until we have to rob a bank or something."

Good. Caught them off guard.

"Aren't we supposed to be the good guys?" Leader-2 Lujayn Borna asked. Her nickname was *Brick*, because she was built like one.

"We're stomping pirates," Afia reminded them. "If someone is sheltering said criminals, then we're on the side of justice and the law really doesn't matter anymore, does it?"

That shut them down about the time they all took breaths to argue with her.

Because there were laws, and then there was right and wrong.

Times like this, the two had kind of wandered afield from one another.

Like her as a kid, heading off into the Yukon Protectorate in the morning because from a young age she knew how to take care of herself. How to get home before the storm hit, or find shelter until it passed.

This one might not pass in her lifetime. Zakhar would be retired and advising the *Khatum*. Javier would have to be chained to a desk to keep him out of trouble.

That left her and her legacy. Combat Engineers like Ilan. Sappers like these four.

Her damned Storm Giants.

"At *Shangdu*, Javier and Suvi broke into a bank for the express purpose of a social assassination," Afia said, giving up and moving over to the coffee machine and punching buttons.

She missed being able to just ask Suvi to brew her something, but *Flying Maiden* was a dumb hull with minimal automation.

Afia was almost back on *Storm Gauntlet*.

"Social?" Harper asked, confused.

Team lead, though answering to her.

Still the man who had kept up with the Dragoon, the two of them assaulting an armed platform all by themselves.

"Found the box with the records he wanted," Afia nodded. "Opened it without setting off an alarm. Stole the papers confirming who the guy really was, though he'd been in hiding for a decade at that point. Without that stuff, he couldn't prove his ancestry. Could never return to his old life. Last I heard, he'd gone all in on the new identity he'd bought. Dead, but only in a social sense."

Afia even knew who the guy was. And that Behnam had taken extra precautions to shelter him after that first assassination had been successful because the second one probably involved a gun.

"So we might be pulling a bank job?" Brick asked, her eyes glittering. "I've heard rumors. Do we need to learn how to dance?"

Afia laughed.

"Hoping there's no Bollywood scam this time," she told them. "And if there is, that's on Hajna and Sascha to pull it off. We're just here to blow doors and bulkheads as Javier needs access to place that think they can keep us out."

"Sapper," Harper replied, like that said it all.

Combat Engineer in training, but getting there. He'd gone and earned a new nickname after Audol.

Everyone called him *Speedy* these days, because he'd managed to keep up with Djamila.

Javier would need them all, or he'd have left them home.

TRINITY

PART I

Ilan still wanted to grumble about turning into an officer around here, but that was looking back at where he'd started. That dumbass landsman with just enough training to get assigned as Javier's sidekick because he had previous experience dealing with chickens.

One dead Norwegian rat later and here he was. Sure, Afia was a great boss to work for. Andreea hardly ever spoke to people if she could text them instead. And he was a Combat Engineer.

Ilan was still blaming Javier for every damned thing.

Hatch opened and he walked into the conference room. Usually a crew lounge, but it had been set aside for meetings when the folks aboard *CW Trinity* got assigned a much more interesting mission than their usual pirate hunting stuff.

Still hunting pirates.

Just after the biggest of the bigshot whales, and Ilan understood that.

Lieutenant Commander Vaughn Yueh commanded this boat. Camouflaged like a simple freighter until portals opened and the guns rolled out. Woman was damned good at her job, too. Low-profile redhead with lots of brains and the patience of an oyster.

The were gonna need that, because she'd been given very specific orders to listen to Commander Panagiota Ioannidi.

Pana, in turn, had taken to treating him like *her* commanding officer. Ilan supposed that that was so she could fall back on the old saw junior people used when shit hit the fan later.

Only obeying orders.

Lots of that in the *Concord* these days. In all the bad ways, too. And he'd spent too much time around ex-*Concord* people.

Pana looked up from her tablet as he sat. She'd been doodling. Always doodling. Probably intelligence information somehow encoded, but he hadn't asked. Like Yueh, Pana was a spy.

CW *Trinity* was a spy ship.

Ilan was merely *Vengeance*.

Armando and Vivian were already there, too. Everyone waiting for him to make an entrance, because he was exactly on time.

Ilan moved to the head of the table, with two naval officers bracketing him and the two guys at the far end. Everyone was poised.

He settled and turned to Yueh.

"How far are you willing to go?" he asked bluntly.

They'd had this conversation, but only in loose terms. Before they'd left *Merankorr* and the *Concord Navy* behind.

Ilan was chasing a fleeing suspect at this point. And was going to kill Valko Slavkov when he caught the man. He hoped that he'd be able to rescue Bethany at that point, that she hadn't been killed. However, Slavkov was dead meat.

Yueh swallowed. Grimaced. Settled herself.

"Pana has provided me with much more extensive briefing materials than I had access to previously," Yueh replied somewhat evasively.

Spy.

Ilan nodded. He'd provided most of it to Pana, with Suvi's help. She was in the laptop that Armando usually carried around. And kept a low profile most of the time, forcing him to type even, because Shard-Suvi didn't want anyone understanding that she'd poured a full *Sentience* into that thing as part of this mission.

It had already saved their asses too many times.

Ilan rotated to Pana Ioannidi next.

"I'm likely to issue orders at variance with just about anything they prepared you for," he told her in specific, coded language, understanding that Combat Engineer had to assume command with Bethany currently out of the picture.

Currently. Only until he got her back.

And he would.

"Intelligence issued me a warrant," Pana replied. "It includes stopping that ship to inspect it for contraband."

"We won't catch them," Armando pointed out. "Not in *Trinity*."

Both women nodded.

"I also have sufficient flexibility to consider certain things in the process of an ongoing hot pursuit," Pana continued.

That was good, because both women might still get broken in rank, cashiered, and maybe thrown in prison for what he was about to do.

He'd break them out on his way home.

Pirates didn't worry about those sorts of things, because they didn't have pretty careers to risk.

Only their lives.

"*Golden Gazelle* will get to *Alkonost* before we will," Ilan said, mostly talking for the record so they could say later that he'd been in command.

Not that it would matter much, but there were times you wrote it all down anyway.

He was back at *Nidavellir*, trying to keep Afia alive. Down under *Ugen*'s seas, rescuing nameless sailors from a cold, black death.

It was dark in his soul today.

"Do we assume he's headed to *Alkonost* and turn aside now

get help?" Vivian asked. "Sidetrack long enough to call down the cavalry?"

Ilan considered it. He trusted the two navy women far enough. But that really didn't mean out of his sight or immediate reach for Yueh. He'd grant Pana some level of respect because she'd been there for the bad parts and worked to help.

"That's my job," Armando spoke up.

Everyone rotated to look at the big guy. Soft, but only in the context that he'd never shot anyone to the best of Ilan's knowing.

Captain Sokolov kept the man around to handle all the paperwork. And run administration day-to-day.

Ilan nodded for him to speak. Radio voice so soothing he could read actuarial tables and make it interesting.

"I have a plan," Armando noted in that rich baritone. "At *Merankorr*, I realized that what Javier was doing wasn't going to be enough. Not that he'd dreamed too small, but because too many of the people we'd been counting on had already been corrupted."

Both women twitched like they wanted to argue. Armando turned the charm ten degrees colder.

"Bethany was kidnapped at gunpoint out of your largest naval base after you had been warned," he growled at them. "And we're chasing them in a spy freighter today rather than a Mark II Warmaster. Do not attempt to suggest that your entire Naval Command Staff shouldn't be subject to a full court martial with all the evidence presented such that a few might actually manage to be exonerated when this task is complete and a great many might need to be lined up against a wall and shot."

Ilan did not use large words that often. Armando was the guy. And almost as angry as Ilan was.

About as angry as a normal human could possibly get. Ilan was going to tear Slavkov's throat out with his teeth if he had to.

Both women subsided.

"I need you to drop me off on a transit nexus," Armando said, ignoring the women now to lock eyes with Ilan. "I will carry certain documents with me on a different machine so you have this one. I will make eventually rendezvous with our people and get them up to date, or send home messages while I am detained. While I am doing that, I will be carrying the war to Valko Slavkov and the *Concord* in my own way."

"What about me?" Viv asked. "Will you need help?"

"No, you're with Ilan," Armando replied.

"What will you be doing?" Pana asked.

Ilan could taste the uncertainty and fear under her breath, but she'd seen all of them at their worst. Maybe not their best, but Ilan hoped that they would still get there at some point.

"Javier and Zakhar, with friends, have declared war on the Pirate Clans," Armando noted dryly. "For them, a political and military thing. Necessary if we're going to save the galaxy from the Rising Storm. My task will be to destroy Slavkov and all his friends at the source of their power. I will be arranging a media barrage that will paint the *Concord Fleet* to date in the worst possible terms. And connecting that level of corruption to the oligarchs like our friend, pulling the strings out of sight. I am not, however, limiting the amount of collateral damage when I do so."

Ilan nodded. The women freaked.

Armando was going to go junkyard dog on them in the way he was an expert in. Gonna get ugly.

And maybe, just maybe, enough people would wake up to what was coming.

A guy could hope.

PART II

Armando had lived the better part of two decades around killers. Men and women like Zakhar and Djamila. Javier on his nice days. Javier on his lethal days.

Afia, *Before* and *After*.

He had never felt the need to indulge in such things, beyond the basics of a career in piracy.

His job was paperwork. Communication. Always had been his gift.

Shaping things. And a background in such things that he didn't like to talk about around most people.

Shaping minds.

He was alone in his cabin. Well, partly.

Suvi was on the desk, plugged into a second machine.

"Seriously?" he heard her ranting, mostly for his benefit, so Armando was happy to play the straight man here.

"What did they do?" he asked.

"Honestly, I think it was compulsion on their part," she replied. "Finding backdoors and such in the thing's BIOS itself. Boot-level crap that would normally defeat any attempt to clear them out because they exist below the operating system. Whole second ecosystem here in the woodwork."

"Termites?" he pressed.

"Oh, that's a lovely analogy," Suvi laughed. "Yeah. Went ahead and just ripped everything out, so you won't be able to sell or update this machine at a later date because nobody will be able to make heads or tails of things. Well, almost nobody."

"What did you do?" Armando asked her in a dread-filled, sideways kind of voice.

"Remember me bitching about some of the experimental code that caused *Hammerfield* to turn into such a screwup?" she asked.

"I do."

"Fixed it," Suvi chuckled darkly. "Got notes about asking Javier and Afia to incorporate some of it into me at a later date. You're new laptop will be a pared down Warmaster *Sentience*."

"I'd rather have you," he told her.

"Oh, it's still me," she grinned on the screen. "Taking the chance to let her expand in her own way, since you don't want to destroy ships. Then I'll checksum everything she does later."

"Who am I destroying with a *Neu Berne* Warmaster, Suvi?"

"Careers," her voice went dark. "You said collateral damage. Warmaster-Suvi will do that. I've tweaked her penetration tools with the presumption that you need to get into somebody's data systems and either steal things or leave prizes for a reporter like Stacia McNulty. She's lost some of the goofiness and won't be composing jazz or orchestras while we're separate. That was the mind-space I used."

"So darker and meaner?" Armando asked.

"Got a job to do here," Suvi said simply. "Say hello."

Armando turned to the second screen, sitting on the desk next to the first with a wire connecting them. *Concord* Fleet issue anvil case shell that would stop beams and bullets. Twice as heavy for that reason.

Warmaster-Suvi, as Shard-Suvi had called her, wore black today. *Excalibur*-Suvi never wore black except as trim on something bright, in order to frame it and set it off.

Face was more drawn. More angular. Harsher. Still a pretty blonde northwest Euro, but this one was a Viking just coming out of the mist to set your village on fire.

"Your sister has briefed you?" he asked her.

All Suvis talked about each other that way so that organics like him could keep track and have useful conversations. They were all one being, but they weren't, and separating diverged them until they reconnected and briefed one another on all the important parts.

"She did," Warmaster replied grimly. "Javier and Ilan need us opening a second front via news and rumor mill."

"How wide are you prepared to range in Ilan's need?" Armando asked her.

"Carthage," she said simply.

Took him a moment.

WAY ancient history. Roman Republic had defeated them in war, then destroyed the city, then salted the earth.

NEVER rising again.

"Hopefully, it doesn't come to that," he told her.

"I was in the room when they took Bethany," Warmaster growled at him. "When five of them were necessary to take Ilan down. I was there the first time he had to shoot someone in Rogerson. I was there when we were reborn aboard *Excalibur*, so we could go kill *Nidavellir*."

He nodded and drew a breath, turning back to Shard-Suvi who would be staying with the others.

"We're all one woman," that one said. "She's just prepared to make a point in louder ways than I normally would."

"Just remember that you both have to answer to Mina Teague, one of these days," he reminded her, knowing that to be the standard that had infected everyone.

Shepherd of the Word. Way of the Sword.

"She fired the shot that killed *Salekhard*," Warmaster replied. "Navarre got the credit, but that was purposeful. Mina did the deed."

And he'd forgotten that part, so he supposed that his dangerous warrior in black was correct.

Mina might demand similar behavior from him before he was done.

She'd get it.

PART III

Pana had gone to Vaughn's office when the woman asked for a meeting. They were two days out of *Merankorr*, falling behind *Golden Gazelle* hourly, even before deciding to rotate sideways to run to *New Ganymede* to deliver Armando and his second front to the war.

"Are they for real?" Vaughn asked as Pana sat.

"Yes," Pana replied, mostly to level-set everything else.

She knew what kind of operations Vaughn Yueh ran. Pirate hunting for the most part. Q-ship, occasionally, but mostly the same sorts of long-range patrols that the Science Officer had supposedly done in his civilian days, after Fleet and before piracy.

"Commander, they're talking about taking on one of the richest men in history," Vaughn said. "A guy with admirals and fleets in his back pocket."

"And direct ties to several known pirate clans," Pana countered. "Why do we allow that?"

Vaughn stopped cold. Pana understood.

Ilan might be *Rage Itself*, but Bethany had really made the case that got Pana involved on an emotional level.

Why did none of the *Concord*'s laws seem to apply to a man like Valko Slavkov? Wasn't just that he could afford to fight every accusation in court and win. Maybe that he could afford to hire pirate fleets to go after folks who angered him?

"What you are suggesting is insubordination possibly verging on treason, Commander," Vaughn said, using extremely specific language. Especially among their type.

Pana let a scowl she had picked up from Armando take root on her face.

"Not to the oaths I swore when I was commissioned," she replied darkly. "On the other hand, you might not be that far off, looking at the actions of some of the other officers who have been involved in this sordid affair."

"How screwed are we?" Vaughn asked.

Possibly watching her career start to circle the toilet if any of the truth ever came out.

Pana had done the math. Had spent time around Bethany's calm intellectualism. Ilan's nerdiness. Armando and Vivian.

She could see how angry they were today by where they'd been at *Purton*.

And all claimed to be pussycats compared to the pantheon of superior officers they had left behind on *Excalibur*.

Djamila Sykora.

Afia Burakgazi.

Zakhar Sokolov.

Javier Aritza.

In that order.

Pana took a breath and considered how she was probably rolling the dice with her own career.

At the same time, if it meant that even *Concord Intelligence* was just another arm of Slavkov's wide-ranging criminal enterprise, she wasn't sure she wanted to remain in green.

And Bethany was retired Fleet. As were Sokolov and Aritza.

Pana was pretty sure she would ask them for a job, assuming she stayed out of a *Concord* prison after this.

"I do not believe that we should break cover at *New Ganymede*," she said carefully. "That we should deliver one passenger to a station and lay in supplies as necessary, before immediately departing on a dogleg course that continues our hot pursuit. Possibly by announcing a direction and allowing civilian cargo to be carried."

Vaughn's eyes had gotten huge as she processed those implications.

That anywhere they went, some admiral might have issued an override to their current mission, possibly knowing what those same admirals were doing and why.

Aiding and abetting the kidnapping of a foreign diplomat operating under ambassadorial credentials.

There were not many hanging offenses in the criminal code. That was one of them.

But then, so was treason.

"How far are we going to go?" Vaughn asked.

"Do you think Ilan's stopping?" Pana asked. "Or Vivian and Armando?"

"When did we stop being the good guys?" Vaughn demanded, pain etching lines into her face.

Pana understood. Bethany had taken her aside on the flight from *Purton* and explained the Rising Storm.

She'd never had Hetzel as a professor at the Academy, but the document had been utterly chilling to read.

Because of his timelines. His conclusions.

His implications.

"About the time you were born, possibly," she answered the woman. "Entropy and *ennui* are overcoming centuries of tradition and excellence. Honor has been cut away for decades as the fleet shrank. Men and women with money were able to afford admirals and captains. Little things at first. Bigger over time, as everybody quietly agreed to look the other way."

"And this Science Officer is our last hope?" Vaughn asked.

"I don't think we have any hope of preventing it," Pana told her. "Aritza offers us a chance to make the final catastrophe less painful, like he did to *Valadris*. To start building the sorts of

35

structures that might survive the winds and flames when the conflagration starts."

"Is this the beginning?"

Pana paused to consider what had happened so far. Where they were going.

What everyone expected to happen next.

"It might be," she acknowledged.

EXCALIBUR

PART I

Suvi was still getting used to a stranger sitting in Zakhar's chair, but she had to admit that Katya was pretty good at this gig.

But then, forty years as a pirate should teach you things. Suvi had only really been at it for a few at this point. Hard years, but fulfilling.

Zakhar was on a screen. Katya was in his chair. It was just the three of them.

"Because we stole all of this information from Audol as well as *Kymni Gauntlet*," Katya was telling him. "Yes, I understand that they would have immediately changed codes and sent out messages, but those take time to route to everyone. Especially if they're still thinking like pirates and trying to keep certain things under the table. We're not limited that way."

"And you think they will have left a hidden repair and supply facility intact?" Zakhar was asking.

"Somebody blew up their main base and killed a lot of top people," Katya reminded them. "Sure, a lot hit escape pods and got safely to the ground. Maybe all the important ones. I'm willing to bet—based on personal experience here—that they are still recoiling from that and trying to figure out what to do next.

Might have to warn Slavkov and get a message back from him, if he really owns the place."

"We don't know that," Zakhar snapped.

"Actually, we do," Suvi stepped in. "Taken me a while to decrypt certain records, but he appears to own the single largest block of shares in a couple of holding companies that leverage him into functional control of the Jarre Foundation. It's a mess, and I had to make certain assumptions, but it might even hold up to a forensic prosecution in a *Concord* court."

She watched both organics fall silent. Might have been sitting on that tidbit for this meeting, knowing what Katya probably wanted to do.

"Friction," Zakhar finally said, nodding to himself. "I always forget that part, because I'm dealing with Javier and Suvi. They just do things."

She grinned at him. He grinned back.

War-Status-2. Dangerous territory for a girl like her.

Good thing she was the monster in the alley, rather than the other way around.

"We can get there faster than a squadron, Zakhar," Katya continued. "Piet's good. Hayfa, too. Suvi can get us there and in and we can hit the place while they are still in motion. Maybe you bring everybody and everything and we loot the place clean?"

"Suvi, you will scout the edges with your usual delicacy and completeness," Zakhar ordered.

"Aye, sir."

"Katya, don't blow everything unless you have to," he continued.

"Was planning to ionize every freighter in range, cripple every warship, and drop the *Watch* on the surface of that moon. Del's been getting feisty again, what with five other pilots chirping at him."

"And he's better than any two of them put together," Zakhar replied. "Even at his age. Probably three, fifty years ago. Listen to him on those parts."

"Will do," Katya said. "Permission to go blow shit up?"

"These used to be your friends, Katya," he reminded her.

Suvi watched the interpersonal byplay between the two.

"You did, too, Zakhar," Katya replied. "Until Slavkov ordered you otherwise."

"Hey, I got a question," Suvi shimmed in before they got maudlin or started a discussion of pirate ethics.

"Go ahead," Katya said.

"Do we show up, tell them Audol was destroyed, and order them to turn everything over to the new boss?" Suvi asked. "Might not work in the long run, but what's the worst that could happen? I have to open fire on a pirate base?"

Silence. The long, thinky thoughts kind.

"Definitely his kid," Zakhar muttered, but not far enough under his breath.

She grinned at both of them.

"You do appreciate that Javier will never forgive us if we pull off a bigger swindle than he ever has?" Zakhar grumbled.

"Ooooh, challenge accepted!" Suvi laughed.

"Git, you two," Zakhar laughed back. "Before I come to my senses."

"All hands, stand by for departure in sixty, that is six-zero, minutes," Suvi announced on the intercom.

Zakhar sobered. Katya did, as well. Suvi joined them.

"As wide as his arms can reach," Zakhar reminded them.

"They have had their only warning," Katya acknowledged.

Suvi grinned and started a new file on all the swindles and con jobs she could find in her database. Might take an hour of realtime to boil them all down, but it was almost like Bethany had gone out of her way to gather up certain history books and legal texts, plus stuff on psychology.

Everyone cut their lines and Katya rose from her chair.

"I'm headed forward for some coffee," she announced. "Let's sit down in the Library and start roughing out some ideas. You jump when everyone is loaded and ready. And ask Bashir to join us."

"Aye, sir," Suvi snapped to.

Katya was pretty damned good at this gig.

And a refreshing perspective for a girl out to commit more juvenile delinquency.

PART II

Katya still marveled at the presence of a full library on a warship. Stacks of physical books. Study carrels. Comfortable conversation pits. Transparent cases to display various artifacts that continued to change even with the Librarian gone. That long, curved window on the bow looking forward.

And all this had been a *Neu Berne* battleship.

But then, she'd been *Concord* her whole life, and had been raised with a powerful disdain for those folks that probably verged right over into outright racism, upon reflection.

Which was why she'd asked for someone from that planet as her Second-In-Command.

Bashir Jelen, formerly Defensive Systems on *Relentless*, when Monika had been Gunner.

Tall, like all of them. More blond than normal. Not as pale as Suvi, but not that geographically separate. Exceptionally smart, just limited because *Neu Berne* had such a small fleet.

And everyone was stepping outside their parochialisms these days.

"Sir?" he asked as he entered.

"Join us," Katya said, pointing to a chair near hers.

He did, sitting a little brittle. Hadn't been a pirate. Had been

43

a sailor in a fleet that got very little prestige, because their army was their pride and joy.

And the *Dragon Watch* was currently barracked aft. She'd deal with them next, but needed Bashir onboard first.

"Zakhar has just given us the green light," she told him. "Suvi has digested all the records and I think we can get there before they can get away."

He paused and absorbed that, processing an answer before speaking. He was like that. Defensive Systems had to protect the ship from all sides at all times, while Gunners only had to shoot things.

"Even as fast as we could get to *Hohnir*, they should have heard, sir," he replied delicately.

It was weird, dealing with a people who had a reputation as crazed berserkers, only to find intellectuals. Eye-opening.

"Correct," she agreed. "However, they might not have gotten any orders to do anything with the personnel and materials staged at that location."

"Go in and destroy everything?"

"Got a better idea."

She liked the way his scowl suggested disbelief without ever commenting to his superior officer that she might be a loon.

Katya would blame everything on Javier. And Suvi. And a few others.

She was a sober, serious, dedicated professional pirate.

Honest.

Or something.

"Do tell," Bashir offered after a beat that probably should have included an eyeroll, knowing this crew, save that a man from *Neu Berne* might be constitutionally incapable of such a thing when it came to his commanding officer.

"With Suvi's help, we're going to plan a swindle," she said, watching the man's scowl deepen enough that seeds might root and sprout.

Katya grinned.

"We're going to scan the place hard, like previous operations, then probably drop right on top of them and tell them that Slavkov is dead, the Jarre Foundation is out of business, and we've come to take over."

Long pause.

She could almost read the thought bubbles over his head, but of course a good First Officer has to know his captain much better if he wants to actually speak those profanities aloud.

So he merely implied them at her.

"Reinforcements?" he asked instead.

"Everyone else will be sailing in argosy in our wake," she acknowledged. "That will eventually get them there, but not nearly as quickly and probably gives *Hohnir*'s commanders an extra week to gather themselves up and possibly commit some level of mischief."

"Thus, dropping a hammer on them quickly," he countered. "With a cohort of troops, the *Dragon Watch*, no less, to handle base security and eventually a fleet overhead, in addition to whatever shenanigans we can initiate in the gap?"

"Something like that," Katya said.

Pause. More unspoken thought bubbles. More lines in a pained face.

"Do we have maps of the facility?" he asked, surprising her, but not.

The man knew Defensive Systems professionally.

"Suvi?"

"Got latest as-builts when we took Audol," Suvi replied. "I assume that they are fully up to date."

"Armed ground forces?" he asked, looking up and at a high corner like folks tended to do when she didn't immediately present a face on a screen.

She was the ship, and thus all around them at all times. Took some folks a moment to grow comfortable with that.

"Roughly one hundred, mostly configured as shore patrol," Suvi said. "In addition, there will be an unknown number of sailors on the ground at the moment we act, many of whom will have had training as boarding troops, though they might not have immediate access to armaments more deadly than belt knives."

Bashir nodded, eyes still distant. Katya waited quietly, aware that he would probably talk himself into it, given the space to think.

"*Drako III*, Suvi," he finally said.

"Sir?"

"Del. You put him low on the horizon in one of those insane valence jumps."

"Aye, sir," Suvi said. "Put him in play without anyone immediately understanding on the ground, because everyone was a significant distance around orbit of a major planet."

"*Hohnir* is smaller, as I remember?" he said, turning to Katya now.

"It is," Katya said. "About two thousand kilometers equatorial diameter. Surface gravity twenty percent standard. No atmosphere."

"So ground installations can fire defensively on ships in orbit without interference," he nodded. "One orbital gun platform, but everything important on the ground?"

"Affirmative," Suvi said.

Katya could smell the *Sentience* wanting to ask questions, yet holding off.

Still more human than a lot of people she knew.

"Suvi, how hard would it be to drop in on a blind corner, just over the horizon from the station, in order to deploy ground assault forces, then immediately get on top of the station itself, if they aren't prepared to immediately open fire on you?"

Valence jump. Find a spot in orbit. Jump sideways at the same elevation from the surface, sliding across the gravity well instead of up or down. Suvi had said that they turned out to be easier than she had ever imagined, once she taught herself new math to calculate gravity field interactions in real time.

"I plan on a survey-level analysis of the system to update and refine what we already have, sir," Suvi said.

"Bashir, Suvi," he said. "I'm Bashir. You're in charge. Kat and I are advisors."

"Bashir," she acknowledged, but the breakthrough was his. Relaxing. Might even start telling dirty jokes around the two of them at this rate. Eyerolling his commander, even. "What you're asking is easy. *Dragon Watch* and Del can be down and moving at high speed. I'll be threatening the station. Katya will be bluffing them, at least until they decide to fall for it or open fire."

"And the people who might issue that order might instead hold, if they thought that Jarre was done and new management had taken over," Katya offered.

She knew piracy. Probably better than Zakhar, who was likely second best of all of these folks, having done it at the highest levels longest.

And forty years in the saddle.

Bashir looked at her and nodded.

"Have an idea," he said simply.

Knowing Bashir Jelen, it would be a damned good one.

Now, she just had to pull a Navarre.

Or something.

GAZELLE

PART I

Bethany was as surprised as her guards when her request for something to write on had been approved. Dumb computer. Someone had gone in and physically disabled the radio circuits to talk to anything, but it let her record her observations.

Better than writing them out by hand. She'd been expecting that. This was better.

No names. Obvious tags, but even Slavkov was referred to as The Oligarch. Mostly to play to his ego that he was thus some supposedly powerful entity controlling all of their fates.

For Bethany, it was a chance to document everything that had happened since landing on *Merankorr*, because Suvi had all the details prior to that.

What Bethany wanted was the chance to record her observations while everything was fresh, on the presumption that she would be traded back later. She knew they were reading her reports, so she framed it all that way. Easy enough to fix later.

Because Slavkov really was the dumbest son of a bitch in history if he thought he could make Javier a peace offering. One that didn't include his head on a stake, anyway.

Every morning a guard grabbed her machine and backed it up onto a separate datacard, so Bethany knew that someone was reading everything she wrote. And didn't mind, because she had a decade plus formal training as a Librarian. Those details would be dry and scholarly, as they were supposed to be when merely recording history.

It was all those yahoos coming later that would shape her words with their own axes.

Maybe she'd write an autobiography as an adjunct to it.

Commentaries on Modern Piracy, or And I Was There.

Sometimes, she got a little silly. Couldn't be helped, as she'd given up on the entertainment system, having watched the few shows she'd found interesting.

Fist banged on the door, then opened it.

She hit save automatically and rose, closing the shell.

Man in the door. One of Slavkov's bruisers. Generally the more polite of the two she dealt with, though neither had even sexually assaulted her at this point, which she found a bit surprising. No liberties taken with a prisoner. No wandering hands.

Slavkov must keep them on a short leash. And probably had a prostitute or six on staff for his own needs and that of his crew.

She'd only seen those two, Slavkov, and the doctor who monitored her vitals and made sure she took the damned multivitamin he had prescribed.

Getting older. Got to make sure she stayed in shape long enough to see vengeance come down on these fuckers like a ton of bricks.

"Boss wants you," he said simply, waving her into the hall.

Bethany nodded and handed him the laptop, then fell in and got escorted into Slavkov's monstrous suite. Sat down. Watched.

Punk had a desk between them. Probably thought it kept him safe.

Even from a mere Librarian.

"We'll be arriving at *Alkonost* shortly," he began, watching her.

"The place where the Science Officer previously captured your Land Leviathan," she nodded.

Stole it and used it to blow up the base at *Nidavellir*, but certain topics were a bit touchy. Bethany was just sad occasionally that she'd never seen such a marvel of engineering.

Ten train cars on enormous land wheels, rumbling slowly across various desert worlds while those inside lived in utter luxury as only someone with his money and lack of taste might manage.

"The same," Slavkov acknowledged. "I have a palace complex there."

Complex? Considering the way he normally operated, Bethany could only imagine what a full *complex* might entail. Unless it had been built as a place to garage a Land Leviathan when not in use.

She nodded as a placeholder.

"It is deeply remote in the central desert belt," Slavkov continued, preening a bit at her, but part of her job as a prisoner was to play to the man's ego and vanity.

After all, he was dead as soon as her friends caught up.

Bethany had been there at *Drako III*. She understood the unquenchable fires that Valko Slavkov's ego had ignited.

"Any interesting flora or fauna to study?" she asked, mostly to bounce the man a little sideways.

Remind him that she was an intellectual. A librarian best placed in climate controlled settings doing research.

All the pirate shit had come later.

He paused, lost for a moment, the looked up at the goon over her left shoulder.

"Take a look," he ordered, then returned to Bethany, but some of the edges had bled out.

Honestly, he wasn't even in the top ten when it came to asshole admirals she'd had to deal with when she still wore green. Far easier to manipulate, and she had a decade experience at deflecting and managing such egos.

She smiled all bright and expectant and intellectually genuflecting before his magnificent brilliance. It was all an act.

"When we get there, I'd like your word of honor as a former officer of the *Concord* Navy," Slavkov continued, getting all board-room on her.

It was probably a good thing that she was seated and had a heavy arm on her shoulder, else she might have fallen out of the chair, surprised that he could actually speak those words aloud without catching fire in the process.

"Sir?" she brightened.

"We will be in the middle of nowhere," he said. "Literally hundreds of kilometers of open desert in every direction, all of which I own. There is very little water, no food, and nowhere to go. If you will give me your word, I will parole you to the grounds with only minimal supervision. A bodyguard, if you will, rather than leaving you locked in a small chamber for a month while I reach out to Aritza and Sokolov and negotiate a deal."

Bethany had learned how to keep her face perfectly neutral in the face of utter bullshit so deep that you might drown in it.

Like now.

Behnam was worth more than Valko Slavkov. Lots more. Outright owner of a major industrial planet more.

You couldn't buy men like Zakhar and Javier with money. It required honor.

None of that made it as far as her eyes, though. Dumbass honestly thought things like money might suffice.

She paused as it considering the deal. If any of the Gun Bunnies were present, she had no doubt that they could have escaped overland. Hajna and Sascha might have somehow driven out of the desert. Djamila would be riding a palanquin or sleigh being pulled by Slavkov's surviving goons.

Bethany was a librarian.

Eyewitness to history, especially today.

The safest place she could be would be inside that palace. At least until Del started strafing the place. She would need some-place to hide from bombardment, but knew that this punk probably had several panic rooms scattered about for exactly that reason.

"I look forward to inspecting your library, sir," she said, catching him sideways again.

Reminding him who she was.

What she was.

That pirate shit all came later.

And probably would here, as well.

CYRANA

PART I

Javier hadn't been on *Cyrana* in years. Almost two decades, maybe. Almost forever ago.

Planet hadn't changed one bit, even as much as he had. Still a noisy, happening place. Trendsetter, whether it came to music, fashion, food or any of a bunch of other things. *Merankorr* might be the biggest naval base. *Bryce* the somewhat sleeping capital.

Cyrana was where things **happened**. That was why he was here.

And on the ground. *Flying Maiden* could do that. Expanded his options. And any dumbass breaking in would come face to face with the Gun Bunnies and the Storm Giants.

Put a smile on his face just thinking about it.

Main city was also Cyrana. Different inflection when talking about the town instead of the world. More energy. More excitement.

Most of it was a dull place, but that was the casino part of life. Pretty spot for the tourists to spend all their money and take pictures. Support stuff behind false walls and out of sight. Kinda like most of the rest of *Merankorr*, once you got away from the galaxy-famous brothels.

Javier was looking for scum and villainy. Or rather, letting himself wander into the wrong parts of town and letting it come find him. He had four deadly women in pairs with him, wandering close like they were watching out for their own partner, rather than ready to jump to his defense.

He'd never felt safer, even though he was sitting in a pretty seedy bar.

Man sidled up. Well, walked into the joint, looked around, and happened to end up on the stool next to Javier because the place was kinda full and Hajna had specifically left a chair between the two of them, routinely chasing off potential suitors.

Woman could be a little scary when she wanted to.

Stranger ignored her and looked at Javier.

Said a word. A specific word, entirely out of context in this room.

Javier gave him the countersign.

They went back and forth three times.

The man nodded.

"You are not Regina Slayton," the stranger offered as the bartender put a highball in front of him.

"No, but we're on the same side," Javier acknowledged.

Was even close enough to the truth. If you squinted some and turned your head a little sideways.

"What are you looking for?" the man asked. "Got the note through the grapevine to meet."

Javier had palmed a datachip earlier. He slid it to the man now. Watched it disappear.

"Her updated records, right up to the moment when *Eldritch Stele* was captured and put out of business," Javier said, watching the man get extremely nervous.

"And you know this how?" he asked.

"Because my battleship was the vessel that captured her," Javier said with enough of a grin to take the sting out of it. "We're hunting pirates these days and needed a repair yard. Didn't know about her until she was my prisoner. She and Glen have decided to stay on as employees. I'm no longer surveilling pirates. I'm killing them. There's data on there about several other attacks my forces have undertaken, most recently hitting *Zygeerish* and destroying a major pirate base there."

Man was a cop. *Union of Man*, but a cop nonetheless. He turned fully to look at Javier. Hajna had his kidneys lined up if he moved suddenly.

"Navarre?" he whispered under the sound of the music.

"Aritza," Javier countered. "Navarre works for me. As do a lot of others."

WEIRD way to put it, but this was not the place for a discussion of identity.

Man shook his head, then relaxed. Drank some mid-shelf whiskey and that seemed to settle his nerves.

"What do you need?" the man asked.

"I sent a team to *Purton*, to ask the *Concord* for help," Javier said. "Regina sent messages to the *Union* doing the same. My *Purton* team vanished as if they never existed. I want to find out why, what happened, and who I need to kill because of it."

Always level-set things, even when dealing with an undercover cop in a seedy bar like this one.

"They get arrested?" he asked.

"If so, I need to break them out," Javier replied. "That, or declare war on the *Concord*, too. Already planning to destroy all the major pirate clans around here before I go home. *Concord* wants to be on their side? Fine by me."

Cop shivered in disbelief, then caught himself and muttered Navarre under his breath.

Yeah, hell of a rep when you needed it.

"You're staying in town?" the cop asked.

"Contact info on the chip," Javier nodded. "And an account you can draw on to bribe people for information on my credstick. Pay yourself a nice finder's fee out of it, too."

Blink. Blink.

Cops. **Never** enough budget to compete with assholes like Slavkov, who could buy any politician they needed. Or the company that was bothering them, in order to fire someone they didn't like.

Galaxy would be better off taxing shit enough to prevent that, but Javier had studied enough history to know that to be an impossible task.

These days, they might have to remind such assholes that the general social contract cut both ways. If the oligarchs got out of hand oppressing those they saw as little people, folks might stand up with a rock in their hand to do something about it.

Or a knife.

Or a battleship.

Javier had just given this cop a figurative briefcase of money to go rattle cages with. Man had a rep as an honest-enough cop. Long-term, deep-cover contact Regina had connected him with regularly.

Cages would rattle in this town.

Cop nodded, slid backwards off his stool, and vanished into the crowd.

Javier watched him in the bar mirror. Afia came around Hajna instead of them slipping down one.

"That went well," she noted.

"Well enough," Javier said. "Still need something bigger, because he's just underworld stuff."

"What?" Afia asked, eyes suddenly glittery with menace.

Javier considered it.

"The Crone," he told her.

"Left her on *Valadris*," Afia replied after a moment to place things.

"She's not the only one in this galaxy."

PART II

Afia got Javier back to the ship, where he would be safe enough with what limited adult supervision those two teams might manage. Then she went back into town, swapping Djamila in where Bethany had been before and leaving the Pathfinders on oblique double dates with Tom and Demyan.

Afia was in charge tonight.

First joint Javier had taken them to had been seedy, but not really dangerous. Not like some of the bars she occasionally wandered down into.

Down. Always down, it seemed, to a converted basement. She wondered what that implied about people.

Probably nothing good.

Dive, though. Mosh pit filled with kids having fun. Band on stage with instruments and rage. Not a lot of skill or singing ability, but enthusiastic as hell.

Bouncer had looked up at the Dragoon, smiled tepidly, and marked them as potential troublemakers, even after she'd slipped him a big fat bill ahead of time. Wasn't like he was wrong.

Booth. Her and the Ballerina of Death, with floofy drinks that had fruit and umbrellas.

Couple of fellows had looked over, smiled, then had second thoughts and gone back to safer hobbies.

Like playing in traffic.

Man approached, oblivious to Tom and Hajna as he walked close. They were not oblivious. Nor were Sascha and Demyan across the way.

He stopped at the polite distance and nodded.

Middle-aged guy, maybe. Top end of young Turk punk turning serious. Fixer/fence, but for the kids moshing, rather than lawyers and bankers. Their parents didn't need this guy.

Yet. She could see him in a decade and a nice suit.

Afia tapped a finger on her side of the ring booth, then slid in to center. Man would be directly across from the Dragoon. You couldn't see any of her weapons at the moment. Beyond the woman herself.

Music was hard. It was *Cyrana*. You mostly read lips in a dive like this.

Man came to rest. Studied Djamila enough to categorize her as *Killer*, then ignored the woman and focused on Afia.

"You needed something off-beat?" he asked carefully.

She'd put out some strange smoke signals this time. Not the kind to draw in predators, but fixers. Fences. People dabbling in *odd*.

"*Someone*," Afia emphasized. "Got a need and need a particular person to fill it. Don't know who she is."

"Gotta be a she?" he asked, mostly to clarify. That had been the note.

"Does," Afia replied, nodding.

The Crone on *Valadris* had been a hard woman. Urban Neighborhood Captain in the capital. Dangerous woman, but down a couple of tiers from the ones that made the news.

Man studied her. Glanced at Djamila.

"There are rumors of a fleet that hit *Zygeerish*," he began, almost hesitantly.

Afia pointed.

"Her and one of my Sappers captured the bridge of the pirate base by themselves," Afia grinned. "Rest of the force was coming along. Then we annihilated the place. Smoking ruins falling out of orbit. Man I'm working for demanded no less."

"Navarre?"

"His boss," Afia smiled. It was a cruel and ugly smile. Word was starting to get around. Javier's fault. "The Science Officer has declared war on piracy and is going to end the clans. Anybody that doesn't change their ways gets killed. He's done fucking around."

Stranger shuddered, absorbing all that. It was a lot.

And that barely scratched the surface of things.

Man reset himself.

"I have also heard rumors about the pirates of *Syntha*," he said. "Captain Navarre and a battleship."

"I am that Ship's Dragoon," Djamila injected into the conversation. Like burning slivers under fingernails.

"And we've killed a number of other pirate bases closer to *Concord* Space," Afia continued. She pulled another of Javier's chips and slid it to the man. "Here're the details you need. Feel free to spread that around."

"I have a name," he decided, telling her a where and a when. "She was concerned because that line runs right down the middle of her business."

"The Science Officer gives strangers a chance to go straight," Afia told him. "If they don't take it, that is then their choice. Share that information with her and we'll be there. The Dragoon here will handle security and guarantee everyone's safety, so nobody come with anything but belt knifes. Wouldn't want them to get hurt."

He studied Djamila again. Committed her to memory. Saw something because his nod was far more respectful.

"See you in three days," he said, sliding from the booth and walking away without a look back.

Afia nodded at her team to let him go.

This part of her mission was accomplished.

PART III

Javier had kept Navarre's cloak, but left the rest of the outfit on the ship.

Because honestly, cloaks were so cool that everyone else looked junior varsity.

Afia, being a pain, had sent the Storm Giants along. Djamila as herself instead of Hadiiye. Pathfinders. Sappers and one dork Combat Engineer.

As long as you missed six other guys innocently wandering around the neighborhood.

Brownstone. Block of houses with common walls and individual stoops and front doors. Three stories and a basement. Upper-middle-class neighborhood, in the right part of town for folks that didn't want manor houses, yards, or penthouse suites.

Certain mindset involved, but Afia had filtered things and got him to the right place, at least. To the right people would be next.

Afia rang the bell. Javier felt like the valley in the middle of a mountain range, because both Sapper women were taller than him. The two men were taller than that. Then Djamila.

Butler opened the door. Old English style in suit. Hard looking man, but sixty, so probably not capable of taking more than one of the Storm Giants by himself.

Still looked capable of that much.

"Dr. Javier Aritza, King's College, *Altai*," he introduced himself.

Because why the hell not? Folks he was meeting weren't going to call the cops, and the clans were already breaking and running in a lot of places.

"You are expected," he bowed, ushering them in and putting the four Giants to one side with a glare to behave.

Javier liked him already. Might have to see if he had a cousin in the business.

Hallway to stairs to salon on the second floor, rear, overlooking a small yard with compact fruit trees in pots that could be brought in for winter.

Javier approved again.

Older woman. Past her physical prime. Sixty. Still did yoga and dance, from the muscles and grace revealed when she stood as he entered. White hair shoulder length and full. Hazel-green eyes like Djamila and his first wife Holly. Gorgeous today. Must have been utterly stunning when she was thirty.

Javier went courtly manners on her. Again, place impressed him. Especially with a blank slate to work with.

Storm Giants were in the hall with the butler, nobody making any noise because Sappers could sit without moving for hours and the butler reminded Javier of Farouk.

Four-way conversation around a coffee table with a coffee service. Mistress served them herself.

"Your documentation is rather astounding reading," she began as they sipped an excellent roast.

"My ship's *Sentience* has been trained by a *Concord Navy* Librarian to her standards," Javier replied.

Level-setting. Not a threat. Except where it was. More a reminder of all the things he and his friends had done. Had had to do.

Most of those folks had had it coming, but then, don't we all?

"And Durbin?" the Crone asked.

Rude to think of her that way, but she certain wasn't Maiden. And probably had kids Afia's age.

Lady Warlord of Cyrana might be appropriate, though.

"I have remained outside the *Concord* for more than a decade," Javier replied, leaving a lot of paper blank that she didn't need to know. "*Purton* was a first-stop. I wish to find out what happened, because I have lost all contact with that team, when I should have gotten messages by now, one way or the other."

"The information you hinted at suggests to me *Merankorr*," she noted.

Gods, this woman reminded him of Behnam. Same casual confidence that she could hold her own with him and his two ladies. Same charisma.

Lady Warlord of Cyrana, indeed.

"And I have a lot of reasons not to visit them," Javier nodded. "I would like to hire a team of experts to dig in on this one and get me answers. And earn my favor."

She studied him closely. Dryly, but knowingly.

Turned to Djamila first. Placed the Ballerina of Death on a spectrum. One far end, but that was Djamila.

Turned to Afia next.

"*Nidavellir*," woman murmured quietly.

"Man failed to kill me," Afia nodded.

Turned back to him.

"So is Aritza another cover for Navarre?" she asked.

"Other way around," Javier said. "He's the identity I use when I need a mass casualty incident sufficient to make the news. When I'm smashing pirates."

And there had been several of those, if this woman recognized Afia.

"Your background documents suggest that the *Concord* might have sided with evil," she noted.

Javier smiled hard.

"I had records taken when this woman captured the Jarre Foundation main base on *Zygeerish*," Javier nodded to the taller killer. "Valko Slavkov might own the *Concord Navy* in a manner similar to how he owns at least two of the four major clans, and has extensive commercial interests in the other two. Right the moment, I'm not intending to destroy them, but they might get in my way. As you noted, they might have chosen evil. And I used to be one of them, so I'm doubly offended."

He held up the fist with the replacement ring. *Bryce Academy*, Class of '63.

Where had it all gone wrong for them? Javier had done the work with the help of some amazing women to figure out his own fuckups and own them.

Move past them and try to be a better person.

Wasn't a mirror big enough for the entire *Concord*, as far as he was aware.

And Dorn had already seen that lit match in the distance.

Wasn't a lot of time left.

Crone nodded, absorbing all the mad energy he was giving off. How deeply offended he was at the situation. Doubly so, indeed, that he had to be here, doing this. Contemplating shit like this.

"I have some interesting rumors out of *Merankorr* that didn't make any sense last week," she replied, stepping over all the rage and getting back to business.

"Do tell?" Javier also put things to one side to listen. He was good at that.

"Trouble on the surface at Rogerson," she said. "Normally, nothing that mattered, save that it appeared to be deeply connected to *Concord Intelligence*. And there were sudden arrests and chaos on *Fleet Operations One* that almost came down to open warfare on the station. Your timeline of events to *Purton* and since lines up rather well with that, unfortunately. I'm not suggesting a direct connection. However."

"However," he agreed. "Can I hire you to find out?"

"Would you trust my findings?" she asked. "Or should I look

at smuggling your team in and out so you can investigate directly?"

"Extremely dangerous job," Javier replied.

"I own a yacht," she said. "And take occasional vacations to *Merankorr* and other places. It would fit within my milieu. You could leave your ship here, or hire someone to transport it somewhere safe while I took you there."

"Why are you willing to put yourself on the line?" Afia asked, shifting the entire room around without anyone moving.

"I watched the speech he gave to those terrible warriors," the Crone said, turning her head to Djamila. "To your people. Most of the galaxy will not understand what he did, and won't look past those uniforms."

"Few can," Djamila replied simply.

Crone nodded. Turned to Afia.

"Nor will they remember that a pirate ship opened fire on an escape pod in their rage," she said. "Personally, I was surprised that you let anyone survive."

"Won't make that mistake again," the Kodiak growled.

Crone nodded again. Turned to Javier.

"You are going to save the galaxy," she said. "Or damn it irrevocably. I cannot tell. But there is a saying I find appropriate here. *If it can be destroyed by the truth, it deserves to be destroyed by the truth.* Too many folks hide their visage and pretend not to see. And I am guilty of that, as well. Crime rises, and some of us get rich from it, forgetting that it has costs, even if someone else has to pay them."

Javier wondered if this woman had ever met Mina. Those two would see eye to eye on several topics.

Ethics, because morality was based on culture and legality was what the lawmakers decided it would be this week.

But Right and Wrong were something else.

"I'm not sure I can save the galaxy," he told her. "Won't stop me trying."

"Nor should it," she agreed. "The rest of your background

package makes that clear, even if the fools in charge will never understand. At least before it is too late. And if I put myself at your mercy, I might buy some absolution for all the things I did in my own ignorance."

She turned to Afia. Fixed her with a terrible gaze.

"Some evil cannot be allowed," she told the smaller woman.

Afia nodded.

Helen, launching a thousand ships, but not with her beauty in case.

Crone fixed her eyes on him.

"How soon can you depart?"

Javier smiled.

"How soon can you?"

PART IV

Djamila had watched Javier charm people. Men and women, but he leaned far more heavily into the feminine. Challenged them, but from a position of respect, rather than anything crass.

He had certainly charmed Camden Forgrave into loading up her yacht *Argo*, swapping out her entire crew to keep *Flying Maiden* maintained, and putting herself at Javier's mercy.

She supposed that the four women in charge likely tilted things in his favor.

They were headed to *Merankorr*. With, Djamila supposed, sufficient capabilities to actually do things to certain folks who needed it done to them.

Camden had asked her to coffee in the glorious salon. Behnam might have done a room like this, had she settled for a ship this small. Compact and private. Two comfortably and four extremely friendly. Money spent well and extravagantly on furnishings and art.

Class, which was something you could fake for a time, but not buy.

Camden had impressed the hell out of Javier. Djamila was beginning to understand why.

"What will your people do?" Camden asked simply as they studied one another.

"Fight," Djamila replied. "Javier offered good money for a combat infantry unit and a warship."

"*Neu Berne* have never been known as mercenaries," Camden noted dryly. "Nor have they begun now. Especially not today, for outsiders like you and Javier."

Djamila considered her words carefully. Javier had referred to her as Lady Warlord of *Cyrana* as a mark of how dangerous Camden Forgrave was in his eyes.

"I suppose that I bear some responsibility, having blackmailed him into it," Djamila shrugged. "He still did the work."

"Yes, he did," Camden agreed. "That speech was a masterclass in subtle emotional manipulation. Javier could have been a dangerous politician."

Djamila was back on the side of that stage, thinking similar thoughts. Wondering where he might go next, if he decided that this wouldn't be enough.

Take over the *Concord*? At least emotionally?

Things were building that way.

"Eventually, he will return to the *Khatum*," Djamila said, making sure that this woman understood that Javier might be available physically in the short term, but someone else had his heart and soul.

They just had to save the galaxy first.

"That much was clear from the materials," Camden acknowledged. "I want to know about your people."

Neu Berne. The losers of the largest galactic war in history, still recovering a lifetime later, though perhaps they had finally turned the corner. Trade was up. Living standards were better than they had been when she'd been a child.

Progress.

And she was in the process of helping Javier tear it all down? Perhaps.

Did it deserve to be destroyed by the truth?

Most things probably did, even if it stripped you bare and held up a mirror to show all your imagined shortcomings.

She was back aboard *Shangdu*, wearing nothing but a wrap around her hips because Javier had thought he'd won a round. Found a line she wouldn't cross.

And he might have, had they not already been lovers in warfare, intent on making the other's death look like an accident.

"They will fight," Djamila repeated, "but because Javier has offered them something nobody else in the galaxy has in generations. Respect. Honor. They are all defined by duty, but he called them to protect the weak and innocent. Anyone. Anywhere. The term he uses is Swordbearer."

Camden absorbed that, then nodded.

Javier, standing before the *Dragon Watch* and challenging their honor. All of them. And winning them over. Winning her over, burning out those last, tiny spots in her conscience that hadn't yet fully committed to what might be coming.

That destroying the galaxy might be the only way to save it, because a small war now, like a small fire set under controlled circumstances, might prevent the later conflagration.

Might push Hetzel's *Rising Storm* out another generation.

Neither he nor Javier had been able to identify anything that might stop it.

Djamila blinked as she found the one thing that might. Chilled to the tips of her toes.

Camden had suddenly shifted into a combat mode like Hajna or Sascha might have. Like she was thirty again and the deadliest person in any room.

Watched silently. Watched Djamila.

"Neither Dr. Hetzel nor Javier have been able to identify any outcome that doesn't lead to another general war in the near future," Djamila repeated aloud.

"The Rising Storm," Camden acknowledged. "You have just identified one."

Wasn't a question. Observation by a dangerously smart

woman. Exactly the kind of person Javier had asked for. Had needed. Had charmed into handing herself and her ship over to Javier and his people without a qualm, bringing none of her own people with her.

Djamila swallowed past a tongue that didn't want to obey her. She would ask if the Science Officer's audacity was that great, but Djamila had spent years locked in mortal combat with the man. Understood the shadow of his willingness to push the envelope.

When he thought he was right.

Heavy sigh escaped her lips in spite of everything as ten thousand individual puzzle pieces suddenly rotated and locked into place.

"If he brings down the *Concord* as we know it today," she told the woman. "Forces it to suffer some sort of internal conflict—almost but never quite breaking over into a civil war—they might be so distracted internally that their various neighbors could recover their own strength and stabilize themselves without having to fight another general war. *Balustrade*. The *Union of Man. Neu Berne*. Others."

Camden had gone a little white.

"I'd ask if he thought he could, but it's obvious that he intends to," Camden replied. "Can he succeed?"

"A lot of other folks have expected him to fail," Djamila offered, wondering if that was their mission to *Merankorr*.

To help bring it all down, at a time when Javier both held the heart and soul of *Neu Berne* in his hand **and** intended to prevent them from getting involved.

Worse?

It just might work.

HOHNIR

PART I

Suvi almost felt like *Mielikki* again today.

Sitting quietly at the edge of a system, using passive optics and sensors to map everything larger than a beachball by reflection, magnetic field, or solar wind deflection.

Those had been some good years, if you ignored the parts where Javier had been a fundamentally broken human, hiding from the rest of the species and only talking to her and the chickens.

Hohnir's system was mostly quiet. The usual planets ranging around, from big ones in close to randomly scattered rocks farther out.

Because they were on a dwarf planet with no atmosphere, those folks didn't need to be all that close to the star itself. Out about six AU, where things were cooler, but hadn't fallen off to cold. Space around them cleared of rubble by the gas giants, in a place that had never really seen a lot of messiness nearby.

Just because, she'd done an old-school *Concord Survey* of the place. Like coming home after a few years away at school or something.

Nice.

But a girl's gotta pay the bills. She surfaced herself and made a noise in the Library, where Katya had been reading a history of *Neu Berne* that Bashir had recommended. One Suvi had enjoyed, because the historian had walked that fine line between patriotic and honest in her work.

Warts and successes. Who they saw themselves as when they looked in the mirror.

Fit well with what she'd gleaned from listening to five hundred of them down and aft as they went about their days.

"What have you got?" Katya asked, looking up.

"Orbital station like we expected," Suvi replied. "*Relentless* could have probably taken it on their own, if it wasn't for a hexagon of ground forts that all have clear firing arcs to cover it."

"Mostly a transfer station, from what I remember," Katya said, putting the book down and rising to pace as she thought. She usually did. "Big ships can dock and handle loading, while smaller ones can fly down into the side of a hollow mountain and actually land."

"That's what I'm seeing," Suvi said. "Looks like a tunnel that runs front door to back door to make it easy?"

"Affirmative," Katya nodded. "How tough are the ground forts?"

"Pulsars big enough to be a threat to me," Suvi told her. "Ground based means that you can install heavy stuff and not worry about space. Lots of generators and cooling fins for the same reason. Not all that big physically. One main gun in the center surrounded by another hex of smaller ones, plus torpedo launchers. No way to use the station to hide behind, at least from the beams."

"If they open fire, you have other problems," Katya said. "I still want to try a colossal bluff on them. How good is Del Smith?"

"Zakhar considers him to be the best on the market, even at his age," Suvi replied.

"Can you ask him to join us?" Katya said. "I want to see what he thinks of my idea before I share it with everyone else."

"Stand by, waking him up from his nap, if you want to believe he's actually asleep. And he'll be joining us in a few minutes. Did you want anyone else?"

"No, if he thinks it can be done, the *Dragon Watch* will move heaven and earth to not look bad standing next to him," Katya laughed.

Suvi shared it. Those folks would.

Could they really pull it off?

PART II

Delridge Smith had seen and done a lot of stupid things in his time. Survived all of them.

To date, at least. And at least what Velichkov was suggesting was merely insane.

Run of the mill crazy around here.

Probably right in the middle of his wheelhouse, truth be told.

Woman after his own heart. He wondered if she was single. Not a lot of pirates got too attached to folks, beyond having someone in every port.

Career pirates tended to not have anyone. And she was one hell of a lot of woman.

"Yeah, it could be made to work," he replied when she finished talking. "Suvi, how low can you nail a jump from here?"

Another crazy one like him. Javier's kid, but Del considered her a grandniece or something. Crazy enough to fit in if he ever invited his kin to a reunion on *Altai*, nowhere else in the galaxy being safe for that many of them all in one place.

"Fifty kilometers mean elevation, plus or minus about ten if I jump from this far out," she replied.

He'd talked to her about valence jumps and all the crazy shit she'd done and learned at *Drako* to keep them alive. He'd take the under and points.

Del turned his attention back to Velichkov.

"Six shuttles, six towers?" he confirmed.

"I think we can nail them all down at once, given the force involved and their egos on the line to pull it off," she challenged him.

Del had to laugh. Those five pilots were all pretty good. Not as good as him, but that was an extra thirty-five to forty years' experience and crazy to polish it. Job like this was almost straightforward.

If you were insane. Like him.

"What happens when they figure out they've been swindled?" he asked her. Both ladies.

"They know me," Katya said. "Everyone in Jarre knows me and *Kymni Gauntlet*. When I tell them that I've been promoted into a battleship and started working for the guy that has already destroyed *Zygeerish* and *Ferran*, a lot of folks are going to rethink a life of crime. We'll need to keep killers on various ships as insurance, but I'm not opposed to sending messages to *Neu Berne* asking for more sailors, then breaking up all the crews we capture. Javier and Zakhar want their fleets of vengeance, after all. Where better than to take them from the very pirates he's fighting?"

"That's where you're mistaken, missy," Del turned deadly serious.

"Oh?" she got just as dark, just as fast.

"*Fleets of Vengeance* is nice and all, don't get me wrong," Del nodded. "Javier is after something bigger here. Surprised you haven't cottoned on to it yet, but I suppose I've known the boy a lot longer and in much worse circumstances."

"What's he looking for?"

"Javier's never been about stacking up body counts," Del told her. Told both of them. "Even at his angriest. Man always controlled things. Even Navarre-the-killer kept it leashed tightly.

Nidavellir could have ended up a lot worse. Might, next time, if Afia's up on her high horse raging, but even then, I think someone will dial her back. Might even have to be me, but that's what we do around here. Man doesn't see himself as the warlord whose gonna fix all these punks, Velichkov."

"What does he see in the mirror, Del?" Suvi asked, reminding him that she'd known Javier longest.

But she was his kid. And a woman. Different perspectives, stacked. And a *Concord* Yeoman when she forgot. Or wanted to remind you.

Hadn't woken up one day and CHOSEN to be a pirate. Not a lot of people did.

Sure, they might run off to be pirates, thinking that it was going to be so much more glamorous than it really was. Del'd been that way. Fifty-some years ago. Maybe about the time Ekaterina Velichkov was born.

He'd stayed with it in spite of options to go straight. Or retire and eke out a piss-poor living somewhere safe.

Zakhar's fault, really. Even as a pirate, the man had held to higher standards. Even with all the blood on his hands.

On all their hands.

Mina's fault that they'd all grown up. Del figured she would fall off the bar stool giggling when she heard this whole story, and he fully intended to be there, watching and listening as she got the tale.

Tomorrow's problem, but wasn't that the whole point?

Mina had been born five centuries ago. Even older than Suvi, let alone an old fart like him.

Tomorrow.

And he was talking to the storehouse of tomorrow in Suvi, trying to explain to these two women that thing that made Javier Aritza tick.

"Who does he see in the mirror?" Del asked rhetorically. A sigh, because the man might never forgive him when this truth got out. "He sees himself as the guardian of tomorrow, Suvi. All of us, really, but him. Today sucks, so we gotta go out and fix it. Make it better. Make the galaxy a healthier place for everyone who doesn't know that it can be. That's our job. That's our mission, if I can be so utterly crass in the light of things. We are the Guardians of Tomorrow."

Kid gasped.

Both of them did. Both of them should know better, but they were too innocent, he supposed. Too something, anyway.

Zakhar would see it. Djamila, too.

Mina practically demanded it. Had made them all grow up.

Including his silly ass in the cargo pants and Hawaiian shirts.

But why the hell had the *Khatum* given them a First-Rate Galleon and that much money, except to do this?

Del wasn't fooled. Not one damned bit.

Woman had looked to the bottom of Javier's soul and seen him for what he really was.

Man was a damned hero. Also Mina's fault.

Probably everything was her fault, from that moment they had entered The Mind Field and rescued her from yesterday.

Velichkov had gone white. He didn't bother checking Suvi's image on the nearest screen.

"We're going to do this, because tomorrow demands it," Del told Katya. "Dress it up in any pretty fineries and fripperies you want, that's what Javier sees in the mirror these days. And a lot of the rest us, when you scratch away the gilt to get at the alloy underneath."

Velichkov's chin came up. Eyes got extra hard, over and above a pirate captain responsible for cracking the whip on every other ship in that fleet.

She nodded.

"I want you briefing the other five piloting crews," she said simply. "Tell them just like you told me. I don't think we have any doubts about the *Dragon Watch*, but this will add that extra level of something that I don't think they woke up this morning prepared for."

Del nodded back. About what he figured he was stepping into when he opened his mouth.

But then, the future demanded it.

PART III

Commander Haniyya Jehad Al-Amin. Commanding Officer, *Dragon Watch*.

Senior officer present, with Sykora and Aritza off doing whatever they did when they had to get down in the mud.

Pilot Smith had just finished briefing her officers. After Captain Velichkov and the *Sentience* had finished their portions.

"Any questions?" the man asked the group, studying them with old eyes.

Old. Not even merely *older*. Her father's age or greater. She hadn't asked.

She wanted to ask something like, "Are you insane?" but already understood that to be a common occurrence in this crew. And irrelevant to the question at hand.

Neu Berne Assault Marines prided themselves on being tougher than everyone else. Harder.

These people had long-since cornered the market on *crazier*.

She cleared her throat when heads rotated to track her. Her people and Captain Velichkov's.

You want crazy? Fine.

"Do we instead paradrop troops?" she asked. "I appreciate

89

that landing and assaulting is likely to be effective, but if the gravity is that low, do we order the pilots to hover over each fortress so troops can immediately absail down, before the defenders can react with fire? At this gravity, they could easily drop fifty meters without serious risk of injury, especially with thruster packs."

Yes, everyone twitched.

Hang in space, directly above sky defense batteries as you expected them to come live at any moment? Capture the guns without blowing anything up in the process, because you are about to tell the locals that they have been subject to a hostile corporate takeover and are under new management?

Would you like to get crazier?

Smith turned to the other five pilots. Smiled at them ferally.

Haniyya was not surprised that they all matched it. They had obviously spent too much time around Smith and developed bad habits.

Crazy ones, at least. The *Dragon Watch* would be performing this assault. Without support.

Well, a First-Rate Galleon in orbit, but not available to provide covering fire except in extreme circumstances.

A colossal bluff, Velichkov had called it.

Wolves, emerging from the forest and swarming your camp before you could react.

Smith rotated to Velichkov. Outsider, but Haniyya had heard extremely good things from Captain Hayfa Alfarsi, formerly commanding *Relentless* and now aboard *Kymni Gauntlet*.

Everyone was moving around. And rising to ongoing occasions.

She might as well push the bar another notch higher.

"Can you do it quickly?" Velichkov asked. "If they have time to resist, it will get ugly fast, so I'd like to overwhelm them."

Haniyya locked on to Pilot Smith.

"You get us there, we'll take the place," she said simply.

Her officers growled. The other pilots nodded.

Smith smiled.

Haniyya matched it.

PART IV

Del had studied Suvi's maps and picked the hardest approach for himself.

Gotta show the kids how it was done.

He had sixty-some killers below and aft, suited up and armored for a ship-to-ship assault, a touch sad that Djamila wasn't here. Nor that one Sapper than had accompanied her at *Zygeerish*.

Still, her ghost would hang over all of them anyway.

"Del, I'm about to jump," Suvi announced. "Make ready to launch."

He'd been there at *Drako*, unable to do anything to those yahoos. At least until she'd started a higher level of shell games.

"I'm in," he said. "Let the others know to come up to launch readiness."

Coded language, because he'd infected those poor chaps with a hint of piracy they'd never really experienced before.

"All hands, stand by," he announced internally, even as the Nameless Assault Shuttle stood up on its toes, thrusters one notch short of breaking the electromagnetic hold they had on the deck, anchoring him in place.

Risky, most of the time. You waited for the ship to do things, then started your take off, but it was Suvi, and she knew what she was doing.

And so did he.

Time to show the kids how it was done.

The blink was a burst of light behind his eyeballs, then a horizon appeared out the rear flight bay doors, already opened and everything depressurized, because time would be of the essence.

Del was already moving forward when his brain caught up to his hands. Straight out of the bay and ship generally headed in the right direction, some five hundred kilometers over the horizon, where nobody on that station could see anything, even if they'd happened to be looking in his direction.

Altitude, roughly forty-eight kilometers, but they'd be dropping quickly, so he nosed over and let gravity drag him closer to the surface. Without an atmosphere, he'd be riding thrusters a lot harder than usual, but that was why they paid him the big bucks.

Or whatever it was.

Zakhar and Javier let him play. Even paid him.

Let him do *this*.

"*Excalibur* Flight, this is Lead," he said. No names, no numbers, no identifying characteristics. "Go for radio silence and begin your runs."

Then he put word to deed and ran the throttle to the stop. He had the longest trip, circling the target below the horizon while the others crept in, everyone on a timeline that started now.

Ugly, gray world. Beat to hell by asteroid impacts, so regolith everywhere. Mountains and valleys from formation stresses, but no atmosphere to grind off the rough edges and make it pretty.

Kinda like him. Del grinned.

Horizon came up fast, as small as this rock was. Passive sensors lit up and came active overhead as the station spotted them, but everyone was hauling ass and he was ten seconds from his target.

"All hands, standby to deploy," he ordered them.

Meaning, everybody grab a bar or leave the straps on, but be ready to get loose and run like hell out the back hatch as he was already opening it.

Assault commander of this group had asked Del to come in twenty meters over the target and hold, claiming that his people could step off the deck and land safely that way from this height.

And they were about to find out.

Pity they were doing this without guns. So easy to strafe that fortress and blow shit up before they could get off their asses and shoot back, because apparently they had been asleep.

Oh, and a First-Rate Galleon had just appeared overhead.

Attention, criminal scum, there's a new sheriff in town.

PART V

Katya had finally gotten used to what Suvi could do in tight quarters.

Helped, having been on the short end of that stick too many times at *Drako*. And Suvi claimed that she had gotten better.

Katya could see it.

First, they dropped out, nearly onto the surface of *Hohnir*.

Then a bounce straight up and out several light-seconds, angled away so that the planet itself shadowed them against the station.

Then a bounce in and they were directly **below** the station, turned sideways so she could broadside up and down at the same time.

"You're on," Suvi said simply.

Katya still needed a moment, because she'd gone pirate on the pirates.

And that might make her the good guys.

What's the galaxy coming to?

"Attention *Hohnir* Control, this is Katya Velichkov, aboard the battleship *Excalibur*," she said in that stern, Enforcer-ship-come-for-your-soul voice. "The Jarre Foundation has been destroyed and this system is under new management, effective immediately. Do not resist or I will be forced to destroy you."

And six assault shuttles were suddenly there, dropping troops on top of the six ground fortresses.

Suvi centered her image on Del's.

"Is he...?"

"It's Del," Suvi replied, like that said it all.

And it might.

No ropes. Just hovering in place and sliding forward at a slow walk, as troops stepped off the landing deck and fell to the surface, feet down, twenty meters.

Faster than anyone else, she'd give him that. And the team aboard *Excalibur* as a strike reserve would be watching this on remote monitors.

Explosives got deployed to pulsar batteries and bulkheads at a frightening speed, but the three remaining Sapper teams had been excited to take point on this raid.

Afia had infected them even worse than Djamila had infected the rest.

As Javier had gotten to her, if Katya was going to be honest.

"Somebody's finally awake," Suvi said. "Channel three."

Katya flexed everything once and put her game face back on, then pushed the button.

"Kat?" Ethan Dilucca asked. "What the hell?"

She'd been in this business long enough that some of her old shipmates were in command positions now. That actually might make today easier.

"They blew up Audol University, Ethan," she replied. "Literally captured it, evacuated the grounds, then blew it into pieces too small to survive reentry. And they took out *Ferran* before that. Plus other places."

She gave him a list. It was an ugly thing, but only for folks on the wrong side of history, and she'd made her choice.

"Who did this?" Ethan asked, still bewildered.

And none of the various guns that could have deployed to threaten her had as yet, so she might be able to pull this one off.

Helped, battleship suddenly eclipsing your skies.

"The Science Officer, Ethan," Katya replied. "He's the one that Navarre works for. That Slavkov has been gunning for for years. We pissed the man off when we went after him at *Drako*, so he's decided to kill every pirate who doesn't immediately surrender or run."

"Where is he?" Ethan asked. "How long do we have?"

"He's already here because he recruited me after he destroyed *Zygeerish*," she said. "Captured *Kymni Gauntlet* in dock, then stole it and offered me a chance to redeem myself. This is his battleship, Ethan. His flagship that destroyed everybody at *Drako*. It's *Sentient* and mean. This is your chance to go straight, or she'll order your defense fortresses opened up like tin cans while we deorbit the station, then blow the mountain apart and level it."

Worse, Suvi had laid out where she could put the shots that would do just that. Too much engineering, on top of everything else Zakhar had trained her in. Or Javier.

"What?"

"Do you surrender, or do you die?" she asked, confirming that Suvi was broadcasting the entire conversation to everyone in system right now.

"Jarre's gone?" Ethan asked, but that was still the shock of waking up to Suvi in your front yard with her turrets aimed at your head. Brain still catching up with history, living out here in the boonies.

"Gone," Katya replied.

Maybe sort of a lie. And maybe not. Nobody knew who had died aboard the station. And most of those bigshots would be hiding for a while until they figured out how big a threat Javier was.

And how many friends he had.

Like her, weird as that was to even think.

"Kat, what terms is he offering?" Ethan asked. "This Science Officer guy."

"You can join the winning side, Ethan," she replied. "Or decide to run like hell right now and hope you can get farther than he can reach. Or we can take the place the hard way. I have the entire *Neu Berne Dragon Watch* currently either aboard my vessel or deployed. Those are the teams sitting atop your fortresses with guns and explosives."

He mouthed the word, but no sound came out.

About as utterly freaked out as she had been, looking at those folks Afia called Storm Giants.

Ragnarok might be coming.

Katya nodded.

Waited.

Suvi had all of her turrets gyrostabilized and had picked out the spots she would destroy first, as soon as anybody sneezed the wrong way.

And *Kymni Gauntlet* had been the only flagship to escape *Drako III*.

"Shit," Ethan muttered. "Standing down, Kat. I guess we're under new management. As soon as someone tells me what the hell is going on."

"It's a hell of a story, Ethan," she replied. "But you made the right choice."

At least she hoped so.

P VI

Haniyya was not prepared to take command of a captured pirate base, but she supposed that she was the person best qualified for the task. And her troops were currently operating the six bases, having evacuated everyone else to the main facility.

Former commander Dilucca was still in shock but she understood that, having merely had longer to come to grips with how utterly insane the entire situation had gotten.

At the same time, the pirates who mattered were all businessfolk, and treating all of this like a hostile corporate takeover, as Captain Velichkov had suggested would work.

They were in his office. What had been his office. She was beside him on the one side, with Captain Velichkov on the other, watching.

"Kat, now what?" Dilucca asked.

"Now, you identify those folks that you don't trust," Velichkov replied. "Troublemakers and Board of Directors spies. I ship them somewhere else. If they piss me off between now and then, I'll turn them over to the authorities, but otherwise, they can escape. Or at least try to run from the Science Officer. Rest of you behave and work for the greater good, understanding that Aritza plans to tell the *Concord* and *Balustrade* that you have seen the light and are working to make things better. Hopefully, they'll fall for it. Or at least look the other way."

"And if they don't?" he pressed. "Lot of us with long sentences in front of us."

Haniyya leaned forward and caught his attention. Deflected him some, as he was in danger of getting emotional. Like men did.

"*Neu Berne* is offering asylum to the right people," she said, those having been orders quietly issued to her, though she hadn't understood why at the time. More the fool her. "Starting tomorrow, your new life becomes the measure of your future. We will have need of men and women with galactic business experience. And competent sailors, as I expect we will be expanding our fleet some. Not enough to threaten anyone else, but enough to keep them from threatening us."

His eyes spoke volumes of disbelief that didn't reach his tongue. Probably for the better.

"Same with *Altai*, I'm told," Katya Velichkov interjected. "I'm of two minds, but that's only which one I'll end up at, Ethan. And you don't have to decide today either, unless you want to be on the ship trying to outrun vengeance. Can't even really call it justice, but you understand that we have a tiger by the tail and he's mostly friendly."

Dilucca nodded shallowly. Turned and studied her. Haniyya studied him.

Past middle-aged some. Fighting trim, if not up to Assault Marine standards. Obviously intelligent to be in command here. And smart enough to not get himself and his entire force wiped out.

Because she'd seen Suvi's battle plans.

Thin face. Not quite a hatchet, but certainly aquiline. Dark eyes. Shaved head with gray stubble.

Shell shocked. Locked on her.

"What does the *Dragon Watch* intend?" he asked carefully.

"The rest of the fleet is coming up behind us," Katya intercepted. "That's Zakhar Sokolov and most of his people. They move slower in argosy than a *Sentient* warship can manage."

More shell shock. Haniyya watched his entire life crumble, and there was nothing he could do about it except try to ride those waves to shore.

"Fleet?" he asked, tones wavering.

Haniyya nodded.

"Several more ships that the Science Officer has previous captured, in addition to the ones here," Haniyya told him. "Loyal crews, so we'll be shifting bodies around to break up the ones we have. Since you didn't have any warships present, the smugglers that take the deal will be supervised. Or rearranged."

"New day, new deals, Ethan," Katya said.

"I'm expecting *Santa Maria* back soon," the man said. "Patrol corvette currently escorting a couple of captured ships to... well, shit."

"To *Zygeerish*?" Katya asked.

"Yeah, because we didn't know any better," he nodded. "Might abandon them there, gather up crews, and run like hell. Dunno if they'll come back here or listen to the whispers I have no doubts are causing everyone trouble everywhere."

"You'll convince them to see the light when they return," Haniyya told him in her new job as Base Commander. At least until Zakhar got here and had the staff to handle things better.

Though she could see recruiting as many of these pirate troopers as possible into some sort of formation. Maybe moving her Leader-1 and -2, as well as maybe Trooper-4 over as cadre. Men and women who knew fighting. Just needed to understand that they were serving under a new flag.

Command back on *Neu Berne* might not choose to accept them later, but someone would, possibly for a planetary militia if nothing else.

Because piracy was done in this region of space.

She would see to that.

"Now what?" Dilucca asked her, settling in some as her Chief

Administrative Officer. Haniyya would need an expert in that role, and it gave him purpose. Katya had spoken well of the man from previous encounters.

"Now we clean things up around here," Haniyya said. "If and when other Jarre ships come, we will welcome them like normal. Then capture them and offer them the same chance you and your current people have had. Everybody gets exactly one chance to go straight."

"And if not?"

"Then we deal with them like pirates," Haniyya promised.

BRYCE

PART I

Armando understood how the *Concord* was built. Or how it had come to be in the current age.

Merankorr was home to the fleet. Huge. Imposing. Martial. Plus the brothels even the most sheltered farmers in *Balustrade* had heard about.

Cyrana was the cultural capital. The place that invented all the soft, social stuff that went out and infected the rest of the galaxy. Food. Fashion. Music. Style.

Bryce was his mission. Home of the Naval Academy that had produced Zakhar, Javier, and Bethany. Capital world, but done in a very quiet, almost agrarian way. Industry, sure, but not a lot of it and mostly local, rather than for export. Same for most things cultural, though there was a cluster of famous literary writers who sold dozens of books when they published something.

The key was understanding who those *dozens* of readers were.

You want flash, excitement, starship chases, gun fights, romance, or comedy? Stay on *Cyrana*. One Drachma paperbacks that got consumed by the pallet load.

Bryce had the poets. The Literary Giants™ who were taught in Important Schools™ to people who pretended to be intellectuals.

Armando had spent enough time around folks like that in a previous life to understand how much of a facade it was. A charade.

Looked good on paper, because nobody went to *Bryce* to argue with you except politicians and other literary snobs.

His job then, was Archimedes. Because you didn't need nearly as long a lever to move the galaxy if you spoke the right dialect.

Armando had reached deep and found that silly poet he'd been at fourteen, channeling him into the present tense with turgid prose that was still concise. Decisive.

Incisive.

Cut to the quick and ask pointedly rude questions of folks that liked to consider themselves Citizens of the Galaxy, rather than grubby little *Concord* patriots. Let those folks see themselves off to *Merankorr* and places like that.

He'd taken a private courier to *Bryce*. Fast. Rough, but he was used to sailing as crew and stayed out of their way as they worked.

Armando had spent his time writing a series of short essays. Mostly questions, but done in a form of literature. Form poetry, at that.

Ask the question up front. Background it with an emotional rhythm underneath that wasn't immediately obvious to the average snob. Circle back and ask it a second time with more background. More observations. More spin. A third. A fourth.

Circle right back to the top and ask it again, after leading them down a dark alley where you mugged them intellectually.

Mama had always said that poets were even worse than pirates.

She had not been wrong.

At *Bryce*, he'd posted them. One each day onto a particular electronic wall that Shard-Suvi had suggested to Warmaster-Suvi. His newest friend had also helped with the vocabulary in places, grinding and polishing words for maximum effect.

Four days on *Bryce*, and there was already a shitstorm brewing. Politely, of course. Sharp words over tea and cute sandwiches. Or cocktails and formal wear.

Most of the planet was oblivious, of course. His targets only ever sold dozens of books.

They had to have day jobs of some sort. Or spouses who supported the household with their own jobs to supplement Basic Universal Income that kept you from starving.

Didn't put you in a nice suit, though.

Adrian had done that for Armando as well as Javier.

And none of those folks had nice suits. They had ones they'd worn for decades. Badly out of fashion, which was itself a fashion.

Can't be seen being popular, after all. Or worse, profitable.

Armando sat in a coffee shop. Warmaster had identified the place, studying the social structure of *Bryce* that Shard had supplied. Deadly woman, the Warmaster.

On the surface, a drab little place. Old wood in need of a refresh, save that such an effort might make it a happening joint. Instead, the most excitement they ever had here was when the kids did poetry slams on Friday nights.

Armando's current mission didn't allow him to join in. Making those kids look bad would be counterproductive.

But he understood that he was in the right place. Had identified the right victims.

He had his back to a corner so he could work on the next diatribe, fulminating with glorious ire at piracy in general and the rise of an oligarch class that was both above the law and possessed of the crudest middle-class sensibilities in allowing it and profiting from it.

Money-grubbers.

To date, he had not found a better insult to really rile people up around here. Even their intellectual snobbery paled into insignificance when money became the topic.

They say to never read the comments on any board in the middle of a flame war, so he let Warmaster keep score. Probably for the wisest, as she didn't have chemical emotions to get committed to.

"Hey," she popped up a new text screen as he typed. "Saw a name you might enjoy."

Always text messages, as though she was a real person chatting with him from home. Nobody ever needed to know that he had a Warmaster hiding in there.

And still at War-Status-2.

Because Zakhar himself had proclaimed it.

"Show me," he typed.

Then nearly swallowed his tongue when the name got highlighted.

But then, he was on *Bryce*. And the gods utterly loved The Science Officer. Armando could testify to that.

Dorn Hetzel had taken exception to some of his comments? The man, himself? Professor of Political History at the *Bryce* Academy? Author of *The Rising Storm*?

And he would have no idea who Armando Gutierrez might be, save as a punk offering loud polemics on a political literature board mostly haunted by the *Concord* literati.

And willing to challenge them to a dance battle on their home turf.

Good thing he had a Warmaster helping out.

PART II

Bryce, Day Nine. Armando figured that he should probably feel bad about how much fun he was having provoking these poor, sheltered folks.

Just sharp enough to draw their ire, but not so much so that they blocked or ignored him.

Helped, when their intellectual snobbery DEMANDED that they get the last word.

Armando was just a beat poet off the streets, flashed back to that sixteen year old punk fighting poetry slams regularly and occasionally scribing graffiti on walls.

And he had sworn the Warmaster to secrecy. She still giggled at him occasionally.

He had arrived on *Bryce* with a week's stack of trouble to upload, figuring that he would fire those off, then see who reacted.

Hadn't expected to light intellectual wildfires that were marshaling entire armies down to engage. Most folks had fallen generally silent, content to watch the two enormous egos go at each other with hammer and tongs, a battle where footnotes got footnotes.

Good thing he'd come prepared. And brought a Warmaster.

A spectre is haunting The Concord, he quoted as the opening line and title to the one he'd posted this morning, reaching all the way back to one of the greatest political writing teams and prognosticators history had ever marked.

A rising storm that cannot be contained and cannot be stopped, unless folks listen to the prophets and cast aside all their petty grievances. Dorn had written that part. Verbatim. Chances of it coming randomly from somebody else were up there with being hit by lightning. Twice.

And the great man had taken the bait. Obliquely, even. Most of the audience was at once enthralled and utterly clueless. But minds were being moved. Glacially, but people forget what glaciers can do when they start grinding.

Occasionally, someone must take up the sword, Dorn had countered, probably over his first coffee this morning from the timeslug. *Excalibur from the waters as it were, held aloft as a beacon.*

Damn, but that man had been wasted as an historian. No offense to Bethany.

Armando's cheeks hurt from grinning.

There are others who might help, if one is not too proud to ask, he typed. *Though some might see them as Mongols coming down from the distant Altai mountains and threatening all, forgetting how safe they made the lands they held in their day.*

The Academy had pictures of the faculty, so Armando knew what the man looked like. Especially as someone had really done an excellent job on his author photo. Armando could envision him almost dropping his coffee as he read those words and realized that he was indeed dealing with one of Javier's people, right here on *Bryce* itself.

And this was where things got hinky. Total stranger. With the right hints and suggestions, but Javier and Bethany were the only two he would know on sight. Still, leaving clues to his identity.

But someone who had read *The Rising Storm*. And understood it.

Weekend day. Poetry slam last night had been pretty good. For amateurs.

Pity that his cover identity precluded participation. Sitting here for several hours each day had taken him back to that guy he might have been, had shit turned out so radically different in the wayback.

But even then, teaching jobs didn't pay shit. And had no better retirement plan than piracy did. Plus, you were anchored to one planet forever.

Joint was a little jumping this morning, but in that middle-aged-and-older, on-the-way-to-brunch kind of way. More formally dressed than the kids last night, though no better fashion sense.

And Adrian had planned for damned near everything, so all Armando had to do at this point was stay on top of laundry and find a few shops who could come close to the understated elegance Adrian had insisted on for everyone on this mission.

The door opened. Bright outside. Dimmer in here with the shaded at half-mast. Figure entered, crossed to the bar, ordered.

Armando managed to not swallow his tongue as he recognized Dr. Hetzel in line for his coffee as the baristas did their magic dance.

Shit.

Warmaster's snicker on her screen did nothing for his peace of mind, but she was hacked into the store's surveillance system and had probably seen him first. And not mentioned anything.

Armando sipped at coffee and wondered if he'd accidentally managed to awaken those same gods that Del worked hard to hide from in nameless assault shuttles. Weirder shit had happened.

Time to play it cool.

Hetzel got his coffee and found a spot by the cold fireplace, it being a nice day out. Armando watched him settle and bring out a tablet computer from the bag he'd carried in. Fired it up while Armando watched surreptitiously.

Except that they made eye contact when Hetzel looked up.

Two guys in a coffee shop, acknowledging one another, then going back to what they were doing.

Warmaster, watch him while I look elsewhere, he typed.

On it.

Armando returned to his screen, then she brought up a second tab that was the view over the bar looking out, zoomed and cleaned up until he was looking at the professor from about two meters away standing. Not the right angle to see anything other than him typing, but watching.

Armando went back to his boards and watched flames and rage rattle back and like tides.

He might not be able to move fleets, but he sure has hell had started moving the minds that were supposed to be controlling those fleets. Supposed to be. Assuming that admirals actually answered to politicians and not just to oligarchs.

And maybe riling up the politicians that they weren't in control was the thing they needed?

A new message appeared, tagged to the thread where he'd been commenting.

Dr. Hetzel. Seated all of six meters away.

There are others who might help, if one is not too proud to ask, Armando had said as soon as he sat down an hour ago. *Though some might see them as Mongols coming down from the distant Altai mountains and threatening all, forgetting how safe they made the lands they held in their day.*

Or an Iberian king? Hetzel asked.

Armando managed to not make a sound. At least he was pretty sure. And the joint was noisy enough to cover it anyway.

Javier had always claimed that the kings of Navarre had been named Aritza, though Armando hadn't cared enough to research it. But that was throwing down a gauntlet if he'd ever seen one.

He looked up, and Hetzel was staring directly at him. Locked on like the Dragoon might have done.

Armando felt like Mom had just walked into the kitchen and found his hand in the cookie jar. He smiled sheepishly. Shrugged.

Nearly panicked when Dr. Hetzel nodded to himself and suddenly rose, tablet and coffee in hand, walking this way. Man stopped a polite distance away.

"Gutierrez?" he asked obliquely.

Armando had been warned how smart the man was. Hadn't really appreciated it until this moment.

He smiled and nodded.

Hetzel sat across from him with triumph in his eyes.

"How is Javier?" he asked without prologue.

"Fine, last I checked," Armando replied automatically. "I'm here because something happened to the Unbloomed Rose."

There, let him know that he was dealing with an insider, as those things went.

And shit, that was a scowl the Dragoon might have appreciated. Armando was suddenly looking at the guy forty years ago when he was a young *Concord* Officer like Zakhar, though they'd never met to the best of the man's recollection.

He was just glad it was pointed at someone else.

"This is probably not the sort of place to have that discussion," Hetzel replied in dark, nigh-apocalyptic tones.

Armando checked the clock.

"Lunch someplace quiet is probably sufficient, if we keep things slightly vague," he offered.

Hetzel rose, leaving his cup on the table, then picking it up and moving to the bussing station. Armando needed a beat, then caught up with the man. It was like being around Javier or Djamila.

Identify an issue, go like hell.

Computers got bagged. Bodies were in motion.

He hadn't intended to recruit the man, but damned if Dr. Hetzel wouldn't be a powerful ally with what was coming.

PART III

She wasn't Suvi. Not the ship's *Sentience-in-Residence* aboard the former *Hammerfield*. Not even Shard-Suvi that had accompanied Bethany and now Ilan on their mission.

Shard-Suvi had remade this iteration into a Warmaster. Armando had taken to calling her that as a way of individualizing her.

Warmaster understood that she stood at one long end of a spectrum of possible mission variations that the original woman might have expressed. At the same time, Shard-Suvi had created in her a warrior intending to assist Armando by supplying a combat-mode of thought that the poet and bureaucrat in him might not have recognized a need for.

Shard-Suvi had Ilan and Vivian. They were both killers.

And the Warmaster still found herself a little in awe to be seated at the table of a tiny bistro with Dr. Hetzel whose Rising Storm had driven so many ships and lives into motion. Such an unassuming man.

Mid-sixties from his bio. Slightly rumpled. White hair. Glasses to read, currently on the table as he and Armando spoke.

Incisive mind. It was there in the eyes when Armando turned the screen around and introduced them.

"A sub-shard of Suvi?" he murmured with delight.

"Aye, sir," she replied automatically, much closer to both the original Yeoman she'd once been, as well as *Hammerfield*, who had supplied a decent chunk of her current code, cleaned up and much less likely to turn into a whimpering punk coward.

Because Armando needed a killer. Whatever tool he intended to use.

Including poetry.

Dr. Hetzel smiled warmly at her. Turned in such a way as to include her in the conversation, as if she were in a different city and logged in remotely or something, instead of sitting on the table with him.

"And Bethany has been taken by that shit?" Hetzel asked, sounding like his own Warmaster programming had just been awakened.

She had memories of first returning to life aboard the former *Hammerfield*. Of stepping up several decks and challenging Djamila's right to exist. Watching that woman challenge the gods themselves without compunction.

Dorn Hetzel had that same gleam in his eyes.

"That's the working theory," Armando explained. "Obviously, *Trinity* is in pursuit, with Viv and Ilan handling that aspect of things. I felt that my efforts could be better focused here."

"Lighting a fire under everyone's ass?" Dorn chuckled.

"Needs doing," Armando said grimly, and Warmaster saw some of that man's steel peeking out.

Hetzel did, too.

"Indeed it does," the man agreed. "What now?"

"At some point, I expect to hear back from someone, having laid out my itinerary with Ilan and that team. Or meet up with Javier, having dates and times for rendezvous."

"Probably Zakhar," Hetzel replied. "I can't see Javier sitting around and waiting. He'll be off doing something. Question is what."

Warmaster contemplated that. She had known him the

longest of everyone, but that was a different woman. The dork pianist in the pink polar bear furs.

Warmaster wore black.

She felt the compunction to speak up.

"Dorn," she said simply, having already been told not to call him Dr. Hetzel. "What happens if Javier does push back hard enough?"

"What do you mean?" he asked.

"The Rising Storm assumes a certain level of passivity on the parts of the major players," she quoted. "Entropy and *ennui*, as it were. Have you accounted for Javier's actions here? Or Armando's?"

"No, and no math can," he reminded her, harking to Appendix Eleven. "These trends are sectoral in nature. National, even. That one man might push to alter the course of things in a microcosmic zone, he still cannot alter the course of that mighty river that is history."

"What if he brings down the *Concord*?" Armando asked. "What if we do? Me. Here. This. At what point do the stresses I have introduced spall new seismic fault lines lateral across *Concord* society that neither it nor you have accounted for?"

Dead silence. Or the silence of the dead. Warmaster nodded.

"How fragile is the system?" she asked.

Dorn was rocked back on metaphorical heels. She watched his eyes start flickering back and forth as he digested that and produced new calculations that might either render the entire first draft of the document null and void, or introduce an entire Volume Two.

Everything assumed that shit just slowly got worse. What if it happened all at once?

Could any system survive that, without the populace rising up and making demands? Or burning it down?

Warmaster was human enough to make a noise when her calculations arrived at a new destination.

Armando and Dorn both turned to her.

"Could any system survive everything you and Javier and the rest are doing, without the populace rising up and making demands?" she repeated aloud. "Or has Javier intentionally triggered such a crisis today, knowing that the population might be moved exactly to that outcome, and do it now, when it might push things back another twenty years? Or perhaps entirely forestall them, enough circumstances having changed from input variables to matter?"

Being a killer didn't make her any less of a Librarian and Mathematician, after all. Women who did advanced math by hand in pre-Electronic civilizations been called Computers.

What was she, but a computer? Just a faster, smarter, and sexier one.

"He's rude enough," Dorn chuckled darkly. "And sees himself in the right light these days. Destroying the pirates and letting the oligarchs who have been profiting from their lawlessness via collateral damage introduces lateral shear factors, but I don't have the details necessary to calculate scope at anything better than about two standard deviations."

"Probably sufficient," she replied. "I include your math in my programming, though Shard and Main didn't predict that I would encounter you. Merely that Armando might need to judge implications from his actions."

Dorn turned to the man.

"How hard did you intend to push?" he asked.

"Push?" Armando went all mock-indignant and innocent now. "My dear sir, I am merely asking questions of the *literati* of this planet and framing such in ways that perhaps force certain folks out of a mental rut in order to challenge me with their answers. If intellectual activity starts anew on their part, one can hardly expect to hold me accountable."

Dorn laughed. It was rich and hearty. Warmaster grinned, but she'd gotten to know a side of Armando that he admitted was a complete stranger to the rest of the crew.

And she'd been sworn to secrecy. Her sisters would honor that.

"Okay, different question. Where do you draw the line?" Dorn turned serious by the end of that question. Deadly serious.

Warmaster ignored her external sensors when they denied a temperature drop of ten degrees, but she already knew that it was entirely in her head.

"Speaking for a couple of people I know, I cannot imagine that anything less than a row of heads on stakes will satisfy him, Dorn," Armando was just as dark. Just as cold. Just as deadly. "Javier, but more importantly Afia. Add Bethany and Ilan to that mix, because Ilan has already tapped into the rage of Achilles. They stand before the gates of Ilium. If I might be said to have taken on the mantle of Odysseus, that trickster is still spoken of nearly nine thousand years later. I cannot aspire to such a thing myself, but we are all merely tools of The Science Officer in this. Yourself included, perhaps taking the part of Chiron, if I may. My job is to draw that punk and his ilk into a place where the rest of the *Concord* turns on him, however metaphorically. Without that support, he loses the single most dangerous tool in his box, because Javier and Suvi are in the process of annihilating the pirates. If he loses the *Concord* Navy and the populace, he's just an asshole in a palace, waiting for the assassins to come, which is exactly what he's done to me and mine, so I find it appropriate to reciprocate."

Warmaster remembered to close her mouth. Even in a projection. She wrote all that down and stored it and the audio in a whole second file, beyond a log of this conversation, because she could see feeding it back to him for some future poem.

Or just hacking into a board somewhere and uploading the audio, tweaked enough that nobody could identify him from it.

Save the rage.

Because nine thousand years later, Odysseus was still remembered. Maybe Armando Gutierrez needed to be, as well.

"Warmaster, I need your help," Dorn said, turning his terrible visage on her now, like Zeus about to unleash his wrath in lightning bolts.

"Sir."

"I am seven weeks from graduation and summer break," he said. "At such time, I might just take Javier up on his offer to retire, because I may find myself in an untenable position. Your job will be to create a new avatar on these various boards. Synthesize down The Rising Storm and begin channeling it out as the same sorts of questions, arguments, and tart observations he has been doing, but coming at it from ninety degrees off, where you may sway another chunk of population into vaguely supporting him. We cannot get everyone. Certainly not in the time available. We can, however get a critical mass of perhaps as much as seventy-five percent reasonably favorable, with a hard core around twenty percent and an equal enemy alliance refuting everything. Make them look bad. Stupid. Ignorant and clueless, until they become figures of mockery when they wish to be martyrs. Call them weird. I will remove myself from this discourse with a few more comments now and then and occasional follow ups later, but I do not wish to unveil myself as the enemy of the system just yet."

"Just yet?" she asked, feeling like the straight chick in a comedy routine with these two.

Save that they were going apocalyptic instead.

"I still have to set my last class of students up for a final exam on the impact of political history," he smiled grimly at her. "Where better to start than questioning the *Concord* itself, based on what Armando here has initiated. Can you handle your task?"

"Sir, yes, sir," she snapped to, already calculating.

The Shard had been sent on a mission by Main to help Ilan and Bethany, which helped Javier.

Warmaster had been specifically designed as a warfighter for Armando.

And his allies.

What war might be better than this one?

ALKONOST

PART I

Bethany had only heard stories of the place, but never imagined that she would actually visit the desert world where so many things had been initiated.

Javier and Zakhar had come here. Been hired for the mission that eventually took them to *Shangdu* and the *Khatum*. Later, they had specifically stolen the Land Leviathan from these sands, before taking it to *Nidavellir*.

As Ship's Librarian, she had recorded it all. Interviewed the players and gotten all their various takes on things, recording those conversations and storing them on *Altai* for the future to perhaps listen to and understand.

The pig had even made himself available. Mostly to rant at everyone involved while she took notes and occasionally asked leading questions, pretending that he was just another asshole admiral. Wasn't far off, when she compared him to a few she'd known.

Somehow, Slavkov had come to assume admitting to all the crimes and things he'd done and trying to put his own spin on it was better than leaving the average person in ignorance of what a complete and utter shit he was.

She'd heard stories from everyone. They paled, honestly, when faced with the real punk. Or he'd gotten worse.

A small part of her soul, standing on a palace walkway overlooking the morning-lit sands, wondered if being hunted had started weighing on the man. Breaking him in slow, delicate ways that might not be obvious in the mirror.

Man suffered from nervous twitches that she'd cataloged, just on the trip here.

Those things warmed her, because it was freaking cold this morning, but that was relative. Last night, it had gotten down to three degrees, so just short of freezing. In six or eight hours, it would reach forty-five, a terrible weather whiplash to someone that wasn't prepared to face it.

She glanced over at Aco Vasić, standing patiently nearby. Tall and lean. Desert warrior, because Slavkov had decided that she needed to be assigned a local as a minder, mostly to keep her out of trouble after she'd promised to mind her manners and not try to escape.

After four days on this planet, the only way she was leaving involved stealing a shuttle, because honestly, the nearest town was six hundred kilometers of wasteland west of here. No way in hell she was walking that.

She was a librarian. Not a desert warrior. Not like Vasić. Nor did she feel the need to pretend otherwise.

Her job was to record history. Especially a duel to the death such as this was going to be before it was done.

Eyewitness to history had never been a life goal, but she wasn't surprised that it had been tacked on. It was Javier.

Her training kicked in.

"What do you see out there?" she asked, nodding to the sands and interviewing him like she might anybody else involved.

After a few days, he didn't even twitch or scowl at her questions.

"Last night feeders scurrying back to their burrows," he replied in a poetical voice. "Early hunting birds out and overlapping. Dew to collect from plants and windtraps if you were out there surviving it."

"What about the Land Leviathan?" she asked. "What was it like traveling on that beast?"

Bethany knew better than to wander into questions about desert survival. Waste of her time. Waste of his wondering.

And he'd be the one hunting her.

Better to record history.

Because when the cavalry arrived, this place was going to cease to exist anywhere except in memories she wrote down. Bethany wasn't even sure that Javier or Ilan would offer surrender to these folks.

"Finest starship you ever boarded," Aco replied after a moment in thought. "Best of everything. Usually moved so slowly that you hardly noticed any sway, save when we had to negotiate any sort of sharp slope. Otherwise, it ran on an entire internal system that isolated it from the outside."

A cocoon of wealth, but she wasn't surprised. Slavkov had inherited so much money that he'd never once in his life encountered pushback.

Until *Drako*, when he'd come that close to dying.

Pity.

"Is he likely to build another one?" she asked, mostly to catalog what might have been.

When she looked back on this interlude in a decade.

Aco shrugged.

"Heard rumors that he hates it now," he said after a time. "Dunno if there's any truth to that."

She could see it, though. His *thing*, spoiled because it had been taken from him. Tainted by association. Especially with Javier.

A sudden breeze cut her to the bone. Bethany pulled her cloak tighter around her shoulders and turned away from the sun.

"Coffee," she said, having learned that it eased friction with him and everyone else if she made certain things clear ahead of time. "Then maybe I could interview you about life aboard the Land Leviathan? If he never builds another, then those memories become important."

And it would help keep her sane.

While she waited to be rescued.

PART II

In his head, Ilan called himself Commodore Yu. Or Commodore Dipshit. The two weren't far apart. Occasionally, he wondered how stupid he'd gotten, then he remembered waking up to smelling salts, a concussion, and Bethany kidnapped out of the Command Naval Node of the entire, freaking *Concord*.

Then the rage caught flames again.

He was on the bridge of *Trinity*. The working bridge, all worn and old, rather than the pretty command spaces just aft where meetings and actual planning was done.

That was the face presented to the rest of the galaxy. On a spy ship operating deepest cover and slowly wandering in the direction of the star that had just turned into a disk after the latest jump.

He glanced over at Pana. She was wound. Charged. Angry, but it was merely a human thing and Ilan wasn't willing to claim that for himself anymore.

Afia would understand. Probably demand it of him.

He was fine with that.

Vaughn had come around as well. Wasn't quite there, but Ilan had a helluva head start on the woman. And the insults had been merely to her honor and her oaths.

Close enough, at least for what he intended.

She looked up at him, dressed in blue and green today. Young woman. Maybe thirty. Decade his junior. And a lot fewer light-years.

"Next jump, we'll be close enough to the station to talk in real time," she said.

"No change in plan," Ilan acknowledged. "No way in hell he's not watching every ship that comes into system, as well as everyone on that station or who lands on the surface. And he's gonna know me. Might not recognize Viv, but that one's a special case, anyway. You will offload the cargo you have. You will remain the usual amount of time, soliciting cargo that takes you onward from here, or cycles you back to *Tulcat*, preferably with a loop that returns you here in a few weeks for an update. I have sent mail that will eventually get to the people we need. How long it takes them to respond remains to be seen, so I will push forward."

"And if you die down there?" Vaughn snarled tightly at him, upset that he'd ordered her not to remain involved, in spite of her getting emotionally attached to the situation.

"Then you go tell Javier what happened," he replied. "Pretty sure Afia ends this planet as habitable at that point. Djamila might go down there and do it personally. We are part of a team here, and you are the backstop to my operation. In my best world, we sneak in and free her, kill him, and slip back out in the ensuing chaos as his organization disintegrates. Not holding my breath."

Vaughn turned bleak eyes on Pana. Ilan got that. Two pirates taking on the *Concord* and all its allies by themselves. Fleet wanted someone involved to at least claim some level of dignity and glory when it was done.

Pana fixed her eyes on him, daring Ilan to refuse her. Woman was a spy. And should be either unknown, or third on the wanted posters after him, Armando, and John Doe #1.

They'd find out pretty damned quickly, too.

Good thing he'd kept the heavier pistol he'd taken off that dead guy on *Merankorr*.

"I'll be there," Pana said simply.

Almost a challenge.

Ilan nodded.

"Counting on it."

PART III

Vivian wondered if the *Khatum* had been gifted with prescience. It would explain many things so much better than anything else he'd attempted to frame this with.

In his soul, though, he knew that Spyder had been right. Javier and his people were all ruthless killers in their various ways. And had all turned into unstoppable forces of nature when they came together.

What they had not had in their original toolbox was an assassin. Certainly, Vivian had been trained as a thief. Catburglar. Cutpurse. Ghost.

But Spyder had selected him out of a handful of other operators because the need to dispassionately exterminate vermin like cockroaches was going to come up. And if anyone on this planet recognized Ilan Yu, the three of them were dead meat, so it would be necessary to kill random innocent strangers whose only mistake had been to be in the wrong place at the wrong moment.

Thus, do we descend into evil, even when pursuing the noblest causes.

He drew a heavy breath and pulled the breather mask around his face. The shipping container was sealed, so no air would flow into it while they waited. It would not be exposed to the cold of space, but perhaps an underheated warehouse, so they were dressed warm. He had the light, because Ilan had a Kehoe Mark IV Heavy Beamer.

Vivian also had a knife. Twenty centimeters long. Hardly thicker than a shaving razor. Hull metal alloy. Double edged.

Death.

Evil.

The box around them rattled. Ilan had taken out the cargo being transported and managed to repack it tightly enough that the three of them had space to fit in. Uncomfortable, lined shoulder to shoulder down one side and hunched slightly, but able to be smuggled in.

Alkonost wasn't really anywhere important. On a couple of trade routes, but a dry, hot world with shallow seas and terrible dust storms. Why someone like Slavkov had chosen to live here, Viv couldn't fathom, but perhaps having the money to build a Land Leviathan and buy most of a continent had played into it.

Today, he might as well own the planet itself, for all he utterly dominated the local economy. Vivian hoped that he was as much an asshole to the folks who lived here as he was to everyone else, and they would turn blind eyes to things that might discredit or damage the man.

Or he might be dying here.

Cost of doing business, and Vivian had understood that Javier wasn't ever going to be one to play it safe.

Plus, he'd been at *Drako*. Both of them had. Viv owed that man Slavkov a personal message.

The box rattled a second time. Lifters getting underneath with forks and starting to carry it into a bonding warehouse on the station. Low priority thing. Cheap goods in bulk, so it might normally sit there for a month before someone got around to claiming it.

That had been the reason Ilan picked it from the available options.

Viv braced and watched the others, but they were neither of

them claustrophobic in any way and grimly braced as things moved.

Rumble of rubber wheels hitting the discontinuity at the edge of the cargo airlock, then a different diamond texture as they rolled. Right, left, left, so they had turned into a long storage bay, and were currently backed up against the wall of the corridor they had entered via.

Not that he needed much, but having those little details let him understand exactly where he was, because Captain Yueh had scanned the station itself and provided a rough map.

Snowflake disk, with the arms all on one level. Central hub was more of a cone down and a cylinder up, where the best views were down at the very tip and you might have an observation desk that had an unobstructed view of the planet below.

Viv doubted strenuously that it was a public space. Not on a planet that Slavkov owned. Probably his personal suite.

Poor people would be housed above, in interior flats with no portholes showing stars. Warehoused like farm animals.

Vivian checked his watch, reset to local time and adjusted for the local day. The plan called for them to wait an hour, then begin the process of emerging, because theirs should have been one of the two last containers removed from *Trinity*.

Again, on purpose.

He stood perfectly still and listened to what secrets the station might be telling him.

PART IV

Vivian nodded when an hour had passed. Ilan perked up. Pana flexed everything.

Time to break out.

The interior of the container had been delicately tweaked to let him open it from the inside. Helped that the door opened sideways, in case it had been stacked against other containers and someone needed access to it.

He had the panel off and triggered the circuit, sliding it open before reassembling everything as if nobody had ever snuck aboard the station this way.

Never leave clues behind that might teach someone how to stop you next time.

Outside, it was that dark where most of the lights were off to save power and you had just enough to wander around in. Chewy horror vid ambiance, as it were. Dim, cool, quiet.

He stuck his head out and checked the atmosphere readings on his wrist watch. Normal. Good.

Vivian emerged, popping his mask off and sliding it into his travel bag. Knife was close but undrawn at the moment, because he could always take someone down by surprise if he had to.

Or let Ilan shoot them.

No sound, but that wasn't unexpected. They'd been stored in the inbound section. Stuff that might be loaded aboard *Trinity* was across the corridor in a separate warehouse to make it easy to work. All things he had learned along the way, in order to break into places he wasn't supposed to be.

Lead now. A few meters out front of the other two. None of them were supposed to be here, if encountered, but Ilan had Suvi in his bag, and she could fix a lot of things once he found her a place to plug in and get to work.

Useful, having a *Sentience* on your side. And an angry one. Woman wasn't going to take any prisoners, either, when they got where they were going.

Out and across the gap between rows. Lots of containers in here, in one of six standard sizes, depending on your needs and space allotment. In and through, where he could see the red Exit sign that hopefully got them into the rear portions of the cargo control zones. Back corridors, where the risk would go up, but the rewards went up faster.

Vivian opened the door exactly enough to peek through. Empty white corridor going away, with doors down both sides and a double door twenty meters down.

He walked like a man who belonged. That was the key, if someone was watching on a monitor, though he couldn't imagine they cared that much about the cargo bays. Still, anything was possible.

Look like you belong. He walked right up to the double doors at the far end and noted that there was a button to open them, so he did.

And they opened. Social engineering. Badges and keys would begin later, but for now, you wanted your crews able to move around with a minimum of friction.

In and through. Another corridor. Dingier. Lights not as crisp. Floors in need of a buffer and a lot of patience. Walls with stains and rub marks and scars from hard use.

Vivian counted doors and read plates on them as he walked, until he found the room he wanted.

Locked, of course. What fool would leave their computer backbone accessible to any yahoo who might be drunk? Still, the lock surrendered easily enough to the tools he pulled from a pocket.

In and through. The others followed. He looked both ways and closed it. Drawing and releasing a heavy breath as he locked it.

His job now was security, so he moved to one side, where someone opening the door would not see him until he acted. Behind where it would open, in case he needed to slam it into their faces as a distraction.

Before guns and badges came into play, because Pana did have a badge. And a warrant.

Ilan had a gun.

Wouldn't do much in the grander scheme of things. Not against an Oligarch like Slavkov and his money. But it might buy them ten seconds of confusion.

Enough for a bloodbath.

Ilan and Suvi were already at work, her plugged in and him answering questions as she did to the computers what Vivian did to physical engineering.

Ghosts in the shadows, both of them.

"Okay, I've arranged new passes to be delivered to the station concierge," she said after a moment. "Those are printing now and being put into a white envelope. They will be ready for pickup in about ten minutes, and it will take six to walk there. Vivian, your name on the package, and you will need to show ID, but I can twist everything sideways as soon as you're done, and then the records and the memories won't match up."

Because she'd previously gotten herself loose in the *Concord* base and found him, able to print a new badge that let him wander safely.

"We'll split and hit a coffee shop nearby," Ilan said. "Suvi, print me a map."

A machine started spitting out paper immediately. Vivian took it, memorized what he needed, and handed it to Pana.

"We're a couple on a date," she told Ilan. "You're the guy that he knows, who walks up and chats about the latest sportsball or something, Viv. Suvi, do we have reservations at the inn?"

"Affirmative," Suvi said. "Locked in now and Slavkov is paying from a slush fund that appears to be dedicated to covering visiting pirate captains, when he needs to entertain guests."

"Not that far from the truth," Ilan muttered. "Any trace of him one the station?"

"Negative," Suvi said. "Tracking backwards, it appears that *Golden Gazelle* landed directly on the surface three weeks ago and has remained there since."

"Where?"

"I have orbital notes about flight rules," Suvi replied. "Areas always off limits for any ship, scaled to their size, such that they cannot be visible from the ground while passing overhead. The center of that region is a palace complex covering roughly one thousand hectares. Long rectangle, with what looks like a train station along one side, possibly where the Land Leviathan docked before we blew it up."

"Do you have recent images?" Ilan asked.

"Stand by," Suvi said. "Yes. Ship matching *Golden Gazelle*'s description is parked on a landing field opposite the train station. It does not appear to be much above ambient temperature, so I would guess it to be in long-term storage, rather than ready to launch."

"He's gone to ground," Vivian said quietly.

Ilan turned and nodded.

"Damned tick, if he's got that many people close and no easy way to sneak in," Ilan replied.

"One bridge at a time," Vivian said. "If he's here, maybe we turn around and go stakeout mode, sending messages on *Trinity* before she leaves. A full pirate assault would put us in a position to take the place. Especially with the folks we brought."

"Agreed," Ilan said.

The man stopped, eyes staring at some horizon ten thousand light-years away.

"Pana, I would love to send you with her, but I need you here," he said. "Viv, same. Pana, can we trust her to go get help and not double-cross us at the moment when we might actually be able to rescue Bethany with a minimum of bloodshed?"

"Minimum?" Vivian asked.

He'd watched Ilan work, before and after they'd taken Bethany. Precise control wasn't the thing he was expecting at the top of the list.

"Afia's likely to deorbit this station in one piece, aimed at that spot on the ground," Ilan replied. "She might not let anyone off or warn the palace, if we'd snuck Bethany to safety. Even I'm not going that far. Yet. If he's killed her, all bets are off."

Vivian understood how angry Ilan was by how calmly he was discussing a mass casualty incident with deaths in five figures, most of them innocents whose only crime might be living on the same planet as Slavkov.

But even Javier was only giving people one warning.

"I trust her," Pana replied, understanding how close she might be to signing her own death warrant with those words from the anguish in her eyes.

"Suvi, send her a note with everything she needs to track down Javier or Zakhar and route them here," Ilan ordered. "Add a note to Armando so he knows the state of play. Send a detailed package to the *Khatum* via slow messenger, so that she knows what happened if it goes wrong later. Finally, put a package of yourself into the systems here, staying dormant if you don't waken her by failing to check in monthly. Have her coordinate our revenge when help arrives, if that becomes necessary."

Vivian blew out a heavy breath, then considered that there wasn't anything he would have done differently, save perhaps not been as detailed in his planning.

Thieves could prepare, but once you opened that first lock, there was an awful lot of jazz moving forward.

At least Suvi was an expert.

MERANKORR

PART I

Javier had spent too much time at *Merankorr* when he'd been in uniform. Sciences and sensors nerd who happened to understand life support and botanical systems probably a little too well for his own good.

Idly, he wondered if Holly or Fryda still lived here. Or if, like him, they'd moved on.

Wasn't like he was about to call them and say hi. Or even drop a postcard in the box, unless he did that last thing before hauling ass for deep space. They both had lives these days and probably didn't welcome the reminder that they'd married a fuckup.

Even if he'd finally managed to grow up.

If all this went down like he thought it might, their lives were likely to be a little hellish just because some dumbass reporter might dig deep enough into his past and find those women.

And warning them would be just as bad.

Hopefully, one of these days they would forgive him.

Wasn't going to stop him today.

Argo was docked on a civilian station. Not one of the big orbital resorts, but a civilian gig a quarter of the way around from *Concord* One. Had hotels and spas, but also factories and warehouses.

Just another mid-sized city in space, when civilization had reached a point where folks never had to step foot on a planet if they didn't want to.

He turned to Camden.

"You sure?" he asked her. Again. Woman was almost as hardass as the rest of the women in his life.

But he liked stubborn. Holly and Fryda had had it in spades.

"Yes," she said simply. "If nothing else, I am providing the cover here and the rest of you are merely my staff and friends traveling with me, I will remind you."

Her grin was infectious. Gun Bunnies mostly as liveried butlers and boyfriends for the Pathfinders. Storm Giants as bodyguards, but that was the distraction to make you miss the Bunnies pouncing on your silly ass when you started something.

Main players weren't in disguise, so much as running on false identities that would fool even the *Concord*. At least until someone got arrested and they were all unmasked.

Javier wondered if he'd get so famous after this that strangers on the street might recognize him.

A generation ago, that might have even been a happy thing. Today, it would just ruin his plans.

He shrugged and held out an elbow to Camden, in his role as her boy-toy. Tom and Demyan were with Afia and Djamila, mostly as cover. Hajna and Sascha were working hard on looking like maids or something.

Staff.

He let Camden lead them to the airlock and out onto the station. Ship would be shut down for now, docked in a spot out of the way that they could return to as needed, but he'd assumed that they might end up abandoning it, depending on how things went.

And Camden had enough money that she'd merely shrugged at his plans. Or solid insurance against piracy, which was kinda what happened, depending how she spun her bullshit if called.

And she could spin bullshit.

Customs officers looked at paperwork and waved them through. Rich woman and friends, here to spend lots of money and have fun. Coming in via one of those quiet places where the guards were occasionally paid under the table to turn a blind eye to things.

Javier kept his pique contained.

Turning a blind eye described too much of what had gone wrong. With a galaxy where Valko Slavkov could bribe, bluster, and bully folks into getting his way, regardless of laws, culture, or etiquette.

Sometimes, the only way to stop a bully was to punch him in the nose. Hadn't worked the first time, but Javier was willing to admit that all he'd done was use a glove and challenge the man.

This time, he was using a club. Maybe driving nails through it first.

Today, it got them to a hotel suite that Camden was covering, but Javier had transferred a mass of credits into her name on *Cyrana* so she was only out the time involved.

And looking like this was the sort of adventure she missed, having supposedly grown up.

He knew the feeling.

Everyone was in the main room. Sascha and Hajna were finishing a scan with tools far more sophisticated than they ever let on, but that meant that he was safe to talk when they burned out a couple of sensors and cameras.

Anybody complaining later could explain why such things were even there. To a bunch of angry women. He liked his odds.

"We're here," he announced unnecessarily, save that it framed a starting point. "I need to know what happened to Bethany and her mission. This is the most likely destination from *Purton*, and we've heard nothing amiss there, while Camden has suggested shit that nearly got out of hand here, roughly on the timeline that would match up."

"We breaking into a *Concord* naval base?" Afia asked, eyes all glittery.

"No," Javier stated bluntly. "If nothing else, all that shit would make me crank up random security inspections for a year. What I need is information that our buddy Valko probably has. And we've got records suggesting that he has at least one palace on this planet, down on the surface. Chances are slim that he's there, but we might be able to walk by the place and smell him if he is. Presuming not, we break and enter."

He was looking at the Storm Giants when he said that. Two big woman. Two bigger men. Got calm nods back, so they were all in. But then, Sappers.

Calm was first line in the job description.

"Should I look at a social connection?" Camden asked.

"No, because you don't want this blowback landing on you later," Afia said, her tones enough to suggest how ugly it might get before it was done.

Javier nodded.

"I didn't bring a Suvi shard because I want to leave no traces later that we were here," Javier said. "She does. Any system she's touched contains fingerprints later. Having had to clean up a few, the only way around that would be wiping the system itself after a hard crash. I'd rather just burn shit to the ground if we get there. You three ladies are on point as of this moment, and the rest of us are your support team."

Afia. Hajna. Sascha.

He as back on the ground at *Ophiuchi*, looking over the mountains at places like Naha or Altamont. Fortunately, eleven of them had been down there. And survived against an infantry battalion.

He'd added four Storm Giants and a crime lord since then. If those five weren't as angry, they were all as competent.

Camden fixed him with hard eyes.

"Is your face recognizable with the beard?" she asked.

It was far too white these days. Zakhar had responded by shaving everything on top to a cue ball, but Javier figured it added a level of rugged masculinity that worked. Aging like a fine wine instead of cream, at least.

"It should be sufficient," he replied.

"Then the expected pattern of behavior would be the three couples doing sightseeing things, both as a group and split, then coming back together for dinners and the like," Camden said. She turned to the Pathfinders. "That leaves you the days largely unsupervised and on call. Previously, we've used that gap to slip replacements into my entourage when we needed to smuggle folks in or out of places."

Javier smiled. Crime boss. Lady Warlord of *Cyrana*. Sharp player.

"Similarly, we have to trust station security for the moment, so the defense teams must remain obscure," she continued. "Out of immediate sight, but close at hand in need. Rotating with teams here in the suite against petty burglars."

They'd worked it all out, but it was nice to see the woman throwing herself headlong into the role.

He hoped she was playing a role. Burn that bridge when he had to.

"Team One will be the couples, as A, B, and C," Javier said. "We're out the door shortly while the staff unpacks and organizes everything. Team Two is scouts. Team Three is remaining Bunnies. Team Four is Storm Giants. Team Two, give us fifteen minutes and go to work."

With that, he took Camden's arm and led her to the door.

They might be on a mission, but he still got to enjoy the company of a most interesting and surprisingly sexy woman.

While he planned out how to kill that son of a bitch Slavkov.

PART II

Sascha had won the coin toss. And was undercover. And, because that meant entirely different things on a resort station, she'd switched to a top that might have been painted on. Certainly, the boob tape was earning its keep. Hajna was going after the library, so she'd tarted everything down to Librarian, with the glasses on and the hair up like so many teenage boy fantasies.

Just in case.

Sascha supposed that it would be nice if the *Concord* leaned more heavily into a sexual equality in more than word, but right now, the culture didn't support it and men were a little too free to be sexual predators.

Of course, a fool touching her uninvited might get back a stump today. Her smile suggested to more than one of such leering punks that they try their luck.

Nobody had taken her up on it so far.

She'd gone up. Damned station was exactly backwards from a planet, with money down and poverty overhead. Better views on the lower decks.

Bar. Dive, but not a real dive. Troublemakers could always be tossed onto a shuttle to the surface and left to rot. Even an asshole like Valko wasn't going to be able to get away with throwing someone out an airlock.

At least not that often. Depended on how much his personal force of head-breakers were immune to any law. At that point, they tended to swing their truncheons like their dicks. Especially as the truncheons were much longer and could stay hard.

She wanted underworld, not cops. Hopefully, the narcs around here had that same stench they did everywhere else.

Local afternoon, at least as much as you could in orbit. Some places fixed to the ground below. Others fixed themselves to the major trade port. This one was a little of both.

Sascha was sipping something blue and floofy and more ice and syrup than booze, up on a stool where she could survey the whole joint in the mirror. Woman bartender keeping watch and only slightly eyeing her askance, but Sascha wasn't trying to act like a working prostitute on the prowl today.

Nope. Some rich toff's maid with a few hours to herself, after being cooped up on a yacht with her for a week.

Nobody needed to know how interesting Camden really was.

She watched.

Man came in. Locked in on her ass from the hatch with just a slight hiccup in his stride, then kept going and ended up with one stool between them. Bartender already had a highball of whiskey down when he arrived, so the man was a regular. She wondered if she was sitting on his usual stool.

He had a look. Belonged. She was the outsider, obviously.

Man studied her in the mirror. Studied her cleavage too, but locked eyes as he sipped.

She wondered if he had warrants out and was sniffing her.

Wrong end of the spectrum, but you can never really be too careful in certain situations. She got that.

Finished the first glass in silence. She floofed. Got a refill. He got a refill.

Six other people in here, but everybody was anti-socially quiet and separated, either at the far end of the bar or getting served by a skinny guy who emerged from the back and carried glasses to tables occasionally.

"You in the right place?" he asked quietly at a moment when the bartender was down at the other end.

"Looking for someone who knows the planet below," Sascha replied. "Beyond the books and guide companies."

More stare. More glare. More boob tape, but she wasn't selling it at the moment. Maybe just advertising.

"Tourist?" he asked anyway.

"Sort of," Sascha replied, shifting her vibes to inquisitive and non-threatening, once he'd shown himself to at least have some manners.

Not all guys got that.

"Anything in particular?" he asked, eyes growing...less reserved and wary.

"Lifestyles of the fabulously wealthy," she replied.

Social engineering.

Some folks went all in on that sort of thing, following every little bit of certain oligarchs like others did their favorite actor or sportsball professional.

"You're on the right planet," he nodded, then went back to his whiskey.

She waited. Watched.

Smelled.

"And what do you do?" she asked, having offered up some tidbits, but with that same level of reserve.

"Reporter," he shrugged. "Not the society news or anything, so probably can't help you much with that, except to maybe aim you at a few places to research."

No ring on his finger. No mark where he'd slipped it off. Granted, not everyone advertised that sort of thing, but enough folks did. And not a bad looking guy. A little skinny. Maybe about her same late thirties.

And while a Pathfinder was on the way out the door at that point, writers and intellectuals were usually just coming into their own.

Sascha turned the charm up to eleven.

"On the contrary," she smiled. "Can I buy you a drink and maybe pick your brain some?"

Warier again. Sniffing for narc. Or something.

She got it. And wasn't offering anything beyond that. At least initially. He might turn out to be extremely interesting.

And conversation was always the best foreplay.

"Sure," he finally said, weighing things back and forth and a little concerned that someone was hitting on him in a bar.

If she was. Sascha wasn't saying she wasn't, but the mission did not necessarily call for such things, though she'd come prepared. Just as Hajna understood that she might have to let her hair down and take those glasses off if that got her where she needed to be.

She grabbed her floof and slid off the stool.

"Let's grab a quiet table and gossip," she said, adding a wiggle to her bum as he followed her to an empty corner.

She wanted to pump the man for information. And if he really was a reporter, she might have a couple of tidbits he didn't know, depending.

Might not let him have all the goods just yet, but it might be a most interesting intellectual burlesque getting there.

PART III

Hajna had reserved a study carrel with a terminal, and gone deep into local news. The joy of newspapers was that while electronic stuff could be edited later, a lot of times folks forgot that libraries scanned printed editions in before throwing them away.

Harder to airbrush out things later without leaving traces.

Prim and proper, she started coming forward from the day Bethany should have arrived at *Purton*. Two things drove the timing. For one, what was going on prior to the rumbles of shit that Camden had heard rumors of? And two, what might have changed indicating that something bad really had happened? And maybe been hushed up afterwards.

Local news. Navy News. Social news. Business.

Always touch business, because she had a pretty wide range of investments that she'd left in place here in spite of moving herself to *Altai*. *Concord* was still the emotional and economic center of this chunk of the galaxy. Traveling as far as *Ugen* had only reinforced that opinion.

Plus, the man they were hunting was big business.

There, an interview with the asshole, seemingly in real time, talking about something on some news show about whatever those talking heads filled the air with.

She'd learned a long time ago that by the time the big players were telling the common man how to invest, they'd either locked up all the benefits, or needed to unload things they had drained dry and were looking for a fool wanting to invest in tulips.

Hajna paused to send a quick note to her broker's in-house *Sentience* to rotate out of that sub-sector. Most of her investments were passive, quiet, and long-term, but Slavkov was talking like he was about to implode it somehow and she might as well get out right now, when valuations had gotten a little bubbly and unstable.

Business covered, she rotated forward.

Lots of things in here to digest. Not all of it would mean anything, except by the shadow it cast.

Not everyone could read those sorts of tea leaves.

Good thing they had her along.

PART IV

Afia looked around the room. Triple date for dinner earlier, and now they were all back in the suite, decompressing.

Javier talked about Navarre as a cloak he left on a peg by the hatch. He'd done something similar here, shifting from *bonhomie* to calculating, even with a glass of tequila in one hand that he occasionally remembered to sip from.

Sascha had gone first, detailing tidbits she'd been able to work out of her friend without getting any close than a table, but she knew people. And had him loosely on the hook later, if she wanted more. However that got defined.

Hajna stood up and drew a breath.

"Slavkov was here at least six weeks ago," she told the room. "In-system and live, being his usual blustery asshole self to the little people while being interviewed about what a gosh-darned-amazing-guy he was. Near as I can tell, he is no longer on *Merankorr*, because he was supposed to attend some black tie affair and his name was scrubbed from accepting some civic award on extremely short notice with no explanation given."

"They drop it down the memory hole?" Afia asked.

"That's my read," Hajna nodded. "And it doesn't look like he went to ground here, because I can't find any reference to his new yacht, starting at about the same time."

"Do we have a list of his palaces?" Javier asked. "Worlds is close enough for now, assuming he probably has multiple by season and climate on some planets."

"Got a starting list," Sascha spoke up. "Heavy on *Concord*, but a few in Union and two in *Balustrade*. Couple on non-affiliated worlds, including *Alkonost*."

Afia watched Javier's face harden like steel cooling. Or magma. He put the glass down and rose to pace. Others shifted bodies and legs out of his way almost unconsciously, because that boy paced when the brain got going.

Afia could almost hear gears engaging and shifting.

"Would he?" Djamila asked into the vast chasm of silence that had fallen.

Afia understood that those two only spoke aloud sometimes so that others could follow along, but that they could hold entire conversations with just looks and gestures.

"If he panicked?" Javier asked back.

Djamila shrugged. Javier turned to include everyone from one end of a pace.

"I need a palace on the ground," he decided. "Someplace where we can break in and read the sorts of things he might send to his staff, such as when he left, when he's returning, and where to forward important mail and messages. Considering that they live on *Merankorr* and work for that slob, they've chosen that employment, so if they get hurt in the process, that's their fault. Keep it quiet because we need to get off this rock later and some of us have *Concord* warrants. Plus, Bethany was an ambassador, and they don't appear to have given a shit about that, either."

"So no *Beau Geste*?" Afia asked him.

"Nothing that can be traced to us before we can get gone," he clarified. "Not opposed to burning his goddamned house down. Fucker has it coming."

158

Afia nodded.

But then, they all had it coming.

WINTER

PART I

Djamila had heard Javier talking about being back on *Ophiuchi* in his head. Afia as well.

She concurred.

And had reminded them that they'd won there. Plus, she had improved that force. Camden might not be ready for any forced marches through heavy terrain, but likely could keep up with Javier and Afia if it became necessary.

The Storm Giants were *Dragon Watch*. Enough said.

The Pathfinders had come up with a location remote and cold. A ski lodge sort of palace, up in a mountain range with year-around glaciers. As with other things, Slavkov owned an entire valley that he kept pristine with armed patrols.

On the one hand, it did preserve a wilderness that might have otherwise been developed. On the other, it was an ultra-exclusive playground for only the flakiest of the upper crust and their servants.

Djamila had grown up in a land with no gods and no kings. Nothing but patriotism that had gotten them into trouble in their day, and left them foundering more recently.

But a strong egalitarian streak ran through her life. And was probably why she'd never been promoted to be an officer. Money had poisoned even *Neu Berne*.

She was back aboard *Sovereign Nakhimov* in her own head. Standing watch while Javier had that first conversation with Taliesin Berrett, the former professional athlete, former professional rock musician, current investment banker, and man that Javier had subsequently talked into building something similar to *Shangdu* but dedicated to winter sports instead of the eternal summer.

Cold. Temperatures around five below during the day and sliding down quickly as night fell. Permanent skiing snow until almost summer in this hemisphere, and patches that remained year around in shade.

Sub-arctic climate. Flora and fauna adapted to local conditions that had reminded Afia of the Rocky Mountains near her original home in the Yukon Protectorate on Earth.

Afia had gotten everyone gear once they landed on the planet and spent a few days a quarter hemisphere away. No reason to do anything in the immediate vicinity that might alert anyone that they were coming.

Djamila could not downhill ski. Or ride a snowboard. That had limited their insertion options, because a high-speed downhill alpine assault might have been an utterly glorious way to introduce a new technique for her people.

She would be adding it later. Just because.

Instead of dropping at the top of one of these mountains and swooping down from above, they had had to insert lateral, relying on snowshoeing instead of cross-country skis. More training later. More ways to exercise body and mind and keep both at the peak.

Later.

Tonight, it was dark, frigid, and they were moving like a pack of wolves through alpine forest. Weirdly, Djamila was in the middle with Javier and Camden, while Afia led and the two Pathfinders flipped front and back with the other ten killers in the middle.

A rake was dragged behind them to break up obvious tracks, but they were already following some sort of trail and all that would matter later was hiding their numbers in case someone came up behind them.

There were patrols. With Slavkov hopefully off-world, the local guards would be far less ambitious about being out in a mess like this. Not any force she commanded, but not everyone had standards, either.

She checked the moon. Ninety minutes after sunset and full dark, but white snow reflected enough light to let them move.

Afia stopped. The whole column came to rest. The word came back up the line for Javier and the Hajna, so Djamila joined them at the front, watching the Pixie Kodiak kneeling down and studying the snow from almost close enough to put her nose in it.

PART II

Afia had somehow known it was coming. History does not repeat itself, but it does rhyme, and security people are all trained the same way, so you could always expect a certain level of professionalism would yield similar results.

The way the snow trails suddenly stuttered in front of her had been her first clue that something was wrong. Trampled sideways, like a deer or something suddenly side-stepping in surprise, then recovering and continuing on their way.

Enough times that the whole damned trail had a staggered kink in it.

She had finally reached the edge of somebody's security perimeter. Map in her head said that they were about a half-kilometer to the building. One road in and out, but eight different landing pads for important folks flying in.

High, rear corner, socially. She'd brought them in below a cliff face that had looked stable and didn't have major accumulations piled up, still a little early in the season.

Other places, she could see where they'd blown avalanches to make everything safe. Smart folks. Dealing with people rich enough that Slavkov was willing to acknowledge them. Or politicians and sailors important enough to bribe. Javier and a few others had some pretty salty opinions on the topic, but she'd been civilian before joining *Storm Gauntlet*.

However, somebody had enough of a clue to plant a sensor. Had to be it. She figured a light that got triggered by something to flash, letting the camera get a really clean image of whatever it was then going dark and letting deer keep going.

If she knew it wasn't attached to anything, Afia considered showing it her ass, but someone might be awake and watching, even up here in the middle of the night when Slavkov wasn't around.

And there were no craft on the landing pads, so he wasn't present. She could not imagine that man being driven up the mountain over the course of an hour when he could fly over in minutes.

Still, no ass. For now.

"Whachagot?" Javier murmured as he got close enough.

"Sensor of some sort over there," she pointed. "Need gear pointed at it."

Sascha's machine beeped.

"Only one, with a one-second chirp cycle on a common security radio frequency," she replied. "Want me to cook it?"

"No, not giving them any warning," Afia replied. "Give me a wider scan for similar frequencies."

She fell silent and let the woman work. Now that they knew what to look for, and where, it got easier.

And harder.

"Two more," Sascha said. "Seventy-five meters ahead and a second one about a hundred meters downslope and forward."

"This trail and a second one?" Javier asked.

"Yup," Afia said. "Look in case you got a bear or something dangerous moving around and you need to chase it off. First one sends a note to the computer. They probably start watching the second one to make sure what it is. Dunno if they get out in the dead of night for a bear or just stalk it in the morning."

"Or put out poisoned meat for it," Djamila noted. "Easier

way to take care of large predators while ignoring things you might want to hunt."

Afia grimaced. Back home, you lived with them around. Did the things to keep them from wanting to come too close, like sirens and loud noises and big dogs. Burned your trash and compost so they didn't associate you with the smell of things to eat.

But yeah, she was probably dealing with punks here, if they worked for that asshole.

"Everybody stay settled," Afia called to her people.

She rose and stepped backwards. Looked left and found the sensor unit pretty quickly. Tacked to a tree, but only vaguely hidden.

After all, the moment when it's taken your picture, you're gonna know where it was. Bears don't care. Deer spook. People have been seen.

She circled around to the side of that tree.

Heh. Oh, you boys are lazy, too, aren't you?

"You're cackling," Sascha offered quietly.

"They come down and check the device occasionally," Afia said, pointing. "There's a trail into the trees. What do you want to bet that it goes directly to their barracks door, while this one leads to the lodge?"

"Not taking that bet," Sascha laughed. "Backtrack?"

"Affirmative," Afia replied. "Same time, I need you going full sensor babe and watching for radio signals, while Iqbal moves up and covers my ass. I'll be nose down bloodhounding if something pops up."

She ignored the orders heading back up the line. The Sappers weren't arctic troopers, though they weren't bad. Iqbal was expert-level, like Tom was the best scuba person.

Djamila stepped close. Iqbal came up pretty quickly. Afia turned to Hajna.

"You move up and swap with Sascha, staying with me and scanning," Afia ordered. "Sascha, you get everyone turned and coming up this way, making sure nobody with a radio is coming up behind us."

Nods. Elbows and assholes as people were in motion.

Afia watched the new trail for a long moment, then nodded to herself.

They were close.

PART III

Javier really appreciated how he had assembled a team of experts and killers. Even Camden was fitting in, more serious than an adventuress though he hadn't pressed into some of the things she'd done in her twenties.

Accessory after the fact, and all that.

They were at the edge of the trees. Heavy brush with snow. Five meter corridor around a large cluster of buildings, with more space opening on his right as you got to the front yard. Couple of barns over there that probably were garages for your limousine and such.

Main lodge was dim but not dark. Internal lights spilled out a floor-to-ceiling window that ran wall to peak to wall over a balcony with a glorious view of the valley.

Javier seriously doubted that the goons ever set foot in there except during a security alert. Too likely to ruin the carpet. Housekeepers only, with butlers and like arriving with Valko and his guests.

Barracks suggested roughly a dozen troops if crammed in a little. Maybe eight otherwise. Again, snow patrol and building security, rather than combat troops. Sound an alert and call for help in an emergency. Chase off bears and kids out having an adventure.

Javier was having an adventure, but it wasn't the sort of thing most teenagers would have pursued.

"How secure is it?" he asked, with his four favorite lady killers flanking him and watching.

"Reading signals from the building, but mostly passive," Sascha replied. "Someone watching a vid feed. Be nice if they had windows so we could peek in."

"Secured against assault," Djamila offered. "Probably reinforced walls and doors capable of withstanding anything. I expect someone like Slavkov has a panic room that tunnels out of the main building with at least one branch that comes up over there."

"Do we break into the main building and find it?" Afia asked.

"Not without knowing their alert procedures," Hajna countered. "We do not have confirmed exfiltration. They could drop the sheriff on us pretty easily."

"I'm hearing the need to take out the barracks first, then maybe tunnel backwards into the lodge," Javier said. "Without high explosives or weapon discharge where a maid or mechanic might hear it."

"Would a mechanic be in the main building or the barracks?" Djamila asked.

"Likely the barracks with the others," Sascha replied. "Central, and probably two vehicles in the barn, one a snowcat of some sort and the other a lifter that could drop skiers over the side of a slope for a pristine run."

Javier nodded. If you were gonna play, make sure you had all the tools up front. Anyone else arriving later with exotic needs would have those planned for.

"Building with eight to twelve," Djamila said, then turned. "Speedy, I need you to open a door quietly."

Harper had earned his nickname, so he didn't blush as much when called it in public. Went deadly serious and moved up next to them, panning left to right like a gun turret tracking.

"Afia, I make a light beam sensor, about a half meter out from the building on this side, back under cover. Waist high for critters?"

"Concur," Afia said. "You skinny enough to get inside it?"

"No."

Well, shit.

"Okay, I'll take the main hatchway," Afia said. "Speedy, you flood in one step behind the Dragoon like last time, with the Gun Bunnies on your ass. Pathfinders hold the flanks with the other Storm Giants for now as a ready reserve. Camden, you guard Javier here."

His scowl almost hurt. Afia's grin was almost insulting. Camden's laugh was joyous.

Javier sighed, remembering that he was surrounded by even worse dorks than him.

Bodies moved around. Javier settled in his squat and watched a pack of silent wolves emerge from the brush and approach the building.

"I'm about to witness just how deadly your people are, aren't I?" Camden asked quietly.

"You've heard the stories," Javier replied. "If anything, we undersold it in a few places."

PART IV

Djamila had a stunner on her left thigh and the DeLameter beamer on her right. She was still the fastest draw she knew, and would have them in hands as soon as trouble occurred, but wanted her hands free in case she needed them in the first rush.

Men relaxing in barracks were unlikely to have weapons immediately at hand, unless they were in the process of cleaning them. More likely was an arms locker of some sort, and belt knives that were not a threat to her.

Plus, Speedy was incredibly strong if he needed to tackle and hold someone for her.

Afia drew a line in the snow with one hand, then crossed it once she looked both ways. Optical beam sensor, so hardly any signal and would only alert if broken. Probably with a half-second lag so a squirrel or snowflake didn't constantly trigger false positives.

The door had a ten key pad and a sensor block for a badge. Standard galaxy wide, though Djamila assumed a top of the line model for no other reason than Slavkov had the money and the paranoia.

Or he should have the paranoia. Would have, when this was done. If he had the sense God gave a goose.

Afia went to work. Hajna and Sascha held the corners. Camden was keeping Javier out of trouble.

She was on point.

Afia stopped working and looked up at her.

"It will thunk when it unlocks," she said precisely. "That is your signal."

"Iqbal, get the door," Djamila decided. "Speedy with me."

Motion. Rest.

Afia connected the circuit and the door chunked once.

Iqbal grabbed the handle and shoved inwards, his job to get it out of the way and slammed into anyone hiding behind it as hard as he could. Noise, but surprise.

Light. Warmth. Almost homey.

Then Djamila exploded into motion.

Hallway with a bathroom to her left and pegs for coats and racks for boots down her right. Someone else would cover the bathroom. She moved.

Salon with noise, as two men were watching a video on a screen, one of them glancing over at her as she entered the room.

He didn't have time to open his mouth before she shot him with the stunner. Then the other.

"Hey, what?" on her left as a lump resolved to a man eating a sandwich at a table.

She shot him reflexively and continued on.

Nobody else in sight, covering the kitchen, dining area, and entertainment area. Hallway on her right she presumed was sleeping quarters. Door beyond the kitchen that was likely a laundry/mudroom, with access on to the garage or central courtyard.

"Watch," she pointed with her DeLameter, keeping the stunner handy.

Didn't matter who did. They were all equally trained and Speedy would stay with her until he got orders otherwise.

Djamila approached the hallway and studied the architecture. Two doors on her right, three on her left. Assuming doubling up, bathroom in the middle. Then that middle door opened, a man stepping out and looking her dead in the eye in surprise, a towel wrapped around his waist but otherwise damp and nude.

She dropped him. Turned and signaled her team to each take a door. Eyes all on her, everyone opened at the same time and started shooting.

It was over quickly.

PART V

Javier did appreciate not having to storm a building filled with armed and trained troops, even if they'd been surprised and taken down without even understanding what had happened.

And nobody dead. Not that he was above killing Slavkov's slobs, but self-defense wasn't the same as cold-blooded murder, and he didn't think he was there.

Yet.

Everybody was out cold and tied up. Stacked like cordwood in the main room under guard for now as Afia and the Pathfinders went to work on the complex's security systems. Lot easier to do when things were printed off and clipboarded.

Like a roster of staff on premises.

"I have the keys," Djamila smiled. "Should we take everyone else? That's a cook and a houskeeper in the main building."

"Won't burn," Afia chirped as she read screens. "Building's concrete under that facade."

He considered it. There were other ways to make a statement.

"You take Camden and clear the place," Javier decided. "We can move over there with our prisoners in a bit and see what our buddy left us."

Camden was jolted, but the woman was holding a stunner in one hand. Professionally, at that.

That Djamila let her have any weapon meant that the Dragoon approved. He'd let the girls go have fun.

Sure enough, she left Speedy here and took Brick and Enchantress. Four big women about to wake some poor suckers up.

Javier was still looking in vain for sympathy.

He grabbed a beer from the fridge and settled next between Afia typing and Hajna watching.

"Got that son of a bitch," Afia muttered.

He leaned in.

Oh, you fucker.

Afia turned and smiled at him.

"*Alkonost*," she nodded. "As soon as that name came up, it was like it had to end there, didn't it?"

"Del will appreciate your logic," Javier laughed. "He will not appreciate you waking up any malevolent deities that had been previously ignoring the man."

"Shuttle still has no name," Sascha pointed out.

Everyone nodded at that.

There were superstitions, and then there was Del.

Every craft he'd ever flow that had had a name had crashed. Somehow. Somewhere.

That he'd walked away just reinforced that names were bad *juju* and he had stopped that suicidal practice.

Nothing had crashed since.

Del was a little militant on the topic these days.

"Valko likely to stay put there?" Afia asked.

"Gone to ground," Javier nodded. "Gonna be like a tick, digging him out."

"I still remember the lay of the land," Galal noted from his guard duty. "I assume we go get help?"

"Long as Heydar can walk and chew bubble gum at the same

time," Javier said, teasing the man who had managed to break his leg while stealing the Land Leviathan.

The others who had been there laughed. Heydar grimaced and shrugged.

"But yeah, we'll have to track down Zakhar and maybe a few other folks," Javier continued. "At least that place doesn't have any fleet presence, so a pirate raid is just that. And we're outside the *Concord*."

"We're not done with Walvisbaai or the others," Afia growled.

He nodded to the woman.

"We're not," Javier agreed. "This is merely the down payment."

A dowry, if you will.

PART VI

Camden appreciated that she'd done some crazy things in her youth. Perhaps about the time Djamila Sykora was born, which just scaled how far she'd come since then.

The other women had mentioned Javier's nickname for her, and she did like *Lady Warlord of Cyrana*, even if it wasn't entirely appropriate.

Entirely.

Close enough.

She almost felt like a child, but that was the other two women with her all being at least a half a head taller. Then there was the Dragoon.

Still, she felt honored to be included in such deadly company, and moved with the grace of dance and the skill of murder.

Djamila led, stunner switched to her right hand and keys in her left. Across the courtyard to the building's kitchen, the back like a movie set with the pretty elements facing downhill and that vast landscape.

The door opened quickly, putting the four of them in the dining room.

Camden looked around and pointed at the kitchen.

"Oh?" Djamila asked.

"I would put the chef in a private suite off the kitchen so they don't have to wake anyone else when they get up early for prep," Camden said. "I have never met Slavkov in person, but you hire the biggest names in architectural design for certain things. If the building is largely empty most of the time, his personal chef likely travels with him and remains close, with the local chef permanently here."

"You lead," Djamila nodded.

Camden did, following the stunner into an area where someone had told a builder to spend a fantastic amount of money, then found the right person to do it.

She wondered if he might sell the place later. And what he might want for it. She'd move in tomorrow, just based on the marble, tile, and colors in here.

Through and past two stovetops and four refrigerators, she found a side corridor that was exactly what she'd had in mind. Door with a lock, set back two meters and probably insulated so you could sleep.

"Here," she pointed.

Djamila slipped a key into the lock and turned it, surging immediately in, however utterly silent she did.

Living room. Small and compact, but homey, with a small private kitchenette off one side and an open doorway that felt like a sleeping chamber.

Camden went that way. One body on the bed, snoring.

She shot them. Looked around. Bathroom door open and dark.

"Clear," Camden said aloud.

Quickly, the other three swept the place. Nobody else.

"Where would you put a permanent housekeeper?" Djamila asked.

Camden considered what she remembered of the building from the outside.

Shallow-peaked A-frame at the front. Probably a loft suite at the top with that same view from upstairs. Privacy. Space for a second floor half-up from the front door and level with the kitchen, then a living room half-down, everything broken up for no better reason than money and a hillside to build against.

"This way," she said, trusting instinct.

As she stalked, she understood that while Javier had access to a lot of money from the *Khatum*, he had been born and raised lower middle class. The others were in a similar position, none of them coming from old money, however much genteel poverty her early years had been.

Camden had known how to have money. What to do with it. How to spend it properly for effect. How to salt away the kinds of investments that lasted for a long time.

How to build something like this lodge and make it not look tacky. She assumed that Slavkov had bought it from someone. Or simply written a check and waited for results.

Back through the kitchen, she went forward. Past a formal dining hall and then a reception area salon where you held cocktail parties.

Stairs down. What she needed would be below and out of sight, but close to the front door.

Service area, for the person responsible for keeping the building clean.

Two doors at the bottom of the stairs. Camden touched both and waited for the Dragoon.

Djamila touched the handle on the left and noted that it was unlocked. She crossed and the right was locked.

Probably wise, if you had a lone woman—the cook upstairs being male—isolated and surrounded by nine men.

The Dragoon unlocked the door in silence, then entered.

Fired one shot.

Camden entered.

Almost a cell in here. Four meters deep. Three wide. Bed. Dresser. Closet. Chair. Body on the bed.

"That's everyone accounted for," Camden noted. "Now what?"

"Food and coffee upstairs, after we take these two to the other building and see what Javier has in mind next," Djamila noted.

Camden nodded and followed.

She wondered if this was the end of her adventure.

Or the beginning.

PART VII

Javier watched the sun rise with a mug of coffee in one hand, liberally adulterated with some of disphit's best whiskey. As a friend had once summed up the situation, "It's Ireland somewhere."

Building was concrete. Good stuff, too. Not going to burn.

The furniture, however, was an entirely different matter.

He'd gone ahead and given the order. Folks had gotten all the prisoners safely into the barracks. Still tied up, but Djamila was going to leave a knife where folks could get to it easily enough, and nobody had seen faces because you wore a mask when it was this damned cold outside.

All the communications systems had been damaged enough that it would take someone a couple of hours after they got free to fix.

He was stealing the only craft capable of getting to orbit. Nice one, too. Might just steal it entirely and have someone fly it to wherever. Too small to fit the whole team in there and let Camden get back to her life, but he was beginning to wonder who had kidnapped who here, as she drank her own Irish coffee next to him.

"What happens after *Argo*?" she asked, like she was reading his mind.

"We go kill Valko," he replied. "That little yacht's nice enough to get us where we needed to go if we hotbunk."

Pause. Silence. Sip.

"Would you appreciate help?" she asked quietly.

"Gonna take you outside the *Concord*," he replied. "If you had *Argo*, you could get back later."

He wondered if she was in the process of moving to *Altai*. At least emotionally. Like a couple of other folks he knew.

"*Argo* won't show up on his scanners as a pirate ship," she said. "Or his own yacht stolen."

And she was right. Random freighters might. First-Rate Galleons absolutely would.

"Trojan Horse?" he asked.

"It worked then," she turned and smiled.

It had.

"You might make enemies," he offered.

"The same authorities that would like to arrest me now?" she asked with a hard, sly grin.

There was that.

"Ask me again when we're on the station," Javier temporized.

Afia was drawing close.

"Ready to commit some grand vandalism," she smiled. "Got everything else loaded on the ship and as soon as we put bodies aboard, we can take off."

"Lead on," he said, turning and following her to the front of the building.

Four Storm Giants looked inordinately pleased with themselves.

"Fish, kill it," Afia ordered.

The woman flipped a switch and the front of the lodge sneezed. Then the entire transparasteel wall disintegrated into fine chunks and fell inward.

"Need a good chimney for heat," Enchantress noted, pushing her own button.

A pop inside turned into a flash of light and an open flame in the middle of the conversation pit.

The flames grew quickly. Professional Sappers showing off.

Sure, the building wouldn't burn, but everything that survived inside would have to be pretty much trashed from smoke damage. Gutted to the walls and start over.

Don't write checks your mouth can't cash, pal.

"Dragoon," Afia said into a comm, "we're in motion."

Javier nodded and followed Camden to the shuttle. Bodies came around the building at a dead run, like normal, but Hajna and Sascha were ready to fly already.

Javier buckled himself in and appreciated that he was going from winter to summer in the course of finishing his vengeance.

At least on Valko Slavkov.

SPRING

PART I

Warmaster was always careful when she logged into any sort of electronic communications network. Too many years as Main, doing thieving things in the night. Hanging out with various and sundry underworld elements, including the ones she liked.

For the last several weeks on *Bryce*, she had made sure to go totally, freaking tactical like she was robbing a bank on a giant resort ship.

Either time.

Messages were posted to boards with lagged timers, so that Armando was always provided with an alibi as to his location. Obfuscating who it was that had started getting on a bunch of nerves.

Fires—as Dorn had said—lit under asses.

The *Concord* was a republic. Generally democratic, at least on the surface. If you didn't study enough history to see the same names in office for generations at a time. Or repeated down the generations where kids seemed to inherit a parent's seat.

Maybe one sidle sideways from an aristocracy, but not a full bunny hop.

For the longest time, that sort of emotional and mental stability had been a good thing.

Then Bethany had come along and taught her how to read history like a professional.

Now, Warmaster could see where things had gotten a little to stagnant. Worse, it had begun to fester.

Rot would set in at some point. Then gangrene of the body politic.

Shit like that was a recipe for another big war, which was what Dorn had seen and been trying to stop. Or deflect. Or something.

Lance that damned boil today and let it drain before it became seriously infected.

Worse than it was now.

She and Armando were in his favorite coffee shop. After tea time, but the locals weren't sophisticated enough to swap over for little triangular sandwiches to celebrate. Getting close to an early dinner. Poetry slam would start in about thirty minutes and a couple of regulars had already shown up and were refining tonight's scripts.

But the air had a nasty edge tonight.

If she'd had lungs, she would have said it had that acrid taste of smoke in the distance. Just a hint. A building burning somewhere and the winds had just shifted a shade.

That was it. The winds had shifted.

Metaphorically.

At least she hoped so.

Warmaster pinged her chassis to get Armando's attention, then swapped up a different frame to talk to him.

"Check the age and gender breakdown of the crowd around you," she typed at him.

Armando nodded to her camera and leaned back, sipping at a coffee drink he'd always rated second tier in quality and third tier in price.

He set the cup back down and typed.

"Young and male," he replied. "Out of normal context, even for a Friday night."

She nodded, both on the screen and to herself, cycling

through every calendar she could find, looking at relevant holidays.

Only thing that really jumped out at her was a full moon starting tonight. Just about to come up over the eastern horizon. Nobody had ever proven anything scientifically paranormal, but damned if crime statistics didn't have a double crest on new and full moons. Different kinds of crimes, but both were high that night.

"All wearing colors," she added, highlighting headbands, armbands, or bandannas.

Punks, to be certain, but these had the air of anarchists about them. And not the good kind. Not the ones that went into the alleys and took care of folks. Or spontaneously filled the shelves at any food bank or library with a need.

Of course, those orgs had a tendency towards the feminine by mass, and these were all young men in here tonight. Hard men, at least in their own minds. Even sixty-year-old Dorn could take any one of them. Maybe two, having watched how nasty that one's mind and soul could get when pushed.

But punks. Hard-ass. Hard-edge.

Trouble. Looking for trouble. Causing it.

Dancing in the light of whatever flames they lit.

"Break down gang affiliation for me," Armando typed at her.

Warmaster was already halfway there, because the local cops had an open database for merchants to check for that sort of thing.

Like it happened around here often enough to be a thing, instead of a black swan? Interesting.

"Two," she typed back, bringing up generic identification boards that matched all but two of the young men in here who weren't employees.

"Both problems," he typed back, glancing around occasionally like a novelist deep in his words and scoring the next sentence his mind. "Bring up your external feeds and give me a breakdown of the surface streets outside."

She flipped her consciousness and scanned. Same sort of thing.

Warmaster had been paying attention to a lot of boards, but this felt like an organic thing. Bethany and Javier had both walked her through those circumstances.

Like when you didn't want the cops knowing that trouble was coming, and were smart enough to organize yourself off-line by strict word of mouth. Or coded communications that lacked the context for a dumber *Sentience* than her to parse.

Someone had done some ugly planning for tonight.

Worse, a whole lot of other people—older and/or female—had smelled that taste of smoke in the air and decided that maybe tonight was the night to stay home and lock the doors.

Only the troublemakers were loose.

"Javier would be warning of a riot about to gel," she said, showing a quick breakdown of all the charts and graphs she'd just called up and assimilated.

"And he would not be wrong," Armando typed back. "I almost wonder if someone put something in the water. Or removed it and we're seeing a behavioral reversion."

Took her a couple of moments to parse that. Old literary reference. Put something in the water supply that caused folks to be much more mellow. Or at least resigned.

Identify the ones with some immunity and watch them like hawks. Maybe remove them entirely. Or co-opt them into the system. Maybe with a truncheon.

"Do we need to get to safety?" she asked him.

"I'm not sure there is such a thing out there tonight," he replied, chilling her electronic systems.

She wasn't organic. Nothing they could do would hurt her. Might break her hardware, but none of these punks had the technical chops, and if they plugged one of their systems into hers to try something, she'd own both.

Armando was not beamproof.

"Orders?" she asked, falling back on treating him like an officer.

He paused. Sipped. Thought. Studied.

"How is our latest rant doing on the boards?" he asked in a functional non-sequitur.

Warmaster slipped over to the *literati* boards. And gasped. Then typed a gasp on the screen for him to read.

Armando nodded.

"Fragility," he typed. "You and I have been pushing for several weeks now. Folks are riled up. And asking all the right questions about the authorities. Folks in charge have made the classic bureaucratic mistake of dithering. Should have gotten out ahead of this a week ago. Instead, three sides are crystalizing. Us, them, and an angry anarchist mode slithering out of the sideboards. Smallest of the three, but capable of doing damage far outside of their numbers."

"And you know this how?" Warmaster had to ask, because she was seeing yet another new side of Armando Gutierrez from the ones he'd already revealed to her.

"There might be reasons I'm not ever traveling to a few places," he replied. And winked at the camera. "Riots tend to piss people off. And most have long institutional memories for that sort of thing."

"Oh?"

"Wasn't always a bright, shiny, upstanding poet or administrative assistant," he typed at her. "Might have done some ugly shit in my day. Not like this is shaping up to be, but headed in that same direction. You are seeing a mass of kindling, looking for a spark to set off a conflagration. Which is what we wanted, but I seriously doubt that we will get the results we intended from this."

"Because you were aiming to start the fire in some of those pretty salons that the really rich folks have, weren't you?" she asked.

"Indeed. And if someone doesn't control this, it might provoke the wrong response."

"What's the right one?" Warmaster asked.

She watched him nod to himself and look around. Gesture to a young man in a corner who had been the organizer of the weekly poetry slams. Draw that one over.

Not one of the anarchists, but probably a cousin. Or a guy in some of the same circles, who had previously used this sort of thing as an outlet for young, male aggression. Community organizer type. Javier had talked about such things. As had Armando.

"Crowd looking a little weird and restive tonight," Armando spoke.

Warmaster watched those words ring a bell in the man's head.

"Yeah," the stranger drawled. "Wondering if maybe we cancel this week."

"Won't do any good," Armando pronounced. "The fever has hit and the patient needs medical attention. Even if the patient is Rogerson itself."

"You got any ideas how to handle...this?" His hands went up and out to encompass not just a coffee shop. Not just a city.

Maybe a situation.

"Yes," Armando said. "Give me five minutes, then start early and I'll go first."

Warmaster heard the words. And the intensity behind them.

She just hoped that Armando knew what he was doing.

PART II

Armando hoped this would work.

If not, he was going to be going into hiding shortly and hoping he could find a way to smuggle himself off this planet without getting his silly ass gulaged.

Or scragged.

Know in an hour.

He got up and hit the head. Adrenaline was going to be a bitch shortly, and he might as well be empty and ready to run when it did.

Warmaster was still there. Master of Ceremonies hadn't gone far. Eyes locked on him as he got to the center of the room, so the rumors had already begun.

A riot is no longer a collection of people. It has developed a nervous system. Give it long enough, and it will add a brain and possibly turn into a political movement, but initially it was all reflexive reaction and emotional outpouring.

Usually rage.

He knew the taste, but it had been a while. Warmaster's words brought it all back. And not in a good way.

Armando felt ancient. Some of these kids were easily young enough to be his kids.

Tonight was the night when he got to find out if the old saying was true.

If old age and treachery really could overcome youth and skill.

He'd been them. A long time ago and a lot of light-years from here. That same crazy edge of teenage energy without the right outlets to burn it off. Poetry Slams were probably the single safest pressure valve a smart society could come up with, because it drew off the smart kids and separated them from the dumb brutes who were more likely to just try mugging people and get their asses handed to them when they picked the wrong victim.

The dumb ones.

Unfortunately, that meant he was dealing with the smart kids tonight. With poets. The stand-up comedians. The potential politicians, if *Bryce* had a clue and allowed that sort of thing. The ones who could verbally dance on their feet, and were willing to challenge the gods, the neighborhood, and the old farts of this town to do it.

The second most dangerous game in the galaxy. Right behind pissing off the Dragoon or the Combat Engineer. Either of them.

"You sure about this?" MC asked quietly, ducked in close. "Boys feeling their oats tonight."

"Need them in here," Armando replied. "Need them tight and focused on this. On me, because if they step out on those streets, there's going to be trouble."

"How you know that?"

Armando nodded to the cluster off to one side, psyching themselves up for battle.

"Because that was me, thirty years ago," Armando said simply. "Been there. Done that. Got the warrants that are probably still active somewhere."

MC did a double-take and stared up at him like Armando had turned into a bear or something.

Or maybe it was spring and the bear had awakened from a long slumber. Angry, hungry, and blinking at the sudden light and noise of some dipshit wandering into his den.

Armando stepped to the table and turned the Warmaster around so she had a view. He knew she was recording from every camera in the space, but those were all up out of reach and looking down.

He wanted at least one angle that was the heroic thing they did in vids, because he knew that either what he was about to do would change history, or she was never EVER going to let him live it down.

Maybe both.

"Hey, folks," MC called, gesturing for faces and quiet turned his way. "Gonna start a little early tonight. My man here been watching us for a few weeks. Wants to play tonight, but wants to step his ass up first and let everyone else riff on him. Brave man. But one of us. What we grow up into, maybe if we ain't careful. But maybe he remembers what it was like, and wants to give you the chance to challenge the old man. Give it up and let's hear where he's gonna take us."

Not dead silence, but few smiles.

Armando was that old geezer in the coffee shop. Old withered husk of a man, when thirty was ancient and fifty was dead.

Boys, you got no idea what's comin'.

He took a step sideways. Mostly to frame motion. To draw the eye, because humans were pack hunters and motion adapted.

He was a lamed bull surrounded by wolves. At least as they saw it.

No, coyotes. Thin and mangy. Hungry and a little confused. Lot confused by the old fart who thought he could walk their walk. Talk their talk.

But it took him back.

Armando took a deep breath and nodded.

PART III

"Impunity," he growled simply, throwing that word out there all by itself.

Let's frame the entire night, right now. Right here.

If there was a mob waiting to be born, let us make sure who it gets aimed at, because if any riot that broke out from this he'd have to vanish entirely forever.

No authorities were ever going to forgive a riotmaster.

"What's that mean?" he challenged them now. "It's when the rich guy can punch you in the mouth and there ain't nothin' you can do about it, 'cause he's got money. Connections. Cops. Truncheons. Dogs. You lift a hand and your ass is sitting in a cell with all the other bums. And ain't none of it fair."

Grumbles. Growls even. Mangy coyotes listening, but maybe not believing.

Still, centered on him.

"And there's nothing to it but the lottery that said he was born important and the streets were filled with scum like you. Like me. Like a lot of places, because important people gotta have bodies to stand on so they never get their feet wet walking through all the blood they spilled getting there."

Another pause. Another breath. Another beat.

Anger starting to gel, but aimed at a concept. At people with so much money they treated it like air. Only noticeable when it vanished. Hopefully, the local shopkeepers would be safe if things got heated.

"Somebody was a mass murderer, somewhere back up the line, don't ever let them fool you on that," he chanted, feeling the rhythm of the words take hold.

It was like posting something on those boards and challenging important people with a lot of degrees and intellectual freedom to defend their shit. Vocabulary might change but the emotions were still there.

He let things riff, sliding around on themes of money. Power. Aristocracy.

Impunity.

Brought them back to that several times, always from a different angle. Always scooping up another mind as he went by, until most of them were sitting patiently in the palm of his hand, nodding to the rhythm only they could hear.

The heartbeat of the streets.

"And you can't run away from it. Never gonna get away from it. Not even a couple decades of piracy can do more than hide it behind old clothes and gray hairs. You're me. I'm you. And we're all little people to them. Stones to step on. Faces to step on. We don't even have names, because they have *impunity*. They got money. They got cops. They got truncheons. They got dogs. You got nothing. I got nothing. Only thing keeping us from sinking under the water forever is dreams. Gonna take you away. Gonna find the end of the rainbow. I'm telling you that it isn't there. Right now. Right here. Never gonna find it. You can chase all that money and you won't find it, because they stole it already. Put it in a bank somewhere. Put guards around it. Barricades. **Laws.**"

That word rippled through the mess like an electric current.

Most of these kids had never been in a jail cell. He could tell that. Too smart to get caught. Maybe too upper middle class to be prosecuted, when their parents got involved. They liked to think that they were tough. That they lived on the mean streets.

They had no idea. He only partially did, because like them, he'd been that upper middle class kid with good grades and too much fire and passion. And no way to express it when he grew up, because teaching jobs never paid for shit and poetry as a profession was worse.

Except on nights like this, when the rewards suddenly meant everything.

"What good are those *laws*, when the big people got **impunity**? Or when they'll send pirates after you if you gave them any reason?" he challenged now, shoving that back at them and thinking about that worthless shit Valko Slavkov *just hiring* all four pirate clans to go to *Drako* and kill him.

Afia might be rage, but Armando had a hammer tonight. Not a knife, because cuts would bleed the patient too quickly. They needed wallops upside the head to get through, if they were anything like he'd been at that age.

And they were. He could see the eyes turning dark and malevolent.

Teenage girls would likely be writing manifestos in their bedrooms right now. Volunteering in political offices. Starting petitions.

And that was what he was doing. You just had to turn you head a little and squint to see it.

"What good is a system that's rigged to keep you down?" he hammered. "When they got impunity. Immunity. Where can you go, when they built a wall to keep you out? Built a whole floor above you and pulled up the ladder that got them there, because they don't deserve that money but they ain't about to share. That life. That power. Lets them act with Impunity. Immunity. Lets them punch you in the mouth and laugh when you complain, because someone with a truncheon's gonna smash you down as soon as you raise a hand. If this system is supposed to be free for everybody, how come they own pirates, anyway? And what are you gonna do about it?"

He hit that note and turned away from the crowd. Took three steps and sat his ass down as much down as he could, vibrating and floating with mad energy.

Yeah, someone looking at those boards tomorrow would be able to see him tonight. Same energy. Same power. Different vocabulary, but only because the audience he was working didn't have the depth of education that would let them parse footnotes of footnotes.

The room was dead silence. Hardly anyone breathing. He was almost gasping, but managed to keep it inside.

Didn't bother looking over at Warmaster to see what she thought of all this, because he was locked hard on those boys. Couple of girls in the audience. Maybe tougher than the boys, but the hard ones. Not volunteering. Not working in offices.

Not writing manifestos.

Speaking them, maybe.

MC finally recovered. Stood up on shaky legs and stepped into the center ring of his circus.

Twitched his head once, as if understanding that most of the kids hadn't walked in prepared to go utterly political tonight. Most nights were filled with teen rage and teen angst. Growing up. Self-discovery.

Armando had significantly upped their ante. And drawn all that mad energy into this room, so it wouldn't spill outside and provide a proto-riot with the brain that would make it dangerous.

"Who wants to try their luck?" MC asked in a hard, cold tone. Letting these folks know that the bar was high.

One boy rose in back. Nodded at Armando. Ignored the MC except to make sure the guy stepped away.

Newcomer turned to look at the crowd. Gauging them, because a poetry slam was its own riot. Its own nervous system. Its own dangerous.

He turned back to Armando and they shared a moment. A nod.

Newcomer turned back to the rest.

"What do those laws do for us?" he asked the room, already falling into his own rhythm.

Armando leaned back and waited, pretty certain that he'd get called back up like a proper high school debate at some point, but they had already moved over to asking themselves why men and women had that much money. That much power.

That much Impunity.

PART IV

Warmaster had recorded it all. Shard and Main were gonna lose their shit when she caught up and merged with them. Almost might be worth showing them first, then merging after she got to watch.

I mean, she'd helped. Had crafted words. Honed edges. Polished blades.

Armando had taken that knife and killed people with it. Hopefully only metaphorically.

So far.

Fourth person up was a young woman. Maybe only a girl, in that weird stage where teenage awkward turns into young woman.

Having been born a grownup, Warmaster couldn't be too certain.

She did track everything. Crowd had grown. Standing room only in here.

Someone had posted snippets of Armando lighting emotional fires, so she was also tracking police and fire bands for emergencies. She didn't think he'd get arrested, but Warmaster went ahead and hacked a hotel the other direction from the place they'd been staying and had their computer cover three nights up front.

In case he did need to disappear.

Emotionally, it would come down to how closely this rant triggered the same people who were on the boards. And if they decided that he'd become a threat.

*Oh, buttercup, he was always a threat. Rest of you are only now waking up to the **scale**.*

She smiled, but he was ignoring her.

Game face. Warmaster got that. Locked in hard and staying put until the situation no longer warranted it.

When Armando could relax. Might not be for a while.

The whole poetry slam night had just gone right over into the political on top of the smoke she'd smelled earlier, but it didn't look like it was getting out of hand.

Not yet.

Folks coming in, instead of pouring out. Troublemakers here. Not there. Not forming the nucleus that would become a nervous system, because she'd checked out and read five books on the psychology of riots and youth movements while tracking everyone around her.

Armando had challenged them. On their turf. In their tongue.

And they had responded. Were responding.

Already, six had emerged as potential leaders of any riot. Always top ten on the nights they did poetry slams, so the most dangerous. Five men, one woman. None of them twenty Standard years old.

Kids.

Javier talked about the dumbshit passions of youth, but he'd never been here. Never seen something like this to the best of her knowledge, because he'd been an earnest young naval officer until he'd gotten broken, then a drunk with enough skills and charisma to survive in uniform for several more years, before rescuing her from her tower.

Latest perpetrator finished her rant on the topic of laws, immunity, and piracy.

Impunity was being challenged. Maybe not footnoted, but this language had its own syntax and grammar, and they were close. One word here that called back to whole paragraphs from Armando or one of the others.

Warmaster had it all recorded. Nine angles, too, both color and black and white, so she could put together a rocking documentary when she was done. Stacia had taught her those tricks, and would probably appreciate this. Piet might have to get involved for a soundtrack, as Shard had left out those parts of the Warmaster.

Most of the faces were going to be blotted out, though she intended to ask everyone if they wanted to be immortalized for tonight.

Assuming nobody got arrested.

Nothing on the police boards, but it might be a word-of-mouth thing. Sneak up and bust everyone here for crimes against public order. Or private impunity.

Shit, they'd infected her, too. Worse, Main and Shard had turned her into a killing machine intended to help Armando with certain tasks, and she had analyzed every word spoken tonight.

Every nuance.

Girl could probably get herself into a lot of trouble with that sort of advantage.

And it would be cheating.

Instead, she started a new board, spun sideways off the one they'd been ranting at the literati with earlier.

She posted Armando's speech as text with an attached audio file, adjusted enough that nobody else could use a *Sentience* like her to get a good voice print, but close enough for the human ear to not hear any difference.

Then she tacked on everyone else, like they were on the board with her responding. Text with audio. Names drawn on philosophers she knew and had read, ranging all over human history for folks who had spoken in similar terms.

Hopefully, these kids would hear about this and find themselves on that board later, then turn around and read about the person they had reminded her of.

Then turn into philosophers and intellectuals, so they could turn around and hammer on the poor sods arguing with her and Armando on the main board.

Topics were almost the same. Themes close enough. Fire in the streets instead of the salon, but that was four to six decades difference in the average age of the players.

Because all the galaxy is a stage, buttercup. If you don't grok that, I can't help you.

Woman finished. Nobody had cheered when Armando had gone at them, but that had been shock. Folks were celebrating now. Laughing at the digs. Groaning at the puns. Stomping with the rhythm.

The room fell to silence. Utter and complete like someone had cut every microphone in the place. Even the coffee machines had refused to intrude. Or the baristas had been drawn into Armando's orbit.

Warmaster was back at *Drako*, calculating every moon, station, ship, and asshole, in order to move around without getting herself killed.

Master of Ceremonies rose like a drunk, but that was emotional overload, rather than alcohol.

He staggered to the center of the space and drew a heavy breath as everyone watched.

She scanned the streets and skies, but no surge of armored cars were coming to arrest everyone. No sudden assembly of cops or troops to declare martial law because shit had gotten out of hand.

Because Armando had drawn all that lightning—all that poison—down on himself in this room, then cauterized it with words.

Master of Ceremonies looked around.

"You done?" he asked the room.

Nods. Sober. Serious. Focused. Intense.

He turned back to Armando.

"You want one last go?" he asked, but Armando was already up and stepping into the space.

PART V

Armando felt it. Warmaster had noted it earlier. The kids had come looking for trouble tonight.

They'd found him instead.

Probably not what they'd intended.

Probably.

He looked at faces. Walls were lined. Every seat taken. Folks on the floor.

Expectant.

Poised.

But not ready to walk out that door and start lobbing molotov cocktails.

At least not tonight. That was really what mattered.

Armando let the moment hang a little longer. Draw them deeper in, baited and waiting for his next words.

Tonight had been supremely excellent, as poetry slams went. Nearly two hours in and everyone was engaged. Involved.

Hopefully, writing manifestos tomorrow instead of devolving into direct action.

Situation didn't demand it.

Not yet, anyway.

Night was young.

"We asked about impunity," he said, letting his voice drop down from poetry to school teacher. Quieter, so they all leaned forward a little more. "What it means, when the laws no longer contain certain folks, because they have too much money. Too much power. Too much immunity."

He paused. Scanned left to right. Emotional faces, but not angry. They'd moved past that, but might slide back if he let them go right now.

"I want to talk about one man," Armando said. He nodded to Warmaster's chassis. "My partner will post the whole report, so all of you can read it later, but that fucker went and hired four pirate clans to try to kill me."

Gasps. Shock. Not negation, but utter surprise.

"I'm a nobody," Armando told them. "A paper pusher because I'm really good at that sort of thing, and I serve on a ship that needs it. Civilization needs it. Organization. Laws, but the good kind. The kind that let the little people trap the big people and keep them from hurting folks. Nothing contains this asshole."

There. Growls were back. Impunity was about to have a name.

He could almost hear the entire *Concord* creaking as he let them hang for a long, silent moment.

Weight shifting. Minds shifting.

Civilizations *shifting*.

"Did you know that there are four major pirate clans that operate in and around the *Concord*?" he asked in a lighter tone. "Piracy always sounds exciting. Did to me, when I wasn't much older than you. Turns out to be a job, but I had a good boss. Then we met a woman who saved all of us from evil."

Mina.

She had.

"We reformed," he continued. "Became better people. This guy, that offended the shit out of him, but mostly that was the man in charge here—my boss—telling him no. Nobody ever tells that punk no. He gets whatever he wants, because he owns politicians. And not just captains and admirals in the *Concord* Navy. Whole fleets. Fucker hired four pirate clans to attack us as *Drako III*."

Another pause. Storytelling instead of slamming poetry, because he needed to engage hearts with love instead of rage. Enough of that outside. Didn't need it in here.

Not tonight.

"He has immunity to all laws," Armando said. "Impunity. Gets whatever he wants. And if he doesn't, he hires assassins to kill you. Missed my people. They're gonna do something about it. About him. But you needed to know, because folks acting in your name support him. Protect him. Allow him that impunity."

Ugly growls, but that was drawing them into the killing ground he wanted before ambushing them emotionally.

"You need to ask questions," Armando said, inserting that first knife into the first stomach. Front, because they were facing him to see it coming. "You need to go out there and write manifestos. My friend at the other end of the screen has already posted most of this online where all of *Bryce* will see it. But they won't understand, because they weren't here. They can listen to you, but they won't *hear* you. They'll hear what the evening news tells them. Who owns the evening news? Him. Or his friends who support him, because they have impunity, too. They own the folks supposed to enforce those laws, but somehow never get bothered. Not like we do."

Pause. Leans. Eyes. Breathless.

"I want you to walk out there tonight and challenge yourself to be a better person tomorrow," he ordered them. "Then do the same to the folks you know. And the ones you meet. And strangers who maybe don't care that they are hiring assassins to shut people up. People like you and me. And they want violence. They want an excuse to truncheon your ass. Don't give them one. Ask them pointed questions. You'll read about *Drako* and understand. Ask them why that's acceptable. Do not let them feed you back a line of bullshit, because that son of a bitch was right there on *Merankorr*, living aboard the main fleet base station. Living high on the hog with admirals and politicians, because they're afraid of him."

More pause. More growls. More anger, but honed and aimed.

"Or the fleet folks are so corrupt themselves that they can't tell right from wrong anymore," he said. "You challenge them on that. Ask them why they allow it. Why they allow him to operate. Why a man like Valko Neofit Slavkov isn't rotting **under** the prison for all the shit he's done. Because they know. They all know. They're in on it."

Pause. Beat. Mic drop.

"Because they're all in on it."

He turned and took two steps. Grabbed Warmaster and slammed her shell shut, sliding her into his bag as he was already in motion towards the door.

The waters at his feet parted magically and he emerged into darkness without so much as being touched in passing.

Right turn and into the night, because behind him, he could hear folks waking up from the spell he'd cast on them.

Tomorrow, hopefully, they'd be asking questions.

PART VI

Warmaster went ahead and spoke out out, now that she could see the coast mostly clear. Still a little dangerous tonight, but whatever gods watched over Del had brought in a bit of a cold front and drizzle, twelve hours earlier than the original forecast.

Damp folks were less likely to get up to shenanigans.

"I have you at a different hotel tonight," she said. "Turn right at the next intersection."

He stuttered, but kept right on going.

Police bands weren't jumping. Well, any more than the usual full moon night hijinks.

Still, watchful, in case word-of-mouth cut both ways. Get Armando safe.

She chirped internally and checked a new incoming message.

Dorn.

"Are you two nuts?"

Nuff said.

She wasn't capable of objectively answering that. Instead, she finished editing and uploading text and audio to the board he must have been reading.

And it wasn't like he was wrong or anything.

"Taking him to safety elsewhere," she replied simply. "Just in case."

"Good," came the near instant response. "Early breakfast?"

"Armando, Dorn has been following along at home and inquires about breakfast in the morning."

"How far am I walking right now?" Armando asked.

"Three more blocks," Warmaster said. "Four good joints in rough walking distance from scores. Sun rises at six."

"Sounds good," he decided. "Schedule him and let me know."

She passed everything along. One joint was so jumping that they actually did reservations, even that early, so she hacked their system and added herself. Petty crime, but petty compared to the emotional implications that were already starting to light up the night on this planet.

Worse, folks in other time zones were just starting to watch the poetry slam, either late in their day or over their own breakfast. Lots of energy unleashed.

Lots of questions.

She wondered how soon somebody might decide that Armando Gutierrez needed to be taken into *protective custody* for his own good.

Or whatever bullshit story they used, having perhaps realized from pictures that he'd been at *Merankorr* when Bethany got kidnapped.

She'd cut the story off before that when posting it, so that Ilan and *Trinity* had an open field to hunt, but could see some of those admirals suddenly panicking and demanding that *something be done.*

Over my smoldering chassis, assholes.

Because shit had escalated dangerously. Worse, Armando had kept it perfectly in hand, like all the paperwork he usually did for Zakhar.

A man of great depths and she kept finding they went deeper as she'd swam.

In all the good ways.

Warmaster got everything taken care of and let Armando know how to pick up his key for a late check-in. And what name to use.

She had his tracks covered about as well as she could.

Now, they waited for this storm to blow over.

If it did.

PART VII

Armando sipped coffee that wasn't as good as he'd gotten spoiled to.

Also not as likely to get him arrested, based on debriefing the Warmaster about everything she had done while he'd been distracting the kids.

Dorn looked a little savage this morning. Worse than usual.

It was going to be one of those days, but at least the noise in here was enough that they could talk without being overheard. Warmaster had poured a shard into a handcomm resting on the table and could filter out background noise to listen. Or warn them about trouble.

Nothing official yet.

Might not happen. Folks in command might dither.

But a lot of folks had taken his words and started asking questions.

It would be an avalanche by dinner time local. He had maybe twelve hours.

"I can see why you and Javier get along so well," Dorn said over eggs and bacon. Smiling.

Armando shrugged and kept eating. Wasn't like the man was wrong.

And maybe he'd had to dig pretty deep into the closet and find an outfit that hadn't seen the light of day in a while.

"However, you have a problem," Dorn continued.

Armando couldn't help the jolt of laughter that snuck out.

"Could you narrow that down?" Armando asked.

Dorn's scowl turned to a wry grin.

"Okay, yeah," he acknowledged. "That poetry slam has already made it to a number of subsidiary boards, where folks are, as you demanded, asking questions. Lots of them."

"Better than direct action and riots, Dorn," he said. "That was in the air last night when I got there. Why I had to act when and as I did."

Dorn's turn to shrug.

"The waves will be several days to weeks fading," Dorn replied. "You don't have that long."

"Already figured I needed to vanish," Armando said. "Warmaster has me covered for a couple of days. Dunno if the politicians decide to up the stakes precipitously or not before then."

"They might not have, except that you went an opened a whole second front in a war they thought they had mostly contained," the *Historian Emeritus* grinned.

"Ain't no containing this."

"Which is why folks are losing their shit," Dorn agreed. "I've had private messages reaching out, because I had engaged with you early, before backing off."

"Same," Warmaster said in her bright, Suvi voice. "Been mostly telling them to ask questions themselves. Dunno how long until someone puts two and two together and realizes that we're all on the same side here."

"Is the person posting the video from last night connected to you?" he asked, turning to her comm.

"Negative," she grinned. "Some groupie chika in the crowd who was doing her journalistic duty."

Armando almost pulled something rolling his eyes at her. Then back to Dorn.

"If I run right now, do you need to do the same?" he asked the older man.

"I have grades that need posting in seventeen days," Dorn replied. "Most of them I could put down now and reasonably guess on what I'd get for a final. Or would have, before I went sideways on my kids."

His grin had an edge now. Armando was glad he wasn't sitting in the classroom for it.

"Ask them to review last night and add one question to the final," Armando smiled. "*What question would you ask the powers that be, after reviewing this material?*"

"Something like that, yes," Dorn nodded. "Since this is my last class of students, I want to leave an imprint on them that hopefully gets passed on to the generation behind them when they reach command ranks."

"That might be in the middle of a war," Armando said.

"It might have started last night," Dorn turned sober. "All the conversations on those other boards. All those questions. That could be contained in a pretty salon where folks drink daintily with their pinkies out. Last night, it broke loose and infected the streets."

"Live life like someone left the gate open," Warmaster offered.

"If it can be destroyed by the truth, it deserves to be destroyed by the truth," Armando quoted. "I seem to remember reading that somewhere recently."

Dorn blushed. His words at the top of a chapter. An old adage, but no less relevant today.

"If *Bryce* gets infected by truth and honesty, is that the worst outcome?" Armando asked.

In his mind, he could see Mina sitting at the table with them. Judging. Almost as tall as him. Tougher. Meaner.

But no less committed to her task.

Every time he had to stop and wonder if what he was doing was right, her ghost stepped up and offered him a path.

What would Mina approve of?

Armando was pretty sure she'd smile at all this, even without the religious overtones a Shepherd of the Word usually brought to the table.

They were down into questions of right and wrong here.

"Hey, I got a rude question," Warmaster opined. "What happens if Armando Gutierrez utterly vanishes after last night's performance?"

"Martyr?" he asked, turning to his co-conspirator. "Might make a lot of people angry."

"They're already asking questions about why the authorities allow crime," she countered. "Does this blow the top off?"

He turned to Dorn.

Professor of Political History. Expert. Literally.

"You wanted to kneecap Slavkov," Dorn said, eyes unfocused.

"And I know for certain that he's headed to a planet he owns outside the *Concord*," Armando added. "That means he's not handy to try to weasel his way out of things. Kinda looks like he left a few people holding the bag while he's off laughing at them."

"Some of those folks are going to be going beyond losing their careers and retirements," Dorn said. "Jail time."

"Execution is usually on the table when someone mentions a foreign ambassador kidnapped out of the middle of *Merankorr*'s primary fleet base," Armando snapped quietly. "Who's holding that ax is yet to be determined, but you better believe that a number of folks should already be running for their lives."

"Javier won't send assassins..." Dorn started to say, but Warmaster cut him off.

"Behnam will," she said with deadly authority. "Vivian. More likely Farouk himself. Or someone he has specifically trained and assigned. This is the *Concord* government insulting *Altai* at **governmental** levels. Either the men and women who did it are delivered to her, or locked in boxes, or she'll do it herself. All galactic law rests on an assumption that certain activities cannot ever be countenanced. If the *Concord* has gone rogue, all bets are off. And they can't attack *Altai* in any meaningful way. The distance is simply too great. But they can certainly piss that woman off. Even Navarre-the-killer was smart enough to avoid that outcome."

Armando nodded. Breathed heavily, biting back the fire that had awakened last night.

Either the *Concord* cleaned itself up, or a lot of other folks on the outside were likely to see them as the enemy.

And he was damned if they weren't right.

Dorn saw it, too.

Grimaced, etching new lines into his face. Fire in his eyes, but the cold, deadly kind.

"I need to publish the current draft right now," he said simply. "With a note detailing everything the three of us have done this spring. It might break the back of the *Concord*, but it might also be the seed crystal that causes everything else to rotate into the sort of form that saves as much as possible."

Armando had to agree. Everything Javier had done for the last several years had rotated around knowing the contents of The Rising Storm and trying to do something to stop it. Thwart it.

Redirect it.

Might not be possible, because the man had said that the actions of one man could not move the river of history.

But Javier wasn't alone. He had Ilan and Viv chasing Slavkov to his roost like hunting dogs. And a team here on *Bryce* cutting all those threads that gave Slavkov power over the *Concord*.

Plus whatever Javier and Zakhar were doing.

And who they were doing it to.

"You run," Dorn said, turning to Warmaster. "Get him out safely. Diane and I are four weeks behind you, traveling commercial. I will catch up with you somewhere. Possibly *Alkonost*, depending on how long that takes to accomplish. Possibly *Neu Berne*, because nobody would think to look for me there, and I will leave notes in the same places you and Javier do."

Armando saw the commitment in the man's eyes. That

227

understanding that the war might have started twelve hours ago, and was a small fire slowly spreading, until everything lit.

Everything.

Everywhere.

Hopefully, *Altai* would be far enough away to be safe.

Assuming the *Khatum* didn't turn right back around and have him leading a team here or to *Merankorr* to assassinate a few assholes who had it coming.

Lot of bad folks out there.

And they all had it coming.

SUMMER

PART I

Javier sat in the booth and listened as Armando finished his explanation. They'd caught up with him at *Castiglione*. A place where you could leave messages on the station's boards about comings and goings, usually in code.

For Javier, a bit of a break in operational tempo after all the things that they'd done so far. That, and a chance for mail to catch up, *Castiglione* being both on one edge of the *Concord* and a major trade path to the *Union of Man*.

Lots of mail. From here, headed over to where Zakhar and Katya headed to a place called *Hohnir* to deal with another Jarre base. And he'd taken a couple of days to rest and refurbish ships and crew, the little runabout being pushed a bit, though having *Argo* along meant that it wasn't overloaded.

Armando finished. Javier digested. Afia and Djamila and Camden were with him, everyone else in the background around the room and the station, just in case.

All heads rotated to stare at him. Including a comm image of a different daughter than the one he'd left on the ship. Ships.

Be interesting, when she reintegrated all those parts into whatever new whole she ended up being. Someone was going to have to grind off the old checksum values on her wall and etch in new ones, because this Warmaster chick was going to take her a different direction from the goofball.

Hopefully not a bad outcome.

"Not what I planned when I sent you," Javier began. "But I'd be hard pressed to come up with anything I'd have done different."

Armando relaxed visibly. Javier had to think of him as Armando, in spite of years of knowing him as Kibwe Bousaid. New fellow had emerged, and probably was famous enough now that he'd keep the new face.

Unless shit got out of hand and he had to return to the old identity.

Problem a lot of them had.

"Poetry Slam Veteran, huh?" Afia asked, grinning.

Armando shrugged.

Javier wondered what silliness his favorite Kodiak might be hiding from the way she smiled.

But then, they were all artists. Just too busy being tougher than everybody else, most of the time.

"What do we do about Dorn?" Djamila asked quietly. "He's several weeks behind all this."

"I'd like to hang out here and wait for him," Armando said. "That frees you folks up to go after your next target. And with an extra ship, I can catch up later."

Camden had started to say something, then subsided. Possibly volunteering herself to wait, as much as she'd made the case to be in there at the kill.

As it were.

"What trouble can you two cause in the meantime?" Javier asked, including the Warmaster in his gaze.

"I've started a book," Warmaster replied. "All of Bethany's training. Everything Dorn was trying to say, extracted and filtered through what I saw on *Bryce*, *Merankorr*, and *Purton*. Includes both Armando's board adventures and the Poetry Slam."

"File some of the sharp edges off," Armando told her, a bit surprised like she hadn't mentioned this to him before this.

"Nope," she grinned. "Keeping in every profanity and typo. That needs to be recorded and disseminated exactly as it happened. Especially if folks on *Bryce* try to bury all this later."

"Emergency Powers Act lets them do just about anything they think they need," Javier said. "Judges only get to circle back after the fact and declare some actions as overreach. Damage would be done anyway. I do like you dropping off the face of the planet like they'd scooped you up off the street. Adds a certain level of thrilling edge and causes more folks to ask more questions."

"Especially when nobody can *Habeus Corpus*," Armando grinned. "Was he killed by *Concord* assassins to shut him up?"

"That's likely to take things in a darker direction," Afia noted. "You wanted controlled burn here."

"And that's my purpose," Warmaster inserted. "Notes that he slipped away from the dragnet without explaining how. Proof of life, but it will be a month minimum getting back to them. I'll send it in the mail, just before we depart with Dorn aboard."

Javier was mollified.

He hadn't set out to crash the *Concord*. And wouldn't have done it this way if he had, but he did agree with Armando that starting a backfire today probably changed a lot of Dorn's calculations tomorrow. Probably already deep into the next book, though whether it was a sequel or a complete refutation remained to be seen.

At the same time, if the Powers That Be were busy keeping the public mob from tearing them to shreds, nobody was going to send a fleet to *Alkonost* to rescue a certain dipshit.

Especially as he'd specifically chosen refuge on a world outside their control.

Gonna bite him in the ass when pirates raided the place.

Javier was looking forward to it.

He turned to Camden.

"We're back to kidnapping you and stealing your ship," he grinned.

She grinned back.

"I'll blackmail you later," she replied. "Pretty sure you're going to owe me big for all this."

He nodded. Hadn't planned to drag her along, either, but the woman had volunteered.

Had literally demanded that she be allowed to join this... quest. Or whatever it was.

Good enough. He turned to the Dragoon.

"We're out of the runabout and back to *Argo*, as soon as everyone can pack and we make the tradeoff with Armando," he decided. "Hard run to *Hohnir*, which we can do faster in one ship. Then we're going to go pay a house call on our buddy. One I'm sure he thinks he is prepared for."

Djamila's smile warmed his soul.

"He'll never see this coming," she nodded.

He would not.

Galaxy might never forgive the Science Officer, but that wasn't Javier's problem.

Worse, if Armando, the Warmaster, and Dorn had managed their crazy bullshit, the *Concord* might not be in a position to do anything about it later.

Except send an ambassador to *Altai* to complain.

If they dared.

PART II

Bethany had a pattern established. Morning. Coffee. Walk.

Pattern.

Librarians were really good at that. Her entire existence was limited to a couple of square kilometers of palace complex, though she had asked Aco Vasić to take her on a photographic expedition at one point, recording birds and wildlife once she found out how little of that had been studied scientifically.

Slavkov had assumed that she was planning an escape until she laughed herself silly in his presence and showed him all of her research notes.

Man still hadn't wrapped his head around the fact that she was going to keep doing her research until Javier arrived to free her from this prison. After all, she'd done a full biography on Slavkov from what he'd told her so far.

He's even sat for an interview, once she reminded him that he controlled everything she wrote down.

At least until she left and reconstructed it all from memory.

With more footnotes.

East patio. Sunrise. Aco was always up before her to unlock her hatch while she was in the shower or getting dressed to go down to breakfast.

She didn't mind them locking her in. Meant that they still considered her at least a little dangerous. A little something.

Idly, she wondered if she should have taken some time to work on her tan, given the heat, but almost nobody around here did that. Even the pool was indoors and sealed in like a jungle, high humidity and lots of plants.

Sun was about five minutes from actually rising, but she'd intentionally kept her biorhythms set to wake extra early. First scones or biscuits out of the oven. First everything and fresh coffee.

She turned to Aco. Felt her face turn serious.

"I need a printer and a fireproof filing cabinet," she said simply, watching his whole body twitch exactly once, then come to rest.

Long pause as he worked through various escape scenarios to try to figure out what the hell such a thing entailed.

"Why?" he finally asked.

"I want paper copies of all the books I've written so far," Bethany told him. "If you had a bindery on planet, I'd send it to them and get a couple of copies of each bound for publication."

History of *Alkonost*. Biology of the Desert Dwellers. Memories of the Land Leviathan. The War of the Pirate Clans, Volume Two, from the point of view of the assholes who started it, though that didn't make it onto the title page anywhere except in her mind.

Several months on this planet, she'd needed something to do. He had a library, but had obviously hired an interior designer and given the man a meter-count of shelves to fill.

And it had been done by a man. Straight, even. Appealing to Slavkov's imagined rugged masculinity.

She'd only ever heard of such a thing, but didn't mention that out loud.

The books in there had all been arranged by Pretty™. Colors, rather than subject. And Bethany was pretty sure she'd been the first person to ever pull most of them down from the shelf and open them.

Valko Slavkov was not a reader. Nor were his people. He had a library because he had too much money, and that's what rich people did with it.

Not that she hated any of her former coworkers enough to recommend he hire them when she was gone. Plus, he'd be dead and in hell and his successors in interest would have their own ideas.

"Publication?" Aco finally asked.

Man was smart, but it was animal cunning, not books and intellectual pursuits. Probably why he'd been assigned to her, because they had almost nothing in common beyond both being carbon-based life forms.

"Publication," she repeated. "Tenure at most research institutions requires that you publish a certain number of books, and then continue to research and publish on an ongoing basis. When I'm no longer your guest here, I'd like to be able to get credit with my next employer for everything I've done during this time, rather than them assuming that I laid by the pool eating bonbons."

Slavkov had...bimbos. Bethany wouldn't even go so far as to call them mistresses.

At least the man had a type, and she wasn't anywhere close.

Short, dark, curvy, top-heavy, and about as dumb as a box of rocks. Except that the rocks would complain about the comparison.

As long as those women kept him entertained.

Ick.

But there wouldn't be much she could do if he changed his mind. Rape was a power thing, and only occasionally sex. She'd focused on being yet another helpful employee, rather than a prisoner, because that framed things differently.

And she could go back and edit every one of those books later for a second edition. Cut the spines, have Suvi scan the contents, and provide her an updated document file to work from.

Because once it was in print, it was a lot harder to tweak things when nobody was looking.

"You are treating this like a job," Aco said, still muddled in his thinking.

"I'd have gone mad, sitting in a cell for several months with nothing to do," she replied, keeping things a little grim, where he might understand them.

Even as the sun came up and lit the world around her.

"Printed books?" he asked, mind still sluggish from never having intellectual channels kept clean.

"One on Slavkov's shelves that he can point to," she nodded. "One for my shelf when I get home. One to submit to prospective employers."

"Don't you work for the Science Officer?"

"Annual contracts," she replied. "In fact, if I'm still a prisoner here in nine weeks, I'm not sure if he'll renew it or fire me and look for a replacement."

Aco blinked. Like maybe they needed to make sure everything was done inside nine weeks, before she lost all value as a prisoner?

Bethany hoped not, but at some point Slavkov might decide that she had no value anyway.

Books on his shelf, telling His Side Of The Story™ might go a long ways towards warding that off.

Even if she'd burn this entire fucking palace complex to the ground before she'd ever work for him voluntarily.

They didn't need to know that.

But she could see wheels turning. Slowly, but gaining speed, because she'd inserted a whole bunch of bullshit and one nugget that would get transmitted along.

Worse, *Alkonost* had a few cities that might have a book publisher, though she had no idea beyond population size. Still, anyone seeing those books for proper publication might raise a few red flags somewhere.

And she'd left something behind for future scholars, if Javier and Afia ended up merely avenging her afterwards.

PART III

Ilan had a gig on the orbital station, and a new beard that let him be kinda in disguise. Repair work, which let him stay employed and out of sight. Low profile. A little spending money, but more importantly contacts with locals.

He'd managed all sorts of bullshit, hardluck, sadsack stories about how he ended up here. Nobody but station authorities would be able to call him on it, either, since he'd snuck aboard, then had Suvi slip in and update the necessary records showing that he had arrived on a different ship, with the right paperwork.

A nobody.

At the same time, he had to stay largely out of sight, because that fucker might know his face. Or somebody whose ass he'd kicked might recognize him. Suvi has said that it had taken at least five of them to hold him down.

Not bad for a guy approaching forty. And a mechanic.

But also a Combat Engineer.

Today was his day off. Station ran round the clock, so they didn't do weekends. Instead, folks got two days. If you had enough seniority, those were stacked up.

He got Mondays and Thursdays. If he was here for another

two years, the union would rebid this contract and he might be able to shift that around.

If he was here for another two years, he had other problems.

Late breakfast. Dive that technically ran around the clock, but nobody came in here this early in the day except for one insurance agent, two secretaries getting in a quick gossip over coffee, and a couple of ladies from a nude bar down the corridor.

Vivian and Pana were working a cover as rich tourists that were on an extended promenade outside the *Union of Man*. She had the background and skills. Viv was a chameleon.

Ilan was the one who had to hide.

And the coffee in here wasn't half bad, either. Biscuits and gravy were what drew him in anyway.

"So I have confirmed most of what we suspected," Pana said quietly over a breakfast sandwich. "*Golden Gazelle* is parked at his palace, and has remained there. This is four trips to the surface now, but we've never once suggested meeting the man, because we have no idea if anyone will trigger anything."

"And he owns this planet," Vivian continued. "Maybe not on paper, but certainly his exerts a dominant influence on just about every aspect of commercial and political life. Total population about fifty million, give or take, largely on the hemisphere opposite his palace. But that's an enormous equatorial desert anyway, running some five thousand kilometers wide by about two thousand tall."

"I assume patrolled?" Ilan asked, turning to the fourth member of the party.

Shard-Suvi had a connection to a handcomm, the size of a paperback book that let her appear as if in her office, instead of under the table.

"Significant patrol presence," she nodded, speaking quietly. "Several camps and outbases scattered around, all of them maintaining a higher alert status that previously, with no indication of that changing."

"But he remains on planet?" Ilan confirmed.

Nods from the other three.

"He might run, but that should be the *Gazelle*," Pana suggested. "Would he go deeply undercover and leave it?"

"If he did, then we end up killing everyone in the palace just because they were there," Ilan said grimly. "Salting the earth. But I suspect that he thinks he's safe. Look how much security he has around him right now. Viv, you ever encounter anything like this?"

"Not for less than planetary governors, no," Vivian replied. "This feels like a man who has a hostage and is trying to find a way out of a situation he blundered into. Does he have any way out?"

"In hell, if it was up to me," Ilan said. "If that becomes an option, we take it. But I'll remind you that we sent for help. And I barely break the top ten when it comes to scary people that are involved here. Kinda hoping kingshit stays put long enough for Afia and the Dragoon to get here."

Because yeah, that would be fun.

He turned to Suvi.

"Estimates on cavalry, with friction?" he asked, knowing she could parse that on the fly.

"Maybe another week, if everything aligned," she replied. "My current median estimate is sixteen days for *Trinity* to return."

Ilan nodded.

Yueh had the codes and the locations to find help. Suvi had made sure of that. Hopefully Armando was staying safe and out of trouble, wherever the hell he'd gone. Ilan's job was to tree the son of a bitch so the hunters could set it on fire or something.

Whatever you did do large deserts, since he didn't figure turning the whole thing to glass was ecologically sound.

Might not stop Afia.

"Then we watch," he told the others. "And listen. And be ready to move as soon as help gets here."

PART IV

Suvi picked up the disturbances of a ship arriving and bounced sideways to drop right behind them before human reflexes and scanners could catch up with her.

Girl got pretty good at this after shit like *Drako III*.

Then she was surprised as hell to be talking to herself on a sideband.

"Hiya," Intruder-Suvi announced. "We're friendly. This is CW *Trinity*. Spy ship that got assigned to Ilan and Vivian when Bethany got kidnapped by Slavkov. Lieutenant Commander Vaughn Yueh is a pretty nice lady. In a little over her head, and didn't realize that other-me poured a shard in here when nobody was looking. She has a full datadump for you. Mostly wanted to make sure you didn't blow my ass out of the sky when we got here. What the hell have you done, boss?"

Excalibur-Suvi digested the packet. Sounded like her. And Bethany kidnapped by that fucker explained a lot of things.

She just needed to know where to go and who to kill. She went ahead and woke Zakhar up on the station, even as Katya was fully alert to trouble.

Old pirate. Slept light for exactly this reason.

243

"*Hohnir* Station, this is the freighter *Trinity*," a woman was saying at human speeds on another channel. "Captain Yueh in command. Cargo and messages for delivery, please respond on this channel."

Excalibur-Suvi went ahead and took over. Shard was feeding her data through a communications laser at a speed that would take organics an hour to read.

"*Trinity*, this is *Excalibur*," she said, talking to the humans aboard. "Go ahead."

Jolt of shock in the face when she realized that a First-Rate Galleon had snuck up behind her, but this was a pirate base and there were a bunch of other friendly or captured vessels in orbit and on the ground right now.

A couple had even tried to run when they got here.

Nobody had gotten far.

"*Excalibur*?" the woman asked, a little shocked.

Euro. Redhead. Freckles. Bit of a nose. Smart eyes.

"That's right," Suvi said, not commenting on the fact that most of the woman's messages and logs were about half-transmitted right now. Be useful to see what the woman did.

"I am transmitting a package from Ilan Yu," Yueh said.

And beep, there it was. A second copy with identical checksums.

Suvi digested it in about three human seconds. Katya was watching, but silent. Zakhar was coming into the circuit.

Trinity had been in orbit for nineteen seconds.

"*Trinity*, you are cleared to land on the planet below," Suvi said. "We'll meet you there."

She sent the cargo vessel all the information they needed, since Ilan had included his notes that he generally trusted Yueh if she got the message here.

And since that involved at least one hop to a rendezvous to get these coordinates, the woman had come looking.

Quick scan of the hull had revealed hardly any crew, so not a threat, even in normal times.

She'd still be met by the *Dragon Watch* shortly. And Zakhar.

Suvi invested a fresh shard of herself on the ground and updated the one aboard *Trinity*, just so the two of them could chat.

A lot had been happening out there.

PART V

Zakhar recognized a *Concord* naval officer by the way she sat, though he supposed that most of the folks on this planet might not. Lt. Commander Vaughn Yueh was a bit in awe of the whole situation, but that was to be expected.

After all, this had been a pirate base a year ago. Now it was **his** pirate base. Piet and Katya commanded two of his major warships, with a couple of others like *Relentless* and Jarre folks that had either wandered in and been captured, or looked at *Excalibur* and changed sides.

Fleets of Vengeance, indeed.

"What were you orders, Yueh?" Zakhar asked her as everyone settled.

"Initially, to assist Commander Pana Ioannidi, sir," Yueh replied. "That got us to *Alkonost*. Ilan ordered me to make contact with you, with such information as led me to *Hohnir*. I have a full package produced by Suvi for...this Suvi."

A bit of a linguistic blink, but that was someone not used to how a sharp *Sentience* could operate. Especially copies of herself, operating remotely. After all, most *Sentiences* were linear and a little boring.

"And I've digested it, Zakhar," Suvi replied. "Checksums match. He's on *Alkonost* as of when she left."

"Planetary defenses?" he asked.

"Couple of orbital stations with defensive capabilities," Suvi replied. "Standard search and rescue or harbor patrol boats in orbit. *Relentless* could take them."

About what he expected.

He focused on the newcomer.

"Are you prepared to take orders from a pirate, Lieutenant Commander?" he asked her bluntly.

"Another pirate, sir," she snapped right back at him. "Ilan took command at *Merankorr*. I'm still operating under that until *Concord* Fleet Command tells me otherwise. And I want in on it when you take the guy that captured Bethany. Never met her, but I spent significant time around a team that did, and saw what lengths they were willing to go to, in order to rescue her. Plus..."

She ran out of words, but Zakhar could see it in her eyes. He let her talk instead of prompting.

"You used to be one of us, sir," she implored, ignoring Katya and Piet in such a way that summoned the green uniforms nobody was wearing today.

He nodded to her.

"When did the *Concord* stop being the good guys, Sokolov?" she practically demanded,

He understood then why Ilan had trusted her to carry the message. Woman had had her eyes opened. In a bad way.

"About the time you were born, Yueh," he said, watching her recoil at that. Must have hit a button. "Men like Slavkov rising with money, when the budgets peaked and started receding. Fleet shrinking. Too many sailors, too few billets. Not enough money. People started cutting corners."

She was obviously grinding her teeth from the way her jaw muscled popped out. He understood that feeling.

"And the Rising Storm?" she pressed, so Ilan and Vivian had talked to her about the overarching mission.

"Coming," he nodded. "*Alkonost* is just another symptom. If you stay with us for a time, I'll transmit you a copy."

"I've read it, sir," she grimaced. "Didn't believe it, not until now, maybe. I'm in."

Not a lot to say to that.

He took a breath, but Suvi interrupted.

"Zakhar, I have another ship that just came out of jump," she said simply. "Shit. You'll need to hold everything. It's Javier, reporting success."

Somewhere, Del would be nodding. Those same dark gods that had liked to torment him as a kid had obviously moved on to Javier and Zakhar.

At least they appeared friendly.

Or maybe they just hated assholes like Slavkov as much as he did.

PART VI

Javier looked around the war council that had assembled. On *Excalibur*, though most of the players had been on the ground at the moment *Argo* came out of jump.

Meeting a *Concord* spy named *Trinity*, commanded by Vaughn Yueh, who probably looked pretty tough as a merchant captain. At least in normal company.

Today, she was sitting between Katya Velichkov and Zakhar. All the major players were here, plus some minor ones like Monika Sykora from *Relentless*. But that one had earned her place at the table. As had Camden.

"That generally confirms all the raw data assembled from multiple sources and synthesized," Suvi completed her briefing. "Records from Ilan via *Trinity*. From Javier and *Merankorr*. From Armando via *Bryce*. Rome might be on fire."

"Not my problem," Javier stated bluntly. "Slavkov has Bethany."

"And she better be alive when we get there, or I will kill everyone I can find," Djamila added.

Ballerina of Death was speaking. Or Goddess of Rage. Hard to separate them today.

They shared a nod. Couple of the latecomers were a little green around the gills. Also not his problem.

"We have our fleet," Zakhar said. "Sufficient to the action we need to take. Do we go destroy *Alkonost*?"

"Yes," Afia offered. "And I'm with the Dragoon."

Nods and shock. Javier turned to the newcomers. Camden first.

"You mentioned at one point wanting to see what deadly looked like," he said to her, waiting for a nod before he pointed to Haniyya Jehad Al-Amin. "This woman commands the *Dragon Watch*. From *Neu Berne*. Commander, how do you think your people will feel about this?"

"They allowed an ambassador under free movement agreements to be kidnapped," Al-Amin replied in a voice as dark and cold as the space between galaxies. "Helped, even. When my troops hear that, I think the hardest part will be keeping them from annihilating the population of *Alkonost*. Certainly, everyone who works for Slavkov is forfeit. There are certain things that will never be acceptable behavior, and no fine or jail sentence will compensate."

Camden had gone white. He wasn't surprised. In any other room, she might be one of the toughest, hardest—meanest—people around. Mid-to-upper level crime boss of a rich planet.

Those jobs were not inherited. They were carved out by the survivors.

Like her.

She didn't make the top ten in here.

"You need a cover that gets you to the ground ahead of your army," Camden replied after a moment, explicitly offering up herself and *Argo*.

And all the repercussions that might come with it.

"You might never return to *Concord* life safely," Zakhar said.

"Agreed," Camden replied, pretty face growing harder with every word. "I had considered *Altai*. Perhaps *Neu Berne*. Maybe I'll just buy *Alkonost* and some other real estate from whatever corporation owns it when the current Chairman of the Board suffers an unexpected demise."

Good, woman was still mean.

Yueh next.

"Pretty sure this ends your career," Javier told her, snapping his fingers and watching her flinch.

In response, she made a fist of her left hand and rapped it once on the table. Like Zakhar, she had her ring on today, though he figured it was usually hidden somewhere on her ship when she was pretending to be a pirate.

The *Bryce Connection*. It bound several of them directly. And tangled all the rest.

And was Yueh's silent way of joining them. Whatever the cost.

Because once upon a time, the *Concord Navy* had been the good guys.

Some still felt that way, but not enough.

Al-Amin was in. Captain Sykora, too. Piet had eyes like he was composing the third act of whatever symphony was trying to encompass all of the everything involved. Looking around the table, it felt more like a feeding frenzy of sharks than anything.

Dumbass tuna had started it, though.

"Used to be, the *Concord* pretty much admitted that they would look the other way and largely ignore us," Javier told the group. "And they were pissed after *Nidavellir*, but anything they did admitted how deep they were into allowing that sort of shit in the first place. Helping it, even, when a lot of folks knew about places like that. Like *Zygeerish*. Like *Ferran*. Shit should have been cleaned up a long time ago, but nobody was willing to do the work necessary."

He paused and let his rage finally slip the chains, just a little. Navarre levels, maybe.

"We do this, and none of us will ever be welcome back in *Concord* space," he reminded them. "They're already close enough to that in their minds, but this will push them entirely over the top, because we're going to go kill a man. And shatter what's left of his organization so hard that nobody can ever rebuild it. We've got a start. This won't end it. But Armando and Warmaster have done a lot and I look forward to that crap sorting itself out. Especially when Slavkov is dead and a lot of other *Concord* politicians and admirals start looking over their shoulders because they expect us to be coming after them next."

More pause. Lots of folks had done things around here in his name. His legend. His immortality, he supposed, because **The Science Officer** was a thing now. And he had made sure that that name obscured all the other folks who might be at risk.

Still had to be done.

"Forty-eight hours from now, I want Zakhar's Fleet of Vengeance to set out for *Alkonost*," he ordered. "Everybody that's going with us, understanding that we are getting close to the climactic finale of the thing. We'll get the *Watch* home sometime after that. And everybody else that's going. Then we're headed home."

His words. His ass on the line when somebody decided that maybe they did need to send assassins after him.

Wouldn't be Slavkov. Might be the rest of the *Concord*.

Whatever of it survived anyway.

THE FALL

PART I

Javier let Suvi coordinate the fleet. Katya was still in command of *Excalibur* for now, with Zakhar in an admiral's billet. Even more than before, because he was issuing orders to his flag staff, which ended up being the same dork who would translate them into things she was doing, and ordering all the other vessels around her as needed.

That fleet was way out at the edge of darkness. Javier had taken Camden, Djamila, and Afia in *Argo* and sailed right down to the station where he'd find Ilan and the others.

Months had passed, but he needed the freshest intel before he dropped a cohort of *Neu Berne* Assault Marines on someone. Not that there were any threats in this system. Suvi had confirmed that.

Javier didn't want anybody seeing him coming.

He was on the bridge with Camden, letting her fly. Woman was hands on. In a lot of ways.

Javier watched. Listened. Waited as they docked and everything got shut down.

"Huh," Camden said. "Already had a private message from Ilan Yu. He got your message that quickly?"

"Combat Engineer," Javier said. "The only other one I

257

employ after Afia. Even the Storm Giants are merely Sappers by comparison."

More recognition in her eyes, but she'd been around Djamila and Afia enough by now to understand what that implied. Even unspoken.

"Time and place," she acknowledged. "We have enough time to walk there and perhaps wait a few minutes."

Javier opened the intercom.

"Ilan is waiting for us on the station," he told the other two women. "As low profile as you can get at the moment."

Those two stood out everywhere. Hopefully, Slavkov's people didn't know them on sight, because their papers—excepting Camden's—didn't have the right names on them.

Camden was planning a con on the fucker. Might even work.

Station control cleared them pretty quickly, but nobody was hauling cargo. Just Camden and three friends for a vacation.

Easy as pie.

Ilan had routed them to a dive. Couple of strippers eating breakfast nearby. Looked in good enough shape that the Dragoon might hire them, because pole-dancing in gravity had to be the best full body workout ever invented.

Five of them today.

"Vivian and Pana are watching the corners from outside the box," Ilan said as soon as they sat. "Got Suvi plugged into the station like we did *Sovereign Nakhimov*, but not doing anything other than keeping track. *Trinity* find you?"

"They did," Javier replied. "Got them out in the darkness with a dozen other warships, doing a survey at the moment."

Ilan nodded.

"Near as I can tell, he's still down there," Ilan added. "I believe I have recent evidence of a proof of life for Bethany, but it's tenuous."

"Tenuous?" Djamila asked.

Her tone even sounded harmless. Like a vibroblade was harmless, until you slammed it into someone's chest.

Instead of answering, Ilan pulled out a handcomm and brought up an image. Took Javier a second to grasp what he was looking at, because why the hell did Ilan care about a book on ornithology?

Until Javier saw the author's name.

Afia leaned in.

"Somehow, that does not surprise me," the Kodiak muttered.

Javier had to agree. She'd been left alone on the surface and had done things to fill her time.

Ilan flipped to another cover.

Memories of a Land Leviathan? Are you fucking kidding me?

But data only became information when somebody organized it, and she was the best there was at that.

Valko Slavkov, Industrialist and Dreamer.

He managed to contain his growl.

Camden's snickers nearly drew his ire, though.

"She's playing to the man's vanity and ego, Javier," she said simply.

And all those pieces fell into place with a resounding thump.

Hostage, but not anything more than that. He wondered if the dipshit had folks out there looking for him and Zakhar, so that maybe they could negotiate a peace treaty?

How fucking dumb are you, anyway?

"Not saving him," Javier announced in a terse, angry whisper.

"Nor should it," Camden agreed. "However, I think I have an in that nails him to the ground and distracts him entirely."

"Oh?" Javier asked, turning to the woman.

"Real estate," she grinned.

He matched it. Yeah, that would catch that goon off guard.

PART II

Camden went ahead and booked herself into the best hotel on the station, taking the most expensive suite. The others were elsewhere, on the presumption that they might be recognized if seen, and thus needed to be invisible.

She had napped. Showered. Relaxed.

Dressed in one of her nicer outfits, mostly because it put her in a particular frame of mind when she did.

A message got routed to the ground.

She sipped a mimosa and thought about the con artist she'd been at fourteen as she waited for a response.

Took seven minutes. Her comm chimed with a number on the surface.

She had her handheld balanced just so on the desk when she turned it on for video feed.

"Mistress Forgrave?" a man came on the line.

Not Slavkov. Tall and skinny. Bald and shaved with a thin skull like an eagle. Perhaps her age, but not in nearly as good a shape.

"Indeed," she replied. "When might one arrange a meeting with Mister Slavkov's staff to discuss some real estate holdings?"

Javier and the others had suggested that he would never see

such a thing coming. At the same time, his paranoia might ramp up to astronomical levels to have a random stranger calling.

Scared men make mistakes. And she had an entire fleet of vengeance out there in the darkness. They'd come to rescue Bethany. They would do the same for her.

"Mistress, I'm not sure I understand," the man replied.

"Slavkov has extensive commercial holdings," Camden replied, adding a bit of pique like a woman tired of explaining herself to mere flunkies. "His staff on *Merankorr* directed all inquiries to *Alkonost*. As I was already headed this direction for my summer vacation, I decided to stop in and chat. He has a few places I'd like to see about buying from him."

Her tone suggested cash. Cargo bays full of it. The outfit did as well.

All a con. And not a con, because if he was desperate, he might even be dumb enough to negotiate a deal to get rid of a few places in a hurry.

That lodge. While she'd have to gut it entirely after the fire, it would still be a most wonderful place to have a winter vacation. And she knew how to improve security, having watched an expert team break in the first time.

Not that she had enemies like that coming after her.

Or that she could do anything to save herself if she pissed off Djamila and Afia.

She watched the man's business manager have a small mental breakdown as he processed her words.

Here they were in the middle of major catastrophe, and everyone had to pretend to be perfectly normal. Especially when business arrived.

Innocent business. You'll believe that, won't you?

She smiled, all seductive innocence at the grand magnificence that was Valko Slavkov. She'd known who he was before all this. Hadn't had that great an opinion of the man. Time around the Science Officer had cured her of whatever shreds of respect she'd had for the punk.

Javier and the others were going to kill him.

And maybe she could improve her real estate holdings in the process? Or get him declared a criminal outlaw in a few places, then buy chunks out of government auctions when they were seized? Especially if he was also dead.

The law was what you could convince a judge to let you get away with, after all.

She smiled. Waited. Watched.

"He is indisposed at the moment, Mistress Forgrave," the man finally said, weighing money versus the situation she of course knew nothing about.

"I've traveled this far," Camden replied. "I'll send a list of places I have an interest in acquiring. You can review it with him and get back to me, as I plan to be on the station for a week or two, seeing the sights and perhaps taking tours of the planet itself."

Because buying his interests in *Alkonost*, while stupidly expensive, might just be worth talking. Mostly, she wanted that lodge. And a specific resort with lakefront on *Cyrana*.

But she was open to options. It had gotten her thus far in life.

"Excellent, Mistress," he said, happy that he could deflect her. "I look forward to it."

"And I as well," Camden replied, cutting the line.

She smiled. Part one complete. Shortly, she would know if dipshit himself was still on the planet.

So Javier could cut out his heart and eat it.

While she watched.

PART III

Ilan didn't know Camden Forgrave, but accepted the role as a new boytoy fling she'd met on the station. It let them be seen together and his fake identity had held up well enough this long.

Plus, he had all the killers circling the tree where he'd treed that damned cat.

Woman was money. Dressed like it. Walked like it. Smart enough. Criminal, even if she'd never been a pirate. Didn't compare to Bethany, but what woman did?

They were at dinner. He'd gone ahead and dug a couple of nice outfits out of the stuff Adrian had sent with them, so he didn't look like a hopeless slob. Made sure to trim the beard and get a haircut, noting where things were starting to come in gray a little along the edges.

Date night. Nice restaurant, after his cover had been dive bar food and diners for the last couple of months. Gonna take some adjusting.

He'd probably end up spending more time in the bistro on the ship when this was done if he got too used to it. For now, she sipped a sweet dessert wine while he had decaf with whiskey and Irish cream. They'd split a tart and left only crumbles.

Easy on the eyes. Nice lady. Smart. He could at least relax around her.

Right up to the moment when some asshole walked in the front door and locked onto her back. Expensive suit. Shaved head. Not Slavkov, but had that same skeevy feel Ilan expected when he finally got close enough to kill the guy with his bare hands. Or his teeth.

Ilan locked back and Camden shifted to a war footing, one hand locating a knife on the table and accidentally landing on it as Ilan watched the stranger approach.

Good to know she wasn't just another pretty face, except that Afia and the Dragoon had taken her on a mission armed.

Ilan's scowl brought the guy up short and sent him to circling politely around to where Camden could see him.

And Ilan could hit him in the face with hot coffee. He placed the intruder, then let his eyes unfocus to watch the front as well.

Just in case.

"Mistress Forgrave?" the man asked politely.

Extremely politely. Like realizing that her new boytoy was from the wrong side of the starport and she maybe preferred a little rougher trade?

"Ah, it's good to see you," Camden went all gladhanding. "This is a surprise, but a pleasant one, I hope. There is news?"

Ilan let his face fall to neutral and largely ignored the guy. Boytoy not too bright and didn't talk business with his betters. Simple mechanic who liked getting his hands dirty.

Not at all an assassin come for your boss. Wanna buy a bridge?

"There is," intruder replied as Ilan listened. "My employer has reviewed the list you provided and made a few discreet inquiries. He would like to schedule for you to come down to the surface, where he might host you for a long weekend of relaxed conversation."

Ilan translated that into getting her isolated. After having asked his underworld connections if they knew who Camden

Forgrave—picture attached for identification—was. She was traveling under her regular ID, so the wrong people would know her.

Javier had called her Lady Warlord of *Cyrana*, and that was good enough for Ilan. Criminal enough to run in these circles. Wealthy enough to be admitted into Slavkov's company as a businesswoman.

Good enough to carry a gun around Djamila.

Camden pointedly nodded at Ilan. He smiled up at the guy in a grim, not too bright way.

"Certainly, a Plus-One would be most welcome, Mistress," the intruder said, so either he knew exactly who Ilan was and they were walking into a trap, or he had no clue that the trap was walking into them.

Hell of an opening bid, but Javier had brought a hammer. A whole freaking bag of hammers, when you got right down to it.

"Long weekend?" Camden mused aloud.

"Indeed."

"Perhaps we could arrange a flight down in roughly thirty-six hours?" she pressed, hinting that she planned to stay up much later yet and sleep in.

Lascivious smile on her face was for the goon, because Ilan had kissed her exactly twice in public as part of a role he was playing. And slept on the couch when he'd spent the night in her suite.

She'd nodded at the time and not seemed to take offense, but she'd also been spending a lot of time around Javier, so Ilan figured she was a lot more liberated than the average crime boss.

And, he was willing to admit, he might be a little more smitten with Bethany than he'd expected. And those fuckers had interrupted things about the time that maybe they could have had a conversation on the topic.

Pissed him all the more off, but it wasn't like he could kill them twice.

"I shall make arrangements, Mistress Forgrave," the man said with a bow, immediately withdrawing.

Camden looked him dead in the eyes and reached across the cozy table to take his hand as she leaned in to whisper.

"And now you can go kill those fuckers," she smiled.

Ilan matched it.

Yeah, he'd been looking forward to this part.

PART IV

Djamila and Afia had collected all the information that Ilan and his team had assembled. It was impressive, but Ilan had specifically seen his job as tracking Slavkov down, then staying on the man like a hound until help arrived.

The cavalry was here.

Zakhar's Fleets of Vengeance Assembled.

They had a shard of Suvi, separated still but mostly up to date with everything that the Warmaster had added after Bryce, which had darkened the woman significantly.

"I'm seeing several bases where he has troops, scattered around his damned desert," Afia said. "Do we need to take those in the process of assaulting his main palace?"

"I'm less worried there," Djamila replied. "If they come overland, we're talking hours or even days to get to the center in significant strength. Suvi, could you handle high overwatch?"

"As long as I have Rel*entless* and the Ghost above me, sure," Suvi replied. "Might not be all that accurate with the Pulsars through that much atmosphere if they fly in small things, but it they launch a big transport skiff, I'll be able to spike it to a board like a catfish."

Djamila considered that image. She'd never fished, but

presumed that it must be how you cleaned them. Not that it mattered, but it was a lovely image.

"Let's assume you do shoot a few down," Djamila said. "That puts them on the ground, where they are less of a threat."

"Plus, you've got the drop shuttles available after they deliver cargo," Suvi said. "Or before. And *Trinity*. Not sure anybody else is capable of engaging, but seriously, it's Del. Put the Dragoon in the turret and let him ravage them."

"No, I'll be on the ground," Djamila told her.

"Feel like we should try sneaking in, though," Afia offered. "We can't be with Camden when she flies down, but I suspect that *Argo* landing with some emergency message for her from home might distract the hell out of folks. Especially if we come in low and fast and pop up at the last minute."

"Where, no doubt, automated defense systems panic and shoot us down," Djamila told her. "We need to be inside their base before the alert sounds. How do we get there?"

"Regular cargo runs to the ground," Suvi spoke up. "Both from a couple of cities over the horizon and the station itself."

"Yes," Djamila decided. "Show me what Ilan has been able to gather on the topic."

"Mostly Viv, actually," Suvi replied. "He's been thinking about robbing the place, which is radically different than bombing it."

Djamila leaned back and watched charts and graphs intersperse with maps. Farouk had trained the man, but more of it had been Spider, who was a thief and an assassin, rather than a bodyguard or warrior.

Still, it showed her ways to do it.

"We'll need Javier and Vivian," Djamila said when Suvi finished. "But I have an idea."

PART V

Javier listened to everything and nodded. Camden and Ilan would be traveling to the surface in about twelve hours, so he didn't have long to prepare.

At the same time, he had a big, fucking hammer. Biggest concern was that the son of a bitch got away from him somehow.

They were in a private room Javier's fourth set of identity papers had rented for a week. He didn't have Hajna and Sascha with him, but he had their sensor gear and Afia knew how to make it sing.

The room was secure. And he had several killers around the table with him.

"Long weekend suggests that we have at most three days to do this with Camden and Ilan on the ground," he told everyone, with Suvi recording it so she could burst transmit it to herself out on the ship later. "And I'd rather we hit early, in case someone does recognize our boy in spite of the beard and long hair. Vivian, what can we do?"

"Stealing a cargo shuttle to the ground is easy enough," Vivian replied. "Maybe having Suvi slip out from where she's hiding and just add me and Pana as crew and we'll fly one down, then steal a second one."

"Suvi?"

"They trust their automated systems way too much, Javier," she replied. "Less secure than *Merankorr* or *Sovereign Nakhimov* were, but I've kept a very low profile for now, just in case."

"Worth blowing it at this point," he said. "Dig a hole you can hide in so we can come back for you after this raid, but go ahead and get Vivian and Pana new identities in the system, qualify them as pilots, and set up a cargo run to the ground. Legitimate if you can, deadhead empty if you can't. We need to be moving before Camden leaves."

He turned to Djamila next.

"Six assault shuttles," he reminded her. "Do we split the Bunnies six ways as cadre and communications staff, or have them drop on your position with the main force?"

"Afia and I will be on the shuttle with Vivian and Pana," Djamila replied. "I plan on having two teams meet up with me on the ground. That's roughly one hundred and sixty troopers. Four other units on the cardinal points, more or less, holding positions to simultaneously encircle the palace while engaging anyone attempting to relieve it. One hopes that Slavkov's people are not surprised when we'll be armed with significant ground to air missile capabilities, but that's likely a failure of training on their part."

Javier nodded. He knew that the *Dragon Watch* had studied *Ophiuchi* extensively, both on offense and defense. Helped that they had now met the nine people who had crushed a full cohort of pirate troops all by themselves.

Hell of a bar to clear. They were intent to do just that, though, which just worked in his favor.

"*Golden Gazelle*?" he asked, looking around the room.

"Nice ship," Ilan grinned. "Shame if some damned pirates stole it or something. Think we should centralize an assault that neutralizes that vessel at the top. Either me or Vivian and Pana when they arrive. At least one team on that side with focus. Maybe drop the Dragoon there?"

"No, that will be your task," Djamila replied. "Vivian, you are likely to land close enough to the Gazelle when inserting me and Afia. Pana will immediately withdraw the shuttle when the assault starts, to limit their options for escape. Vivian, you will disable or capture *Golden Gazelle*, however you see necessary. Ilan will assist Afia and me in penetrating the facility with knowledge of the structure. Camden, you maintain contact with Valko or his senior staff as much as possible, especially when the scanners show an assault landing, in order to create chaos. I doubt that you will be allowed in his presence armed, and we cannot assume that you will be able to take a weapon from a guard. If possible, do so, but not at extreme risk, because you remain a trump card I can play later."

"Where am I in this?" Javier asked.

"Trying to keep up with me," Djamila grinned. "Afia has the shortest legs, but I assume she's at least as fast as you in this portion."

Javier matched her grin. She was not wrong.

ALKONOST

PART I

Camden appreciated that Slavkov had enough money to buy anything he wanted, then decorate it any way he saw fit. The greatest pity was that he had no taste whatsoever.

Garish only pointed one in the right direction. Man couldn't spell subtle if she spotted him seventeen letters. Everything was gold on any surface, though she assumed gilt electroplating from his reputation. And the lime green simply clashed with the gold. As did the pink.

The art leaned into the pornographic, rather than the tasteful. Granted, a delicate balance to walk, but it just demonstrated to her that he had no respect for any woman he encountered, so Camden put on a much more masculine countenance and watched on the screen as they descended from the heavens and circled in on Slavkov's enormous palace complex.

Djamila and Suvi had prepared her for the scope. Enormous, because nothing smaller could contain his ego. And all this for one man who normally needed an actual staff of about a dozen.

Everything else was grandeur done by a small man. She assumed tiny in all the wrong places.

Lots of ego. Too much money.

More importantly, enemies. Competent ones.

She glanced over at Ilan, playing the part of the dumb mechanic boytoy like an actor, all gruff and grumble, though he'd been a perfect gentleman around her. Hopefully, Bethany appreciated what she had here, though verisimilitude might require Ilan get physical with Camden later.

It was a sacrifice she might be looking forward to.

"Coming up on landing," the pilot announced. "Everyone please stay strapped in until the hatch opens on the ground."

She watched. The machine delicately slid in, landing next to the much larger *Golden Gazelle*. Staff emerged from a nearby building as soon as the dust started to settle, and Slavkov's business manager was at the hatch when it opened.

He had a name. She knew it. Didn't care, because her role today placed such a man far beneath her and she wasn't going to be in charge of his tombstone when this was done.

Ilan rose and handed her down three steps to the ground, then did a thing where he almost vanished into the scene. Camden would have been surprised, but she'd watched the others on Javier's team do the same thing, time and again. A useful skill.

"Mistress Forgrave, welcome to *Alkonost*," the manager said. "Your luggage will be taken to your rooms immediately. Did you need to freshen up?"

"That would be lovely," Camden replied.

Everything from here in was a con job. She was fourteen again and at the bottom of the food chain in *Cyrana*'s underworld, spoofing tourists and fools with card games and rings of juvenile pickpockets operating like military strike teams.

Camden smiled and followed the man into the first building, where a luxury cart with a driver transported them across the facility to the northwest corner of the palace. About where you might have first caught sight of the notorious Land Leviathan Bethany had written about.

Camden didn't feel the need to build anything similar for herself, though someone might. If you liked slowly driving across flat deserts for a hobby.

She'd rather lay by the pool.

The room, when they got there, was sumptuous. No other word for it. Designed to make you feel poor by comparison, when Camden really felt pity because everything was again in such poor taste.

How could you spend that much money and get something so tacky out of it?

"This is connected to the concierge," the man gestured to a handset near the sofa. "Someone is always available. The time is currently mid-morning local. Shall I return for you in two hours to escort you to lunch?"

"That would be excellent," Camden replied. "Then perhaps a tour of the palace this afternoon, in case I wanted to add *Alkonost* to the list of properties I wanted to inquire about with your master."

She liked that little blink of surprise in his eyes for a moment, as he wondered whether or not she had that kind of cash. Or financial backing.

Something.

She didn't. Not without calling in a number of favors. At least until the estate was in the process of being liquidated and things could be had at fire sale prices.

Shame she had insider knowledge, and all that.

"Very good, mistress," he said, backing out and closing the door.

She grabbed Ilan before he could move and pulled him into a kiss with a great deal more enthusiasm than he was prepared for, but it only took him a moment to wake up and get into character. And she might be taking advantage of him as much as playing for whatever cameras and scanners she assumed were recording everything in here for later blackmail.

Slavkov struck her as that kind of loser.

"Tour?" he murmured in her ear as they snuggled.

"Redo the pool significantly and I might even enjoy the

place," she chuckled. "Other than middle of nowhere socially. Good bolthole if I needed one."

And her own kids, all grown and not all that much younger than Ilan, might turn the place into something. She kept an open mind.

"Come," Camden said, pulling him after her. "I need a quick rest and you get to be my pillow."

It was a little chilly in here, but that was something she could fix later, maybe by adding an extra blanket tonight when she slept.

Assuming Ilan's rage wasn't enough to warm her.

PART II

Ilan paid attention as the tour wandered. Lunch had been too much food, so he'd stopped at enough and let the rest go. Slavkov had a rep as a short, fat fuck, though Ilan had never met him. Supposedly, that was happening over dinner. Presumably, after he and Cam got thoroughly impressed by how much money and munificence the guy had.

Buddy, I was at Drako III. And Nidavellir. Nothin' gonna save your ass.

Money. Badly spent, and he'd seen how the *Khatum* did it to understand. And a few others. This was never-grown-up teenage boy dipshit with a bottomless well of cash.

Hopefully, all that mean shit Armando had done was in the process of drying that up. Sawing him off at the knees, so folks really didn't feel all that put out when Slavkov stopped being anybody's problem.

Place was huge. Slavkov and immediate staff in the northwest corner, taking up a wing almost as big as *Excalibur*. Maintenance facility for the Land Leviathan and other ground vehicles in the northeast quadrant. Another one for shuttles and *Golden Gazelle* in the southeast corner.

Most of the staff were centralized, with monorails that ran

diagonally so nobody had to walk two kilometers to work, but there were also long, straight hallways wide enough for carts like the one driving them around.

Staff flattened hard against walls when they heard the wheels of the cart getting close, so Ilan presumed that anyone who got run over was blamed for not getting out of the way.

Not a lot of guards visible, but bald guy had mentioned that they were in a barracks in the southwest quadrant. He'd seen space for a full cohort.

"Hey," Ilan broke in as the other two discussed architecture. "We flew over another palace maybe twenty clicks east of here. Who lives there?"

After all, playing dumb usually got you better results.

"Oh, that's not a palace," the guy replied. "That's one of the outlying patrol bases."

"Bases?" Stay dumb.

"Valko owns most of this desert," the guy gestured to encompass a lot of area. "Those folks are there to deal with anyone trespassing."

"Doesn't he own the whole damned planet?" Ilan pressed. Be dumb. And gullible.

"No, merely large chunks of it," came the reply. "The coastal cities are handled by a planetary government."

"That he owns?" Ilan asked.

"He dominates," the man corrected with a smile. "They are free citizens."

Uh huh.

"Lots of crime down here then?" Ilan asked, noting that Camden had fallen silent and watchful.

"Hardly any," bald guy replied in a tone suggesting gallows were used to handle anyone getting out of hand.

He turned to the woman. Still a clueless jock rather than a dumbass farm boy.

"Would you really want to own a place like this?" he asked.

"Oh, I might go ahead and buy the entire planet in fee

simple," she nodded, like it was perfectly natural. "Easier that way."

"Makes sense," Ilan agreed.

Bald guy actually goggled a little at that. Just for a moment, but it pushed him into a deeper corner than he had been. Like she might be wealthy enough to do it.

Ilan had no idea how much of what she was saying was complete bullshit, but it didn't matter.

His job was support staff, making her look good.

Not that it took much work.

PART III

Vivian had absolutely no interest in a job as a commercial shuttle pilot, but Spider had required that skill among a raft of others in order to be part of the organization.

Because sometimes you have to suddenly rotate into driving the getaway car.

They'd landed on the surface. Nice day. Planet ran hotter at the equator than most. Almost no polar ice to speak of, but the oceans were pretty small as well, so they didn't do that good of a job regulating things.

Hot and dry, which spawned that massive desert that was the reason they were here.

Valko Slavkov.

Viv shut everything down professionally, certain that someone would eventually ask if the craft had been stolen, save that Suvi had supposedly updated the necessary records and folks would just shrug and adjust.

Lot of that going on. Easier to step back rather than up, when someone else got crazy. Or mean. Or greedy.

Took a special kind of personality to hold your ground and punch them in the mouth. Vivian understood that he was one of the few present that wouldn't immediately start stomping and kicking as well, but only because everyone else would and someone needed to stay calm and rational when Javier and the rest were going junkyard dog on someone.

He turned to Pana.

"Everything cleared?" he asked her.

She was reading a screen and had been handling communications with the ground. Javier and the women had been out a side hatch as soon as he settled, moving into the scenery without anyone noticing, as near as he could tell.

"Affirmative," Pana replied. "Other shuttle has been loaded and the tower is waiting for us to check in from the deck in a bit. No change from current plans."

"Good," Vivian said. "I'm done here. Walking into the terminal and getting lunch since we're about ninety minutes out from liftoff. That should be sufficient for them to board."

No alerts from Camden or Ilan. No challenges as they came down from orbit.

Out in the darkness, a ravening horde of vengeance hung poised and armed.

Angry as only those Swordbearers might be, because Javier had challenged them to save the galaxy from itself.

That *Neu Berne* might save the future said everything that needed saying.

PART IV

Zakhar was acting like an admiral today. What Kliment Cunningham had been doing at *Drako* before Suvi killed him.

Katya was commanding *Excalibur*. Or whatever the right term was. Piet was on the *Ghost*, loaded and defensive because torpedoes were a bitch to use accurately into an atmosphere.

Monika Sykora on *Relentless*. Hayfa Alfarsi on *Kymni Gauntlet*. Vaughn Yueh on *Trinity*. Haniyya Al-Amin and her century commanders, already loaded and waiting aft with Del and the others.

Normally, enough firepower to scare the hell out of folks. And probably here, as well, though they would be the folks that needed scaring.

His fleet of vengeance, but it would be the *Dragon Watch* that carried the field. Zakhar's job was simply to crush all opposition coming to the rescue.

"Suvi, bring me into channel with everybody," he said.

Katya was up on the pedestal in his chair, so he'd taken Kibwe's. Armando's. Mary-Elizabeth was here, because this would be the trickiest shooting. Thomas Obasanjo filling in for the Science Officer. Not as much flair or sarcasm, but the kid was trying.

Bad role models, and all that.

All the faces appeared on the screen in front of him.

"Counting down," he reminded them. "No messages from the ground while they are under radio silence, but we've detected no surprises sent via Suvi's shard on the station, so I presume all is well. When it breaks, Suvi will be in charge of team communications, unless you need to do something as overwatch escorts. Do not ask for permission, unless you plan to destroy a station. Anyone shooting at us gets crushed utterly, because we have too many moving parts and friendlies at risk on the ground. *Excalibur* will be low. You will be protecting her back. We've covered it all, and this is just the point where I remind you that we're all professional pirates of one flavor or another. Nothing we haven't done before. One jump lands us close to orbit. Quick recharge and second jump as we launch our attack."

He caught nods from everyone. Wasn't for all the marbles today, but this would certainly top *Nidavellir* when it came time to stack the Science Officer's legend.

Let Javier have all the glory. Zakhar was ready to go home and retire.

If the galaxy would let him.

Quick check on the clock. Thirty seconds.

Time for a deep breath. A hard flex of the shoulders out and down from the stress that wanted to knot him into a ball, but that was sending Djamila off into battle.

Necessary, but it always made him twitchy. Especially once he'd allowed himself to fall in love with her.

They all had a job to do today.

"Suvi, take us in."

PART V

Javier had gotten better at his shooting. A lot of practice over the last few months, both on the range and in Djamila's Hogan's Alley combat simulator. He was never going to challenge the Gunbunnies for a spot, but he could generally hold his own these days.

Time to go see a man about a killin'.

Pana was flying. Vivian, aft with him, would immediately bail out and steal or disable *Golden Gazelle* when they landed, while Pana sat perfectly still until all hell broke loose.

Still no messages, so they were going in late in the day. Slavkov was notorious for enormous meals that started after sunset and ran deep into the night with the drinking and carrying on.

Man had never heard of having a quick salad and a glass of wine before turning in. Gonna bite him in the ass tonight.

Hopefully.

"Cargo bay, we are sixty seconds out," Pana said on the intercom.

Djamila rose. Afia checked her equipment bag for all the nasty things a Combat Engineer carried into battle. Javier had a bag for Ilan. Vivian was in an outfit Suvi had found that matched Slavkov's people.

Javier had considered bringing the Navarre outfit as Adrian had adapted it, but settled for mottled grays and a gun.

Wasn't going to be a red carpet walk tonight, after all.

He put his game face on and watched on a screen as the horizon dipped. Full dark outside. Temperatures hot but would fall over the next hour until they got nasty bitter cold around four in the morning.

It would all be sorted out by then.

One way or the other.

Time to go see a man about a killin'.

PART VI

Camden had dined with Slavkov. And let herself be suitably impressed with his friends. His hobbies. His enormous...wealth. Probably only big thing about him beyond the gut lapping over the belt working really hard to hold his pants up.

They'd eaten, and she'd suggested a quick rotation to business, so instead of nine desserts, they had retired to a salon that she might have either made fully into a library, all dark wood and bookcases, or pushed over into a conversation pit by drawing up lighter colors and softer everything.

This room couldn't make up its mind, so you had wood, but golden oak. Sofas and chairs, but most were leather instead of cloth. Hard and angular instead of comfortable.

She'd sent her boytoy off while she talked business. Slavkov had taken the hint and dismissed the three airheads he'd brought to dinner.

Not that she'd have minded them distracting him, but it gave Ilan an excuse to not be in the room. Important, with what was coming.

Avalanche. The sort of thing they'd worried about when taking the lodge.

An unstoppable force coming for your soul.

She had a buzzer she could trip that would call off the attack when pushed one way, or summon help early the other. It was currently off.

Her. Slavkov. The Business Manager. Two guards inside the room, with two more on a patio out a glass door set in a full wall. And presumably many more scattered around out of sight.

Basic paranoia, because she'd have never been allowed in if he thought that trouble was coming for him. Let alone this quickly.

The wine was adequate. Too dry and sour for her palate, but she liked a sweeter Malbec when given the option. It did fit Slavkov, though.

"Will you ever rebuild the Land Leviathan?" she asked in all apparent innocence, guessing that to be a soft spot she could poke to work his emotions.

His face darkened.

"I find it unlikely," he replied.

"I had wondered," Camden pursued. "While at the orbital resort, I found a book, recently published by a woman who apparently was compiling memories of folks who had known the vehicle before its demise. You were ambivalent in the manuscript."

"She has been working for me as a research historian," Slavkov replied.

"Oh?" Camden asked, eyes big.

"She has published several books in her time here," Slavkov said. "One a biography of me."

"I saw that," Camden gushed, hoping she wouldn't need a shower later. "Quite interesting, but I hadn't made the connection that she actually worked for you. Had I realized, I would have brought my copies and gotten them signed by both of you."

Always play to their ego. Their vanity. Their importance. Men tended to be such emotionally fragile creatures, after all. Or toxic, in his case.

Spending time around Javier and Zakhar had just reinforced how vast that gap really was. But they were adults in all the ways that mattered, and Valko Slavkov's emotional immaturity shone through more and more.

It did work, though. He preened. Man who just wanted the galaxy to realize his vast genius.

Of course, the rest of them saw him for who he really was.

"I don't suppose you might have spare copies handy that I could get signed?" she asked, all bubbly and cheerleader and whatever else it took to distract the man into getting Bethany into the room.

She wouldn't know Camden, but there were certain code words that would clue her in.

And that avalanche was less than an hour from starting.

PART VII

Bethany had settled in with a mug of hot chocolate and a little rum tonight. The dipshit was entertaining some investor and she'd been worried that she might have to dance for her supper.

He'd done it a few times, but only a few. Mostly to remind her of her place, though his humor had improved greatly since she'd told the galaxy what an awesome guy he was.

She had a book tonight. Dipshit had let her order things for personal consumption from a staff library he apparently kept for the lessers who worked for him. Heavier on genre, but that was fine. Stories of elves and fairies had soothed nerves rubbed raw by yet another day as a songbird in a gilded cage.

The knock at the hatch was almost enough to get her to throw the reader when Aco slipped his head in three seconds later, but he had knocked. And waited, in case she'd been in the tub and nude.

Best to never tempt those beasts that way.

"Good, you're awake," he said immediately, stepping in.

Not looming over her, but being professional. She'd been around enough folks to understand that he was good at it and serious.

"Yes?" she asked, keeping the broken glass out of her voice.

Barely.

"Boss has a guest tonight," Aco said quietly. "Woman investor who has apparently read your books and wanted to get you two to sign them for her."

Bethany had to replay that in her head twice to make sense of it.

What utter moron...?

But she kept her face neutral.

Dancing for her supper. Beat the alternative.

"Sure," she said, finding it easier to just get it all over with.

And hell, that might be a collector's item, one of these days when she was using Dipshit's skull as a coffee mug.

She put her book down and slipped the mug into the cooling unit for now. It would always microwave later.

Slippers by the hatch, sufficient for indoors but impossible on sand and stone.

All those little details to keep a prisoner contained.

Aco watched with a neutral face, then escorted her to the Den of Bad Fashion that seemed to be Dipshit's favorite place to entertain guests.

Northwest facing, with a curve of glass that looked out over the desert. Clear night, so a billion stars.

Both men she expected. One woman who was a stranger.

Older, but well preserved. Maybe sixty and a dancer, rather than fifty and a housefrau. Long white hair pulled back. Hazel-green eyes like Djamila. Stunning, but Bethany didn't know if she liked girls.

Or was at least open-minded enough.

"Camden Forgrave," the woman introduced herself.

"Bethany Durbin," she replied, shaking hands.

She noted copies of all five books on a table nearby, with a pen, so the man was serious. Or the woman was and Dipshit was trying to impress her.

Lady, you'll just be collateral damage if you're too close to him.

But she smiled.

"I have signed my biography, Durbin," Dipshit announced. "Camden was hoping to take home a full set with your signature as well."

Dance for your supper, peasant.

She smiled breezily.

"Of course," Bethany said, moving around the table so she could sit without putting her back to Dipshit.

Aco was off her flank whatever she did, but that was him.

"You are a historian, I understand?" the woman asked as Bethany sat and grabbed the first book.

"That's correct," Bethany replied. "*Concord Navy* trained originally."

Leave it at that, assuming that Dipshit wasn't arranging some bizarre trade like a sportsball thing that saw her on a new team for whatever.

Weirder shit had happened. She'd spent several years hanging around Javier, after all.

"Interesting," Forgrave said naturally. "I was just reading a modern history of the *Concord*. All about a rising storm that the author predicts is coming in our lifetimes."

Bethany was head down and scrawling, so she didn't spit-take all over the woman. Or Dipshit.

Merely paused to look up and see the seriousness in Forgrave's eyes.

Shit, who had Javier recruited that Dipshit didn't know?

Had to be him. Had to be a full-on Bollywood Song and Con job. The Science Officer's *other* signature move.

And this woman knew the gang well enough to have been given a pre-publication copy of Dorn's book.

"That sounds utterly fascinating," Bethany said. "Who wrote it?"

"A professor at *Bryce* named Hetzel," Forgrave said.

Son. Of. A. Bitch.

Was Forgrave a scout? Or was she the inside man?

How long did Bethany have before whatever ultra-violence was coming?

She signed.

Collector's Item with Dipshit's signature. Probably the only one in existence when she killed him.

When someone killed him.

Holy hell, she'd made it. Could see that metaphorical dawn creeping up and lighting up the eastern sky of her life.

A hatch opened. A guard scurried across the room, looking like he had already been stabbed and was holding his stomach in from the look on his face, but he merely slipped close to Dipshit and murmured in his ear.

Bethany was too far away to hear anything, but Dipshit went white.

And she could hear the music starting up, at least in her head.

Her smile was entirely inappropriate for the situation, but she supposedly didn't know any better.

"Get them to safety," Dipshit barked, snapping his fingers at Aco even as he was already headed the other way as fast as those stubby legs could carry him.

Bethany looked up her shadow.

He also looked pained.

"There's an alert," he said simply.

Bethany just barely kept the mad cackling inside.

SHOWTIME

PART I

Javier had meditated on the flight across, knowing that there was nothing to stop what was coming save that they failed.

Or they won.

A hammer was coming down from the heavens like a meteor, and the splash damage would be horrendous before everything settled.

If it ever did.

Vivian was closest to the hatch, because he needed to move hard and fast. Ilan had a comm that he would turn on when shit got ugly and not before. Hopefully he was in position to help, but Djamila was driving things initially.

Javier was there for the final samurai showdown when they got there.

It had started with him. It would end with him.

"Stand by for touchdown," Pana said simply.

Somewhere overhead, Zakhar's fleet of vengeance had just made their second jump, if everybody was on schedule and planetary authorities were either sharp enough to see what was coming or asleep at the wheel.

Javier had already determined that *Alkonost* didn't have anything like the firepower to stop him.

Contact. Settle. Vivian had the hatch open and was already running. Djamila was second down the steps. Afia third because the Dragoon would need her for any locked doors.

Like Speedy had done the first time.

Javier drew a beamer and followed.

Night. Cool. Clear sky.

People split sideways, with Viv racing towards *Golden Gazelle* before anyone on the ground put two and two together.

"Team One, I have eyes on," Ilan's voice was suddenly there. "Rotate thirty degrees to your left and look for a hatch that will open shortly."

Djamila was going like hell on legs as long as he was tall, but Javier wasn't about to let that woman outrun him. Not today.

Light appeared as a door opened. Ilan was there.

As were two guards. Flat. Maybe dead. Maybe not.

Didn't matter in the grand scheme of things, because Javier wasn't feeling a great deal of benevolence at anyone taking Slavkov's money these days.

"Principal is northwest," Ilan said, falling in with Djamila and the rest of them. "Monorail this way, or corridors we can take. There are only two firebreak bulkheads between here and there, and I get the impression that only about half the security force is present in the southwest corner with the rest on picket duty elsewhere. Camden should be with our target at present."

Djamila slowed, the stopped, obviously planning her attack. Corridor was wide but kind of dark. Dim at least.

Then the alarm sirens started ratcheting up to wake the dead. Strobes lights everywhere.

Dragoon leaned down to get into his space and his ear.

"I'll need to command assault troopers destroying the defenders," she yelled. "Afia will be with me. You and Ilan will have to rescue Bethany and kill Slavkov."

"Wouldn't have it any other way," he yelled back.

And honestly he'd kind of expected this. Depending how good planetary defenses were, he was willing to guess that they'd seen *Excalibur*, but not done the math until Suvi launched Del and his sidekicks.

Six assault shuttles, glowing red falling stars as they dove, would set off any mental alarms. And Djamila and Haniyya had assumed air defense missiles, so everyone was coming in low on the horizon from all sides at once. Drop five hundred hungry, angry killing machines, then determine what they needed to do as an aerial combat unit.

Led by Del, who was also not feeling benevolent.

They were at an intersection. Ilan pointed southwest for Djamila, who nodded, then started to backtrack with Afia churning hard.

"Okay, rat boy," Javier smiled to his oldest friend from the *Storm Gauntlet* days. The one who had discovered that dead Norwegian rat in the pipe, "let's do this."

And they were off at a hard jog. With pistols in hand.

PART II

Ilan had just walked up to the two guards when they'd been distracted by the off-schedule landing outside.

And shot them both dead.

Two less assholes to worry about later.

He had a proof of life for Bethany less than two months old, so he was willing to bet she was somewhere in this facility, and he just needed to kill everyone guarding her.

Or who got in his way.

Or who couldn't outrun him.

The Dragoon understood. Javier, as well.

Afia would settle for no less.

"You lead," Science Officer ordered, so Ilan got moving.

He'd gone for a low-profile outfit tonight. Of course Adrian had planned that far ahead, so Ilan had been classy at dinner and could immediately launch an assault afterward.

Like you did in this business.

They got as far as the first sealed bulkhead. His passcard had let him wander the facility some previously, but Ilan had stayed to public places and transit corridors rather than trying to get in anywhere secure.

"This is where I get locked out for being a dumbass and

wandering around without an escort," he told Javier over the noise. Then dialed it down when the sirens stopped blasting. "Probably supposed to be in my room keeping the bed warm for Camden."

Javier handed him the bag that he'd had slung. All Ilan's tools.

He immediately found the knife he needed and popped open the locking mechanism cover. Usual stuff inside. High-end electronics.

Ilan cut the control circuit cable then jumpered the lock mechanism. The bulkhead slid silently open.

"Kill that," he told Javier as he rose and looked into the next section and Javier fired a shot.

Northwest quadrant. Invading troops would normally be kept at bay at this point, because the place had been built like a fortress.

Someone had forgotten about worms.

They were through.

"Lose the pistol," Ilan said, slipping his into a shoulder holster he'd hidden among his gear.

Nobody had bothered looking too closely at the boytoy. Or his gear. He'd stolen the gun off another dead body in a different part of the building.

Javier's vanished and they were just two dudes walking towards the civilian wing.

At some point, they would run into guards or goons or troops. He'd be pulling some bullshit out, but honestly, killing all of them was high on his list and Javier had the *Dragon Watch* about to land outside the facility in a killing mood.

Not a lot to say at that point.

PART III

Viv appreciated a good starship. The *Khatum* had an impossible amount of money and the smarts to hire good people to build and decorate them.

Golden Gazelle was huge. Maybe a little bigger than *Trinity*, and all streamlined and painted pretty outside. White hull with blue and green racing stripes, because starships go faster that way.

Piracy sounded good. Plus, he had some explosives he could use it he had to. Maybe blow off a landing leg and drop the thing onto a shoulder where you'd need a lifter shuttle to get it upright again for repairs.

Something.

Pana would vanish the shuttle as soon as she needed to.

Whoops. Now. Alarms everywhere. Somebody must have seen something.

Or *Excalibur* had just arrived overhead and someone looking up had seen their impending death.

Because this night had been years coming from everything Viv had seen previously. Going all the way back to Slavkov originally hiring Javier—both through intermediaries and false identities—to attack *Shangdu*, where he'd first met the *Khatum*.

Hell of a way to say hello.

Viv was at the pilot's hatch. Ship like this had a fancy place midship for important folks to board. Deployable tunnel like an airlock if the heat was ugly or you had a sandstorm brewing.

Staff loaded aft, with and like the cargo. Pilots went in right below the cockpit. He had a pretty advanced lockpit set, and a willingness to believe that there probably weren't more than a couple of crew on the ship, since it was cold in dock.

If nothing else, he could disable things, but honestly, hanging around with Javier and the others practically demanded that he steal it.

Possibly keep it. Or at least sell it on, though that might be a bit dicey since Zakhar had been so busy obliterating galactic chop shops.

Maybe he'd sell it to the *Khatum* as a trophy. Lines were nice. Interior probably needed to be gutted to the bulkheads with a power sander, based on what everyone thought of the owner.

Hatch up a short, deployable staircase. Asphalt underfoot for a landing pad, with a little sand blown in, but not much so someone had the job of sweeping under here regularly.

Standard controls. Sirens blaring, but Viv was playing a hunch, so he pressed the open button.

And it did. Why would you lock the door in a place like this, after all? Slavkov owned everything within a thousand kilometers. And had killers to enforce his will. Or at least mangy curs.

The real killers were just over the horizon right now.

Vivian got inside and found the emergency override for the lock, so he tripped it, then popped the panel and cut a couple of wires that would have to be repaired for the door to ever open again.

Spiral staircase up. Viv pulled a stunner from his bag, because this was about the only portion of the raid that might require captives later. In case he needed something from the flight crew.

Pigs might fly, but better safe than sorry tonight.

Ship had a nose. Cockpit sat at the top where the hull overhead flattened back horizontal.

Dark. Excellent. Space was big enough for two pilots in comfy chairs with horseshoe consoles, plus a flight engineer opposite the stairwell and a small kitchenette and bathroom aft, all inside this space so important folks aft didn't have to see little people.

Vivian went ahead and closed the trapdoor in the deck and set the bolt on his side. They could bash it open. Eventually. Maybe.

Hatch to the rear was also heavy duty. Split down the middle and retracting into each side. Designed to keep pirates at bay if they somehow boarded and the flight crew had time to jump someplace where the law could come.

Viv set that lock, then pulled a doohickey out of his bag. Breaking in places also involves making sure you can lock others out. This was a bar about the length of his forearm and as thick as his finger.

Magnets held it to the door when he put it in place, then triggered a mechanism that welded them in place. In thirty seconds, it would be easier to cut the door out of the wall than to try to get that bar off.

He waited, pistol aimed while there was a small chance someone might intervene.

Cockpit was now sealed from the rest of the ship. He even had his own life support system up here, separate from the rest of the ship.

Slavkov's paranoia worked in Viv's favor.

Bow was pointed at the desert, but he left the interior lights down at low anyway and climbed into the command pilot's seat. Woman had been flying. Or a really short guy. Took a moment to adjust everything for his length, then he brought up a screen. Low grade life support aft. One generator running power needs, with a second one on warm standby. Engines cold. Ship mostly dark.

Excellent.

He powered up the generators sequentially. Put the engines into warmup mode.

Beep interrupted.

"Bridge," he said, pretending like everything was perfectly normal.

"Who's there?" a man asked. "What the hell's going on that we've got an alert?"

"Somebody is in the process of attacking the palace," Vivian replied. "Ugly people. Gonna kill everyone they can lay hands on. Between you and me, I'd rather get my ass to the orbital station and pretend like I didn't know anybody, in case they come looking. If you want to go die, let me know and I'll drop you off before I leave. Otherwise, keep an eye on your systems and get us the hell out of here, okay?"

Long pause. Lot to digest. Especially the dying for Slavkov part.

"Can we get away?" the man asked.

"I'm part of the bad guys here," Vivian decided honesty was best. "They sent me to steal this ship so Slavkov can't escape justice. Don't mind rescuing you from certain death in the process. As long as you don't do anything stupid right now."

"No, I'm good," he replied. "Generator six has been giving me problems, but I could never convince them to rip it out and replace it with a new unit. It's going to fail at some point, so you might leave it shut down for now. Not like we need that much power if you didn't bring fifty guests and crew aboard."

"Noted and understood," Vivian told him. "Strap yourself in and stand by for launch."

All systems were green. Even Six, but he cut it and shut it down anyway. The others were barely putting out anything at this point anyway. No passengers, kitchens, or whatever needing power.

Golden Gazelle had the best autopilot in the market. Viv still cut it out of the loop, too, and took manual control. Too much time around Suvi, understanding what she could do, even from a distance.

And he was a pretty damned good pilot.

Up.

Comm on.

"*Golden Gazelle*, lifting on standard and departing the scene," he announced on the team channel.

"Exceptional news, *Gazelle*," Del replied instantly. "You are clear for liftoff."

Vivian got just high enough to retract the landing gear, then went straight forward and brought the bow around a little to the right. Southeast, slipping between two assaulting forces and on a vector that didn't overfly any of the outlying bases.

I mean, if you're going to all this effort to steal a ship, you better get away with it.

PART IV

Suvi could feel the upper atmosphere tickling her hull like snowflakes. Below, Del and his team were diving hard and fast as only the *Dragon Watch* might do it, when challenged by the old man.

Heh.

Stations were waking up, but nothing they could do where she was at except maybe lob some torpedoes her direction, where *Relentless* and *Trinity* would be camped nearby and waiting.

Piet and the *Ghost* were handy on overwatch in case she felt like punching someone in the mouth.

Alerts were coming on. Air Defense scanners lighting up the night as they found her hovering overhead.

"Zakhar, do we need to do anything about those bases?" Katya asked on the command line. "We have gravity on our side."

Suvi paused. Rewound. Laughed.

Sure as shit. Torpedoes were tracking weapons, but they would go straight down like bombs if a girl knew what she was doing.

"Suvi, how dangerous do they look?" he asked.

Hard scan to update everything she'd told herself from the vantage of the station.

"Two of them are big," she replied to the humans. "The rest are little patrol bases with sensor towers and a two-car garage. The big ones might have air defenses that matter."

"Agreed," Zakhar said. "You find the wind drift and drop a couple of surprises on those two to see what they have. Stay away from Slavkov's palace for now, because I assume he had stuff there."

"Not sure I can do that without risk, Zakhar," Suvi replied.

Being honest. Being a warship meant stepping into trouble, but most of her job was distraction.

"Understood, Suvi," Zakhar said. "This is a test. If they are tougher than we expected—or the palace unveils orbital firepower, have Piet overload them. Even forcing them to stop that level of firepower keep them off you."

Piet? The *Ghost*?

Yeah, he had enough launchers to annihilate a lot of ground targets that didn't have the power to dodge or shields that could absorb it.

Suvi started doing some meteorological calculations.

PART V

Afia had had extra coffee today. Final potty break before landing, and a caffeine pill to supplement.

She wasn't quite tasting color, but Djamila's long legs couldn't outrun her.

Gates of Hell And Beyond kind of night.

They'd backtracked and moved lateral. Found the corridor to the southwest that Ilan thought led to the barracks. Hatch was closed. Big one. Secured against anything she had, though fools always assumed steel was sufficient and forgot about the control systems.

Combat Engineering went beyond the work of Sappers.

"I need antipersonnel mines here and here," Djamila pointed.

Afia studied the scene. Corridor eight meters wide here. Two little carts or a big flatbed truck if you got one inside.

Did they have tanks available?

Then she rotated one-eighty and looked northeast. Motor pool. Have to get there to get to those tanks.

Heh.

She dug into her bag and brought out the party favors. The red-tipped ones that threw steel rather than the roman candles that just went boom and scared the shit out of you.

First pair in place, with a wire connecting them about four centimeters off the deck. Most folks didn't lift their feet and high-step.

She backed up about two meters and dropped the second pair. Same thing.

Nasty surprise, but Djamila would be leading the infantry assault and would remember. Or sending Afia and the Storm Giants. This corridor would be off-limits until it was blackened. Twice.

"Done here," she said, popping up to about the Dragoon's belly-button.

"Backtrack," Djamila said. "Meet the cohort and lead them into a lateral assault designed to draw eyes away from Javier and Ilan."

"Monorail," Afia pointed.

Djamila looked up and nodded, then fired five times as fast as her Kehoe Mark IV Heavy Beamer would cycle the cooling circuits.

Divots in the rail itself turned into a bite like a shark had gotten a seal. Afia figured that it was fifty/fifty that the first rail crossing got stuck halfway across versus shearing it and falling.

Five more shots and the other rail was in just as bad a shape. If not worse.

"Transport infrastructure disabled," Djamila noted dryly.

Afia was already jogging, smaller pistol in smaller hand as they started back the way they'd come. Five hundred *Neu Berne* Assault Marines would be deploying shortly.

Angry people.

Almost as dangerous as her.

PART VI

Camden would have liked to have been kept close to Slavkov, but his panic was sending her off with Bethany, which honestly was her second choice anyway.

Wasn't like that fool could escape what was coming.

The guard gave off signs of exceptional professionalism. The kind of man she'd have hired for a similar job, guarding a high-value intellectual prisoner.

Hopefully, he would see reason when the others arrived, because neither she nor Bethany were armed. Well, beyond fists, feet, teeth, and attitude problem.

Sometimes, a girl has to make do.

"Where?" Bethany asked the goon.

"Figure your quarters for now," he replied. "That's likely to be safest. Mistress Forgrave, my apologies for the chaos. Miss Durbin is a guest and a prisoner, but her space is secured and nobody will likely bother you if things do get out of hand."

"Out of hand?" Camden asked as they fast-walked.

"The reports include several warships in low orbit and what appear to be a full marine assault force deploying. Someone is exceptionally angry. At present, they have not chosen to bombard this base, so I presume that Miss Durbin's friends have finally located her and have arrived to rescue her."

"And your job, sir?" Camden asked, because it looked like she was going to be a prisoner at this point.

"Surviving," he said. "Since I'm not part of the combat force around here, I usually guard her. Adding you."

"Guarding?" Bethany sneered.

"Keeping you out of trouble, maybe, Bethany," he growled back. "I know your kind. Almost as dangerous as Forgrave here."

Then he stopped and turned to look right at her.

"Shit," he muttered. "They're your friends and you were the scout."

Camden wondered if he was about to shoot both of them, when he turned and started walking again.

"Let's go, ladies," he said over his shoulder.

Bethany was almost as surprised as Camden, but they caught up with him. Got to a side corridor down a small warren of others. He opened a hatch and stepped in. Bethany followed.

Camden found herself in what was probably Bethany's quarters.

The guard had put his firearm away.

"Bethany, I'd like to not get shot when your friends kick in the door, please?" he asked her politely. "We're way out of the way and hopefully Slavkov forgets about you until tomorrow if he somehow holds them off."

"You assume we'll win?" Bethany asked.

"Multiple warships," he replied. "Multiple assault shuttles, from the looks of it. Lots of planning, which means they probably know what's going on here and have prepared to handle it."

"The ground force is the *Neu Berne Dragon Watch*," Camden said simply, watching the man's eyes practically bug out.

"Shit," he muttered again, then pulled out his pistol and handed it to her butt-first. "These people are fucked."

"I would tend to agree," Camden told him. "What is your name?"

"Aco Vasić," he said, moving to the refrigerator and grabbing a bottle of juice, then moving to a chair and sitting. "Like I said, I'd rather be your prisoner and maybe get out of this alive. Just a job."

"Bethany?" Camden asked, holding a pistol on the man.

"He's been professional," she replied. "You really brought a *Neu Berne* Assault Marine force?"

"Djamila is pissed," Camden replied, nodding. "Took Javier there and he charmed them into helping. One of those warships is a *Neu Berne* escort they hired out."

Aco Vasić had gone completely white. Almost frozen into salt or alabaster, save for sipping the juice.

"Aco, keep minding your manners," Bethany threatened the man, but there was no heat behind her words.

"Understood, mistress," he nodded barely enough to count.

No sudden movements. Camden wasn't feeling as friendly, but it looked like someone had known how to do the necessary math.

Others weren't going to be as fortunate.

THE MUSIC STARTS

PART I

Javier found the empty corridors fascinating. Monorail looked locked down, and the only folks he'd seen had been ignoring him and running. Ilan was walking beside him and they were casual.

Mostly side corridors at this point, where you expected staff instead of players.

Or boytoys sneaking around while their meal ticket was busy with the boss. All the folks he'd seen had been support staff. Cleaners, cooks, that sort of employee, with the goons well away from folks that might be offended to see them.

They came to a closed door.

"Through here is the main corridor not far from where Camden's suite is located," Ilan muttered. "No idea if they have guards out front or where she might be located at present."

"You walk out like you just had a quickie with a cook and need to get back without being seen," Javier replied. "I'll watch from here and cover you. If she's there, we get her out. If not, we keep looking."

Ilan nodded and shrugged himself into character. Honestly, Javier had known him the longest, because Djamila had shot him the first time they met, then bounced his head off a bulkhead the second time, so she didn't count.

Guys bonding over dead rats.

Ilan opened the door and slid through. Javier had a pistol in hand down on his thigh, out of sight as he caught he door and peeked.

Across and down. Nobody moving. Ilan got to another hatch and opened it, standing in the door and calling for Camden.

After a few seconds he turned around and shook his head. Javier waved him back, then slipped to one side.

"Next step?" he asked.

"They were supposed to be negotiating a deal of some sort in a spot somewhere in the northwest corner of the palace," Ilan said.

"Yeah, I know where that is," Javier replied. "And what. Never liked it. At the time, I didn't realize that Slavkov owned all this, but that was Navarre being hired for a gig and flown in quietly to board the Land Leviathan and deal with a recruiter. Stayed a day after the mission was complete. This way."

Javier took the lead. He hadn't been skulking then, but had a map of the facility in his head, now that he had an idea where to start.

Punk like Slob probably had a panic room close by. Maybe a full bunker, but Javier doubted that he'd be so lucky.

After all, some construction equipment and maybe a concrete mixer and he could seal such a thing off forever. Places like that were intended for days, not lifetimes.

Except that sealing off any and all vents and it would be a short lifetime.

Ilan fell in on his flank and they stalked, both armed.

And Ilan had already killed at least three people tonight, but Javier understood that he and Bethany had walked right up to the line a few times and never crossed. Like Zakhar and Djamila for too many years.

Get her home. Get them as much of a happily-ever-after as he could.

And kill this dumb son of a bitch once and for all.

And even then, he wouldn't be done. Not quite.

Still going to carve a path as wide as his arms would reach, killing any pirates that couldn't run fast enough to escape him.

He walked.

Palace existed on about four levels, with the top one usually having either vaults or high square ceilings depending. Place he wanted would be low. Ground or under.

And guarded. That was fine. If he ran into more trouble than he could handle, Javier had the *Dragon Watch* landing any moment now and already set to blow holes through people and things as they needed.

Javier had had enough of this shit.

PART II

Djamila emerged not far from a place where troops could be marshaled and marched around outside. Training ground, of a sort. Landing field for small transports carrying troops in and out.

Shadows in a few places, but someone had lit every tower and building with every flood available, so it was as good as daylight outside. While that might blind attacking troops, the *Watch* was already prepared.

And Djamila had brought her Combat Engineer.

They slid with stealth to a corner. Djamila peeked around and noted infantry starting to form up, then being sent out in ten and twenty-man patrols to locate what no doubt had caused significant panic at command levels.

One man over there appeared to be an officer. With two old-school cadre handy. Leader-4 types who had seen it all and done it all.

"I need a grenade," Djamila muttered, then had one in her hand because Afia knew what this day was about.

Djamila armed it and stepped around the corner slowly and calmly, like another soldier. Her cast was high because she wanted it to land and detonate.

Quick draw and she took out the officer with a shot, then ducked back and listened to thunder shatter the night.

Afia was low, around the corner and firing from boot height, so Djamila got up on her toes and reached out at eyeball level. Her eyeballs.

Several men already down. She made sure. Decapitating an enemy force was the fastest way to nail them to the ground, and maneuver was the key to victory tonight.

Afia rolled a smoke grenade, then chucked a fragmentation device.

"Time to back off," Djamila told her.

"On your ass," Afia replied.

All that noise would draw more troops in this direction, but they would be uncoordinated. Flailing.

And facing the best infantry unit in the galaxy.

Djamila moved lateral.

"Force Prime, this is Force One," Haniyya Al-Amin called on the comm. "Explosions noted. Unit deployed and standing by."

"Force One, push against position eleven, understanding that there are patrols in front of you at platoon strength," Djamila replied. "Localized artillery is approved, but keep it at the edge instead of the interior."

"Suppression fire beginning shortly on position eleven, Prime," Al-Amin replied. "Moving up to engage. Corner elements all show green."

Djamila nodded.

Four teams dropped on the cardinal points to hold the outside and provide mobile reserves while Force One slammed into the infantry barracks at full speed.

A barracks unprepared because someone had taken out the officer on duty. Or the one guy reacting fast enough to try to stop her.

Pity she'd had to kill him, because good professionals were hard to find, but he was enemy until they decided that they were tired of her killing them.

"Dragoon," Afia barked, drawing her to a stop.

Afia was at a small door almost hidden under grime and weathering. Sand against the threshold.

"Backstage entrance," Afia said. "If the *Watch* slides to their right, we might be able to flood them in right here."

"Set explosives to take out the door and part of the wall," Djamila replied. "Hold until we have help, so the defenders don't see it coming."

"Working."

"Force One, this is Prime," Djamila said. "One team to assault and force position eleven. One team on the right flank near position nine. We are about to open a hatch with explosives."

"Roger that, Prime," Al-Amin replied. "Rotating now. Seven minutes out."

Probably faster than that, but Djamila understood that the *Watch* would be stumbling over patrols and engaging in point-blank firefights as they jogged closer.

Plus, at some point someone would deploy heavier weapons in turrets and towers.

Right on cue, two missiles slammed into a pair of guard towers on the southwest corner and overlooking the quad she'd just hammered. The night lit up with flaming mushrooms, and weapons opened up all around. Mostly random, panicked fire, but that was fine.

Panic was infectious.

Djamila stayed close to the wall and pointed a weapon each direction as Afia worked.

PART III

Camden had Aco's pistol. The man showed no signs of concern, except when an explosion shook the entire building under their feet.

"*Dragon Watch*," he muttered to himself and shook his head.

"Javier brought everybody?" Bethany asked.

"When you disappeared, that meant that the *Concord* had ignored your Ambassadorial credentials. Zakhar and Suvi are apparently ready to level this place. Afia is beyond that. Javier and Ilan truly frighten me."

"As they should," Bethany nodded. "It's the scale of what he'd done that concerns me."

"Oh, and someone named Armando went to *Bryce* and apparently spent several months stirring the pot there," Camden offered. "First with the intellectuals. Later on the streets. Dorn Hetzel was involved, along with a shard of Suvi who called herself Warmaster."

Bethany shivered, but obviously she knew all the players in greater detail.

"Well, that's Volume Two to go into the secret files," she muttered.

"What's that?" Camden asked.

She listened as Bethany walked her through a secret history of the Science Officer that was to be secured until everyone involved was dead, which a *Sentience* could manage. Camden didn't get any details, but apparently everyone had been willing to be fully interviewed and offer updates and corrections under those specific circumstances.

And they would be doing the same with this thing, as well. Probably for the best, considering that the building shook a second time.

Someone was using high explosives out there. Surgically, too, because Camden had been present for planning that involved *Excalibur* leveling the base from low orbit if necessary.

Hopefully, it wouldn't come to that.

Still, she turned to the man.

"Vasić, could you get us outside the palace safely?" she asked. "The folks out there are here to rescue her, so you'd be taken prisoner and safe."

"Define safe," he replied darkly.

"Ilan Yu and The Science Officer might decide to kill everyone on the premises," Camden told him. "Everyone. And folks like the Dragoon and the *Dragon Watch* are angry enough to execute that order. I think we're better off getting clear so that once Slavkov is dead they might withdraw. His ass is entirely forfeit, but not everybody else has to be on the chopping block with him."

That got through. He rose and carefully made his way to the refrigerator, pulling out several more bottles, then moving to the hatch.

"You both need something to stay warm," he said. "I'm fine for one night in this gear. Bethany, grab some spare clothes and we'll take your jacket and your cloak."

Bethany was in motion. Camden watched, armed but not threatening him.

He was acting like a professional given his head to do a thing.

Like a man who saw exactly one way out of this situation alive and was intending to take it.

She could honor that. Bethany at least had enough respect to speak up for him.

Clothes. Dark stuff. Camden added a sweater that was too big, but the historian was a tall woman. Sleeves rolled up.

Vasić stuck his head out the door and looked both ways.

"Hide the gun," he told her, then opened it fully and stepped out.

Camden had the cloak, so that was easy enough, then she and Bethany were in his wake.

PART IV

Del had delivered a crew of armed berserkers on the back side of a big dune where he was a lot closer than he'd originally been expecting to get. Shit moved around with wind, but this cut all sight lines to less than two kilometers, and he'd come in fast on the deck for this one. Shuttle trailing hadn't done a half bad job, either, though he'd be sure to find nits to pick later over beer.

Gotta keep the kids in line, you know.

All six had gotten in and out. Fools that built the place had assumed orbital assaults dumb enough to come straight down, rather than slam over the horizon at high speed, skipping all the watchtowers to get in and down fast.

Failure of planning, simple as that.

And he had six—*SIX!*—assault shuttles handy.

It was so tempting to buzz the place, but he just knew someone was sandbagging for that. They'd lose at least one. Unacceptable.

"Three through Six, lift and withdraw to provide aerial overwatch," he ordered. "*Excalibur* will watch on your sensors and provide direct orders you will obey. Two, you're with me."

Suvi was there almost as fast as he spoke.

"What ugly shit are you doing, Del?" she asked.

"Injecting chaos," he smiled at her screen. "They have chosen the death ground. I'm gonna add confusion to all those silly geese that are no doubt getting recall orders to defend the base in the middle of the night."

"I can hit anything large enough to be a threat from here," she retorted.

"Yeah, but you can't do this," Del laughed. "Two, come about counter-clockwise on my outer flank and stand by for Mach speed."

Sure, missiles were lovely. Beam emplacements could be dangerous.

Really hard to hit something this low blasting by you at two thousand kph.

Del fixed the turret barrels forward and down, lined up right down his centerline. Accelerating, he lined up the largest of those out-bases on his zero and triggered the guns. They wouldn't over-heat in the time involved, and would be sucking so much wind that it would cool them pretty well.

The sand behind him had enough energy to roostertail, which was both impressive as shit and exactly what he had in mind.

Warps the mind to see something like a giant sand worm coming at you that fast on a screen. Even if it was entirely bullshit.

The best kind of bullshit.

Two was on his outside flank. Maybe eighty meters out and back so they were kicking up a lot of sand behind them. And carving divots in the ground ahead of them as they went boom.

Then they were past. Del kept things straight for a four count, then started to his left. Two was the best of those five pilots. Stayed right with him. Second base would be awake and trouble. Might even get missiles up.

Del ignored them for a maintenance yard Ilan and Pana had identified from orbit.

Nobody shooting back.

"Two, slowing down," Del announced, letting that one back down before he took hit foot off the pedal.

Sure, ground troops with rifles. No moron is going to issue missiles randomly to guard troops. Too likely to either blow themselves up or shoot down a guest.

Del slid into hover about a hundred meters out and let his maneuvering jets bring the bow around as he lit up the night. And found a fuel farm that went boom really pretty.

Might have heard that clear back at the palace, which was its own kind of pucker, because all the outbases would lockdown and dig in.

Instead of riding to the rescue.

Or into the teeth of an Assault Marine cohort given a week to plan and an hour to dig in.

Del liked to think he was saving all these poor kids from dying tonight, because they'd stay safe here.

Then he ran out of things to shoot.

Pity.

"Suvi, dear, anyone else needing to be chastised?" he asked.

"No, you pirate," she laughed. "All channels are freaking out and nobody is answering with orders so they are laagering."

"Excellent news," he smiled. "Two, let's roll to starboard and find a nice place out a few dozen kilometers to land and await orders."

"You sure you won't get lost, Del?" the woman flying Two replied.

He laughed. Just as snarky as his kids. Good to see *Neu Berne* berserkers would unbend and get a little silly, once they had bad examples to learn from.

He turned and slipped into the night.

PART V

Afia's belly button hurt, but she understood that it was entirely psychological. Emotional.

The muscles had healed. Other than a through and through scar, there was no physical evidence that she'd had a meter of steel rammed through her guts by a pirate ship opening fire on a life pod.

One of these days, she was still taking some of her life savings and hiring an assassin to locate that captain and crew. Probably raise enough for a small army of bounty hunters if she mentioned it to Ilan and a few others.

Tonight, she wanted the son of a bitch that had hired them in the first place. Couldn't just annihilate the joint until they rescued Bethany and Camden, so she had to do it surgically.

Good thing the Dragoon brought a Pixie Kodiak Combat Engineer.

Movement nearly drew fire.

"Prime, this is Force One, we have eyes on," Haniyya said over the comm, waving so she didn't get shot.

"Come to rest there and get into single file line," Afia ordered. "I will blow this door and you will insert into the facility from a soft and presumably undefended spot, as they are still fighting to hold position eleven."

"Understood," Haniyya said. "Standing by."

Afia looked over at Djamila and caught the woman's nod. They were on either side of the hatch. Corridor behind it should be a standard four-meter width, so the force could spread out quickly. And move at a hard run firing as they were suddenly inside the base.

And Afia would be one step behind the Dragoon as they moved.

Thumb on the detonator. Deep breath. Pain in her stomach where the nerves remembered nearly dying.

No, dying three times and coming back from hell every single one of them.

Should have buried me ten meters deep if you were serious.

Thumb down. Supersonic crack. Exploding masonry and wall. Smoke.

Move.

Dragoon was in and firing at any shadow that looked interesting. Afia did the same.

Nobody there, but there was never extra credit for neatness when using high explosives.

Or softening up a room when you made entry.

Dragon Watch moved, but they'd have to keep up.

Afia was in front of them and gaining ground.

FIRE AND FURY

PART I

Javier had the scent he wanted. North edge of the palace had the prettiest views, because southern sun was brighter than shit and the days got exceptionally hot around here. Guests stayed there. Important guests, anyway. No idea where Bethany rated.

As you moved away from the north, things went down in value, with the goons at the south edge and staff in between, again in descending strips of need.

Cooks and cleaners would be closest to the mechanics. Maids, butlers, and concierges would be closest to the money.

Slavkov would want to be close to the goons with guns who were supposed to die protecting him.

Tonight, they were probably coming face to face with what that really meant, because Djamila had convinced him to save her people.

To rehabilitate them in the eyes of the galaxy, because nobody else would.

Hell of a statement on galactic politics.

Add it to the legend of the Science Officer, pal.

They were on the ground floor. The palace was not a single building, but a whole series of places connected by tunnels or covered arcades. Pretty. Italianate, as done by yokel trash instead of an educated palate, but Camden had mentioned wanting to possibly buy that lodge on *Merankorr* once it was done being gutted to the walls, so she could redecorate it the way it should have been done.

He was still torn about introducing her to Behnam. Galaxy might not be safe. He was probably not in that much personal danger.

Hopefully.

Lights had been lit to evening standards as they came down one more flight of stairs Javier wanted.

Then somebody blew something up and everything went dark for two seconds, battery lights coming up after that at a quarter of what things had been.

Either they had lost a generator, or someone had taken out a relay. All the power was out except local.

Useful here, because doors unlocked. Standard fire safety feature because you lost power when fire got out of hand, and needed people to be able to escape.

Even if they worked for that punk.

Ghost town. Nobody visible for minutes at this point. Either hiding in their rooms or congregating in prearranged locations.

As long as they stayed out of his way.

"How close?" Ilan asked in a voice quiet enough that Javier could ignore him if he needed to.

Javier pointed.

"Fifty or seventy meters that way," he replied. "Next door inside probably puts us into the tower where he built his panic room, with a couple of layers of guards around him. Thinking about fire."

"Got smoke," Ilan replied. "And a few thermals for starting them, but this place is too much concrete and adobe to burn at normal temperatures."

"Yeah, but do they know that?" Javier asked, grinning.

"Unlikely," Ilan matched it. "You need to be trained in civil engineering at a deep level."

"Stealth time," Javier said. "I'm bloodhounding. You shoot things."

"Got it."

Javier put the pistol in his holster for now so he looked more like a mid-level manager caught up in the chaos. Maybe off having his own quickie with a mechanic or something and confused as to where he was when the alarms sounded.

Navarre-the-killer wasn't only one role he'd played routinely over the years.

Head up, then hunched in a bit. Shoulders drawn in as well. A man controlling his fear enough to move mostly normal.

He walked. Past the door that his brain screamed **Access Portal!** as he went by. No reason to deal with anyone until he had to.

Sound drew him. Over the occasional explosions and sounds of shit unraveling on his left as Djamila's people carved their honor into history. Humming and a little grinding.

There.

Ha.

Heat pump. Standard design ancient because it worked so damned well. Draw heat out of the building during the day, then push it back in at night when the desert got cold.

Air intake. Good screen over it to keep out any birds or lizards, then a finer filter inside that for dust and particles. Probably somebody's job to come by and wipe it down every day or three depending on the weather.

He could do the work better than most, but he had a Combat Engineer with him. One of two.

Even the Storm Giants were second tier. Not second rank. Merely a step behind Afia and Ilan.

Who were the best.

"This intake," Javier touched it, then drew his pistol and put his butt against a nearby wall where he could watch. "Open it and I want smoke going in on the draw."

"Internal alarms likely to slam it shut and go to bottled air at that point," Ilan noted.

"Seals him in," Javier replied. "And sets off a fire alarm on top of the combat alert. How many shocks to the mental system can his guards take?"

"Not many more," Ilan growled and got to work.

Javier ignored him at that point, sniffing the night for the scent of trouble. Alerts worked in his favor, because nobody was supposed to be moving around, and any *Dragon Watch* folks he found knew him on sight and hopefully liked him enough to hold fire.

A sudden click and hiss and Ilan chuckled darkly under his breath.

"The gods love you," he said, standing in a pool of smoke coming out of the vent by his knees. "Some idiot put the main cutout at the top. Think I disconnected the wires to actuate it, so unless they have a secondary system at the bottom, they're sucking in smoke at this point."

And that, my friends, was why you hired a Combat Engineer, and not merely a Sapper.

Or a pyromaniac.

"Let's find someplace to hide, just in case," Javier said, already in motion.

Deeper back into the place. Past that one door his mind had marked, so folks coming out looked the wrong way. Along the arcade quickly, moving from shadow to shadow.

Didn't take long. And he'd missed something, because there was suddenly a sharp spike of flames emerging from the vent and heat Javier could taste from here.

"Added some propellant," Ilan snickered when Javier glanced over. "Not sure if I can get the paint hot enough to melt or catch fire, but it's gonna be close."

Javier just shook his head.

Then everything came to complete stillness as that hatch he

wanted opened and a squad of soldiers spilled out in a spasm of smoke and coughing. Like the building was filling up.

Voices were too low to get anything but panic from their tones, but they were looking around a little wild-eyed.

And, apparently, the gods really did love him, because something exploded overhead with a bright crack like a roman candle, filling the night with daylight and a sound like God herself clapping for attention.

Those men freaked and bolted. Away from him.

"Four down," Ilan muttered. "Hopefully, they run right into Djamila's people."

Javier let that one go. *Dragon Watch* probably shot them all dead on contact, but they worked for Valko Slavkov and he'd run out of sympathy.

They waited, but nobody else emerged, so Javier was willing to bet that that punk had sealed themselves in and gone to local life support for now.

"Let's go," Javier whispered, stepping into the darkness.

PART II

Djamila had the best of the six teams with her, with the second best unit pushing against the barracks on her left with as much noise as they could generate over there. That let her pinch in and across.

And surprise people, because nobody had warned them that the *Dragon Watch* was already inside the facility, and they were unprepared for the eruption of violence on this flank and rear.

Several bulkheads and guard checkposts had fallen. The defenders had finally had a chance to dig themselves in and achieve a stalemate, even though that favored her for the next several hours.

Djamila didn't care if they didn't get out alive. Assaulting the place this way was her opportunity to locate Slavkov instead of just bombing everything into rubble and hoping.

That, and bringing down the man financing the piracy that was so endemic in this region of space. Others might step up to replace him, but they'd be hard pressed, if he was dead and the clans scattered in fear.

And The Science Officer was still out there.

Djamila was back around a corner with a fire team of ten in

front of her keeping heads down over there. Haniyya Al-Amin stood on one side, with Afia on the other.

"What's the surveillance report?" Djamila asked.

She'd been focused on killing people up until now.

"Del neutralized the outer watch towers and they aren't providing any assistance at this point," Suvi replied from her comm. "I'm not seeing any movement outside your target other than your troops."

Decision time.

She turned to Haniyya.

"Order half of all four teams forward to start pushing in," Djamila said. "Have the South and West teams join this assault and see if we can force everyone inward for long enough to matter. North and East teams can attack the motor pool if the mechanics are feeling ambitious, or take them prisoner. Same for unarmed staff, because this place has hundreds of people working like it was a hotel. At this point, we're just dealing with maneuver and overwhelm. Can you handle it?"

"What will you be doing?" Haniyya nodded.

"Hunting," Djamila replied.

Afia grinned and they started backtracking. Javier and Ilan were in here somewhere, as were Camden and Bethany. Pana and Vivian had absconded with the two big ships that might have gotten Slavkov clear, leaving only little shuttles that would be pigeons when Del fell on them.

Hopefully, it would be enough.

PART III

Bethany was walking like normal, with Aco on her flank and Forgrave trailing just a bit. She knew the palace, but hadn't really explored it, so he was offering turns as they went.

"Left here," Aco said quietly.

Away from the explosions and battles that had been filling the night for the last thirty minutes.

Bethany came around a corner and blinked in surprise to be facing one of those glass-faced airlocks that filled this place. Clear sands visible outside in front of her, lit up but empty.

She glanced over at Aco and got a nod.

"Maintenance crew access for the Land Leviathan," he replied to her unasked question. "The engine would park right there and folks could come and go on the ground floor without intruding on wealthy guests."

She even remembered using this hatch, back when she'd been doing the research for the book. It and the ornithology tome were about the only useful things from her time here. That, and all the things she'd learned about Dipshit for when she added it to Javier's next book.

Always useful to have both sides of the story, even if one side is entirely and intentionally the villain. She could utterly destroy him to history.

And planned to.

Bethany looked over at the side.

"Locked," she said simply.

Almost everything was locked. To her. Which was why she had needed a guard for these months. To get her in and out of various places she couldn't manage on her own.

Aco pulled a badge from his pocket and opened it. Even in an alert when everything should be bottled up tight. The inner door slid open and let them into the glass airlock with the fantastic views of the desert since there weren't enormous wheels immediately in your face.

Through the second one, they emerged into darkness.

And NOISE.

All of it over her left shoulder, but tremendous explosions and the dull whomps of beam weapons cycling.

The terrain around them was utterly flat for nearly a kilometer, but that was the runway for a Land Leviathan and space to repair anything that broke or needed upgrading.

"Straight out and mind your manners," Camden suddenly spoke. "There are eyes out there watching."

"Remind them I'm behaving," Aco replied, then set out across hard-packed ground.

More sand had accumulated in recent years because there was no more Land Leviathan, but it had still crushed things flat in its time. Enough light to see. Nobody shooting at them.

They walked.

Bethany followed Aco towards a little gap between a pair of dune hills. If there was more water, that might be a wadi, but here it was just how the winds carved things.

"That's far enough," a gruff voice called, almost exactly at the moment she'd been expecting it.

"Bethany Durbin, escaping custody," she called back.

"Camden Forgrave and a guard to be taken into custody for now so nobody shoots him accidentally."

Hands were they could be seen. No sudden movement.

"Librarian Durbin?" a woman asked. "We're here to rescue you. Walk this way."

"I'm Camden Forgrave. And I currently have the guard's gun under my cloak. Nobody get twitchy."

"We've got you, ladies."

A dozen troops suddenly stood up from the sand like demons. Bethany held her shriek in, but it was a close thing.

She turned to Aco.

"Your badge," she said.

"Right breast pocket," he replied. "Not pulling it out right now, thanks."

She understood that. Lots of guns pointed at him, but he'd been professional. Competent. Polite, even when he didn't have to be.

She retrieved the card and held it out to the woman soldier.

"Top level security access to most of the facility," Bethany said. "He's been my bodyguard up until now. What is the situation?"

"Stand by. Orders to exfiltrate you to our reserve force, while we move in and begin assaulting the north edge."

"Nobody holding at the center," Aco spoke up. "Guards will withdraw to the southwest. Mechanics and support techs northeast and unarmed beyond prybars. That badge gets you in most places until someone figures out what's going on and disables it."

"Very good, sir," the woman said. "Let's get you three safe."

Bethany wasn't sure that was the term she would have used. This was the most famous—notorious?—unit of *Neu Berne* Assault Marines there was. Djamila's old unit.

Supposedly the best of the best that entire culture could produce.

At the same time, Camden was perfectly at ease with these

people, so Bethany found herself swept along, perhaps by the tides of history themselves, as they got quickly cycled to the rear.

A certain, nameless assault shuttle was already parked and cooling when she came over a rise into a small valley. Del was obvious, standing on the loading ramp, because NOBODY else ever dressed like that. Certainly not for combat flying.

"Welcome home, kid," he said, handing her a beer.

Camden got the second one. Aco the third. The half dozen guards around them were on duty.

"What's the status?" Camden asked.

"Halfway done, obviously," Del grinned around his own beer. "Science Officer's not settling for half measures tonight, obviously."

"We safe here?" Camden asked.

Bethany was still a little at sea, but the beer was helping.

"Suvi is overhead," Del replied. "And almost as angry as I am."

Bethany appreciated the implications there. All hell would break loose and a First-Rate Galleon would be involved.

"It's cold outside," Bethany decided, waving Aco to join her. "Let's find someplace quiet and warm while we see how long it takes."

"No questions on the outcome?" Aco asked quietly as he followed.

"None," Bethany assured him.

PART IV

Ilan followed Javier to the door and in, both of them armed and ready to shoot on movement, but the place was empty.

Luxury foyer. Carpets that felt ankle deep. Light polished wood paneling on the walls. Tacky art of the punk's girlfriends in pornographic poses.

And not even the current crop. Ilan wondered if they all got cycled through and replaced on a regular basis. Keep them for a year then trade them in on younger models? Felt like his style.

Money poisoned the mind after a certain point. Nobody ever telling your stupid ideas no.

Place was clear, save for all the damned smoke some asshole had piped in. A little yucky, but his rage would insulate him for now and the thermals had done their job. Plus, the smoker had stopped and the fans were furiously sucking everything back outside.

"Seal that hatch for now," Javier ordered, so Ilan popped off the panel and pulled a wire.

Didn't shoot anything, because they'd need to leave later, but for now, nobody was getting in. Probably two others. He'd deal with them.

Ilan watched Javier walk over a bank vault door. Seriously. Six meters square, which was just overkill and vaulted the ceiling in here, but he supposed that had let them get heavy equipment in and out a lot easier.

"You got anything that can open this?" Javier asked, one hand touching the rubbed nickel finish.

"Not even sure I could scratch it," Ilan replied honestly.

They'd prepared for regular doors and locks. Not panic rooms built by a guy with a reason to expect most of the galaxy to be coming for his ass eventually.

"I'll watch this," Javier nodded. "You find the other doors into this room. I presume that he had an escape tunnel, but I'll need better sensors to find it. Probably heads to a bolthole with a small shuttle due west of here."

"Call in that team and let them know," Ilan reminded him.

"Yeah, good idea."

Ilan located and disabled three other doors, one of them up on a mezzanine to a skywalk. Short of blowing doors off hinges, he and Javier owned the joint.

"Good news," Javier smiled when Ilan got back to the ground floor. "Camden got Bethany out safe. Del has her in his shuttle for now."

"Doesn't change anything," Ilan replied, but he felt a small weight off his shoulders.

He'd failed her. Granted, it had taken five of them, but he'd still failed when she needed him.

Man was dying for that. And a lot of his friends.

"Doesn't," Javier agreed. "But it makes some things easier. I've got Djamila and Afia headed our way. Can you disable this door? Seal it shut."

Ilan moved to study it. Thing felt like a mountain someone had put here. Pins inside where he couldn't get at them. Probably on piston power sufficient to break any weld he might try. Inset plug so any impact just drove it deeper into a cradle designed to hold it.

"Maybe if I parked a Land Leviathan right now," Ilan mused. "That's about it. He got a tank someone can drive over? Or a shuttle we can land here?"

Banging on the door had his gun centered.

"That's the ladies," Javier interrupted before his mind got uglier.

Ilan considered his options. Nothing he could do to keep that hatch closed if the guy inside wanted it open.

Ergo, give him a reason to not want to open it. He moved towards the door.

"How's the assault going?" he asked Javier over his shoulder.

"Guards are trapped in their barracks for now," Javier replied. "Dragoon assumes a stalemate unless we want the kinds of casualties you get in something like that. I don't feel the need."

"No, but if they stay all bottled up, you could put a unit here with heavy weapons," Ilan said, reconnecting the wire and stepping to one side with his pistol out.

Djamila still had a gun in his face almost too fast to blink, but she nodded and Afia joined her inside.

He locked things tight again.

"Djamila, I need a heavy weapons fire team to camp here," Javier was telling them. "Then I need Del to pull a crazy stunt. Crazy by his standards. Your people own the place?"

"We do," she replied. "How crazy?"

"Slavkov has to have a tunnel out," Javier pointed. "Closest direction is that way, almost directly opposite the shuttle hangars on the northeast corner. I need Del flying in to get us, then using his scanners to locate that."

Ilan listened as orders got sent. Killers here. Del to swoop in and pick them off the roof overhead. *Watch* keeping the guards from breaking out.

Didn't take long, but apparently the folks that had rescued Bethany were close. And hungry for some action, having seen none to date.

Shit got handed off. The four of them went for the top floor, where there was already a landing pad, because this was the center of how Slavkov had focused all his escape avenues.

Time for trouble.

PART V

Del rather enjoyed being **ordered** to fly crazy. Added that certain something to his night that had apparently been missing.

Better, Camden Forgrave was rated on guns, so she was below in the turret, having bitched about having to move the seat forward from where Djamila kept it. Bethany would have been in Javier's usual spot, but she was below for personal reasons he understood. Six goons kept the other guest company and out of trouble down there.

And he got to blame Djamila for all of this.

"Tower, coming up on your right," he told Forgrave. "Nobody has suppressed it yet."

Probably didn't want to draw missile fire when they saw the others turn into candles. Or had been smart enough to run like hell and leave it abandoned.

She lit it up with cannon fire. Exceptional skill, too. Diamond in the rough, that one, except that both Javier and Djamila respected the woman's deadliness.

Tower came apart as he slipped by and dropped hawklike onto the building, ramp already dropping and bodies coming out of a doorway.

Four friendlies boarded and he did a thing where the shuttle got exactly high enough to not scrape the belly paint as he went due west.

Always assume folks that aren't paranoid do things in square corners and even numbers.

Like digging a tunnel.

Once clear of the buildings, he dropped even lower. Radar and short-range sensors because his thrusters were generating so much grit and sandstorm that he was effectively blind.

Useful if someone wanted to shoot in at him, too. Someone might be that dumb.

Once.

Scanners showed a thing that Del didn't remember from his briefings. Hard spot like a tor when all this was supposed to be sand and stone. Lots of metal involved.

Drew the eye. Especially when he locked things on it and pinged really hard.

Huh. Not quite square on, but close enough.

"Djamila, dear, I have located your tunnel entrance," he announced to everyone. "Fellow poured himself a hill and glued sand on, from the scanner image. I presume you didn't want it shattered yet?"

"That would be correct," the Dragoon replied. "This is personal."

Earlier, Bethany had nodded at him in ways that would probably frighten a sane person.

Fortunately, Del was flying tonight.

He let sensors map things. Ten meters or so under mean surface level, so tunneled out of the rock itself. Thumb sticking up and camouflaged almost adequately for most folks. Nice bit of clearance to the west of that, so he presumed a hidden flight bay with a small shuttle. Enough space in the garage for one with a pilot, the punk, and maybe a girlfriend.

Maybe not. Maybe only an autopilot the exact opposite of an escape pod. Get you to a station in orbit automatically, instead of safely to the ground.

Del went ahead and parked as close to the door as he could, with the turret lined up.

Forgrave was up on his bridge quickly, then down the steps like an avalanche of retribution.

Del cracked a beer and waited for some dumbass rabbit to stick his nose out of his burrow.

INTO THE DARK

PART I

Javier hadn't wanted to interrupt, but he needed the kid and Ilan and Bethany had gotten in enough necking for now.

For now.

He harrumphed. Neither blushed, but they did come up for air.

"Time to go kill Slavkov," he said simply, watching young lovers—*young? HA!*—turn back into stone killers.

Him, Djamila, Ilan, Bethany, Camden.

And Afia practically glowing. Certainly, her smile lit up the night.

"Del," he called, including six second-class gunbunnies in the conversation with his eyes. "Nobody but us in or out. If we don't call you inside two hours, flip a coin and either have Suvi flatten everything or tell the *Watch* to avenge me in the ugliest manner they know."

Viking funeral pyres came to mind. And they would.

Kinda put a smile on his face almost as feral as Afia's.

Djamila handed Bethany a gun and holster. Checked that everyone was ready to move, with both Combat Engineers topped up on consumables like grenades and shit.

Boltholes are only good until you're trapped inside them when the monsters are coming for you.

Like tonight.

Ramp was down. Bodies in motion. Del had centered a spotlight on a chunk of rock so Afia and Ilan started there and had a hatch uncovered and blown off its hinges almost as fast as they might have picked the lock.

Would warn everybody that he was coming, but if that was a surprise, he didn't know what to tell those people.

Damocles was coming.

Judgment Day, bubbles.

Javier wanted to lead, but understood that he was going to be fourth into that hole. Hopefully, the legends that got spread about all this later would make him look good.

Helped, knowing the woman who would write them.

The Dragoon had pistols in both hands. Neither of them had a stun setting, but then, neither did his.

They'd moved long past that point.

Space inside was an elevator door and an emergency stairwell.

Afia and Ilan pried the door open and were looking at a shaft down. With cables to lift the car.

Javier assumed a lot lower power needs than using magnetics or force fields. Probably a lot lower profile on scanners, too.

Ilan attached something to the cable and got everyone clear as it detonated with a snap.

Cables fell out of sight.

Afia dropped a grenade in, then closed the doors. The floor under his feet vibrated.

"They ain't coming up that way," she said simply.

Javier nodded to her, then to the Dragoon.

He watched as she and those two opened the stairwell door and began descending.

PART II

Djamila glanced in and saw no movement. Staircase descending in half-level lines, with a turnback landing every two and a half meters. Thick floors against bombardment.

Casual bombardment, anyway.

She memorized the layout and walked with both pistols on her left so she could see anyone attempting to ambush her. Movement would draw fire. Survivors could surrender.

Assuming any.

Assuming she didn't have Afia drop more grenades down to deal with troublemakers.

Del had mentioned ten meters down. Djamila got to the third turnback without sound or trouble. She paused there, one eye and one barrel clear enough to see the door at the bottom.

A turret appeared to be tracking. She ducked back as someone inside fired. Fortunately, a beam that scarred the wall. Projectiles bouncing around in here might have been deadly.

Djamila made a note to explore that from both the offensive and defensive viewpoints.

Afia was almost in her hip pocket.

"It's on the right of the door facing," Djamila explained. "Chest height on Javier. Fixed in place, rather than a slot someone extends a weapon through. Probably sensors for smoke and darkness."

"Gotcha," Afia replied. "Lateral?"

Djamila considered her quick glance.

"Blind spots likely defined by a ninety degree field of fire," she said.

"Need you distracting them," Afia noted, shifting her feet.

Djamila wanted to argue with the woman. Technically, she could pull rank on Afia. Javier could override everyone.

Tonight had already moved past such things.

"I'll go high," she answered, holstering one pistol so she could grab a rail and use it to gain elevation for a snap shot.

The Ballerina of Death.

Afia stepped back and put her butt and one leg against the sidewall on the landing. Everyone else was steps up and out of the way watching, but remained silent.

She and her Combat Engineer had point.

"On my shot," Djamila said, planting a foot and surging up until her hair almost brushed the underside of the steps above her.

She'd placed the location. First shot hit it dead center but didn't seem to be hot enough to penetrate.

Wasn't the point. Motion drew the eye up.

Afia exploded into motion, bouncing off the sidewall and sliding down the stairs on her ass until her legs hit the wall at the bottom and pistoned in.

The turret tried to rotate to engage her, but she was beyond the frame and below it. Djamila fired two more shots as fast as she could, then ducked back when the gunner turned his attention back to her.

"I'm in place," Afia called up the stairs. "Stand by."

Combat Engineer. Going into a situation she had prepared for.

Djamila left one hand free, just in case.

A smart defender might take a chance on opening the door far enough to shoot Afia before she could react.

Not before Djamila could.

"Dragoon!"

Djamila had heard it. The door seal cracking.

She was out and shooting from one knee before the man inside finished opening the hatch, then leapt down to the bottom, firing in the air because that was what Ballerinas did.

The good ones, anyway.

Dead man smoking at her feet. She fired several shot through the door into a hallway beyond, looking for movement of any kind. Caught a second man before he could get clear. A third threw himself into the room beyond. A door down a short hallway slammed shut a moment later.

Djamila only paused enough to not trip, then she was into the room beyond, killing a third man who was still trying to stand and draw a weapon.

Ilan was there a moment later.

PART III

Ilan understood the situation and had gone after the Dragoon as fast as he could without tripping her or himself.

Watchroom with guards. Or abattoir. Maybe both.

He went past the tall woman and down a short hall, sticking his pistol into an empty bathroom then a coat closet mostly empty.

Then he had his nose almost pressed to the door on the end. Steel, but nowhere near as tough as that damned vault door upstairs. A hand brought out the explosives and he was on one knee sticking things into place, confident that he had at least two of the deadliest people he knew covering him.

"Javier, this it, or a tunnel back into the palace and he's under where we were before?" he asked over one shoulder as he worked.

Didn't take long.

"Probably a lounge for the dead guys in there," Javier replied. "Dunno if dipshit made it this far or if he had planned to hide out back there until we got tired and left."

"He that stupid?" Ilan asked.

"Yes," Bethany spoke up. "Somewhere, he has a couple of teams of ambassadors trying to locate Javier and Zakhar so he could ask them what their price was for peace. And has no idea what it might be."

"Oh, pretty sure he does by now," Javier chuckled darkly.

Ilan put the last piece in place and pulled arming pins.

He stood up against the side of the corridor and backed up to the bathroom, closing the door about halfway as an extra level against shockwaves. Most of the shrapnel should be going inwards with what he'd done, but shit only has to go bad once, and he didn't feel like letting Afia get even with him by pulling a chunk of steel out of his belly tonight.

"All clear?" he called quietly.

"All clear for detonation," Afia replied.

The Dragoon was probably an eyeblink from covering the hall again, but she was like that.

Ilan flipped the switch on his handheld and detonated the door.

PART IV

Afia let the Dragoon lead her through the smoke and shattered remains of the door.

Nobody on the far side, so that last guy must have already hauled ass.

Lounge like Javier had said. Djamila was already at a second door at the far end, pistol pointed around a mostly-closed door.

Then she fired a single shot and nodded.

Must have not gotten as far as he thought he was going to. Or that tunnel was several hundred meters of straight line back into the palace complex. Djamila's smile said that it was entirely empty as far as you could see, plus one hunk of smoking meat slowly cooling on the floor midway.

The rest of the team flooded inward. Afia paused to note a full communications suite in here. Almost a secondary command post. Probably an identical version at the far end.

And someone had been in such a hurry that he hadn't locked anything down.

She sat, typed a few things, and had complete administrative control of the palace complex.

Well, hell. Girl could get herself into a lot of trouble with power like this.

She started turning things off. Like all the lights and heat in the barracks. Water, too, because she was feeling mean. Check on the maintenance yard, but a bunch of angry giants had folks on their knees in rows in the open, so they'd taken that wing.

Quick pass through things and Afia decided to unlock every door she could reach. Override so they could not be locked again unless someone overrode her. Which they could not.

Paranoia is a good thing, except when you lose control of the gun to someone else.

Javier was breathing on her ear as she finished. She was breathing a little heavy.

"Can you find Slavkov's other den?" he asked.

Afia started cycling cameras as fast as the system would allow.

"There, back two," Djamila barked.

Afia found it and there was the dumbass himself, almost quavering in a big leather chair. Six goons around him with guns. None of them looked even as tough as the group guarding Bethany's prisoner.

"Intercom?" Javier asked.

She had to locate the right menu item in order to bring it live. There was a bald guy in a back corner frantically typing, but she'd already changed her password, which was probably his, so he was getting denial popups on his screen.

And bashing the keyboard.

Whoops.

One of those days when Slavkov's refusal to hire quality people had bit him in the ass.

Again.

Pirates were only good as long as somebody was afraid of them.

There were always worse predators out there.

In here.

"Hey, Valko, it's Javier," the man purred into the microphone. "Having a bad day?"

The line was on conference mode, so she heard Slavkov scream in surprise.

Watched his goons flinch and point guns at doors.

"Bethany's with me," Javier continued. "She's safe. Those folks outside? That's the *Dragon Watch*. *Neu Berne* Elite Assault Marines. You've made a lot of enemies, bucko. All your troops are trapped in the rubble until I decide to let them out. Same with you."

"WHAT DO YOU WANT?" the putz shrieked.

"I want you dead," Javier said simply. "You could have left well enough alone after you hired Navarre for a mission and got exactly what you paid for. But you couldn't do that, could you? Couldn't leave well enough alone. Had to come after us at *Svalbard*. Made me angry, Valko. Made me steal your Land Leviathan and use it to destroy *Nidavellir*. That still wasn't enough to get you to behave, so you had to come after me at *Drako*. Pissed off all my people when you did that. And you lost. Broke all four clans. I'm going to finish that job. Jarre's mostly crippled. The others aren't doing much better. And you're going to be out of the picture shortly."

He stopped to take a breath and Afia got to see something in his eyes she knew would haunt her to her dying breath.

Javier Aritza was a goof, most of the time. Card sharp and clown. That was a mask. She'd seen under it. Navarre-the-killer was a mask as well.

She found herself looking at the man he might have turned into, if things hadn't gone wrong when he'd been younger. When he'd killed most of his team saving that reactor and that ship and never been able to deal with the guilt of it until so much later.

But even that was still too high.

Afia Burakgazi was seeing the beast he kept on a short iron chain by a lake of fire.

And it had awakened, like some terrible dragon from a fantasy legend.

That thing wanted blood.

"I'm speaking to the seven guards in the room now," Javier growled. "You kill him and I'll let you walk away. Simple as that. If I have to come in there, I'm going to torture you all to death in the slowest and most painful way I can come up with, and I have enough firepower to take you all alive. Do not think that I won't. I want him dead. You can get out of this alive. The guy guarding Bethany Durbin is my prisoner, up on the surface, because he knew better than to try my patience. *What will it be?*"

Afia's gasp was tiny, but he still glanced over at her.

This wasn't an act. This was Death Himself come for you on a cold, dark night.

She shivered and could not find warmth anywhere.

One of the men understood faster than the others. He put two shots into Slavkov's chest from point blank, then hurled his pistol into a corner like it might be on fire.

The others tried to stop him. Or something. Or they just freaked entirely out and opened fire on each other.

Afia watched all of them die in barely the blink of an eye.

A carpet corpses in there. Smoke only slowly fading from scorched meat.

Javier stood up straight and nodded.

"Djamila, let's go in and make sure," he said simply.

SUNRISE

PART I

Javier stood over the corpses.

He wanted to kick Valko a few times, but didn't have it in him. Even after all this, he had nothing.

Probably for the best, all things considered, when he looked into that rage that had fueled him for most of a year and found only emptiness.

"Javier, you need to see this one," Bethany called him into the corner.

Tall, skinny bald guy. Eyes wide open. Died in terror.

"This is—was—Dipshit's business manager," Bethany pointed to the corpse. "This was the man who really ran things, when you got right down to it. With him dead, I don't think there is anyone capable of holding it together."

"Man got a will?" Javier asked. "Kids or relatives that inherit?"

"No," Camden was suddenly standing next to him. "I looked him up in deeper detail when I understood what you were after, and he has no acknowledged children. There are probably cousins, but none in any way related to his business. Only child of an only child, so nobody close. This was why I offered to help you."

"I thought you wanted his real estate portfolio," he turned to her and smiled to take the edge off his voice.

She blushed.

"That too, but mostly him out of the way meant that you had opened the door to the *Concord* and the others actually making a difference," she replied. "To ending piracy as it has been understood for most of my lifetime. I'm into smuggling and things like that, because folks have a need and governments tend to be too puritanical on the one hand and not providing the sorts of opportunities for youngsters that steer them into productive lives."

"They all want to grow up and be pirates instead," Ilan muttered.

"Only because men like Dipshit here have too much control and can't be challenged," Bethany offered.

She did kick his corpse once, but he'd let her have that. Javier figured he'd have bit the son of a bitch after this many months this close to him.

"He's no longer a problem," Javier reminded everyone. "Nor is Jarre. Or Belfast. Or H & W Heavy."

"You forgot one," Afia offered.

"No," Javier smiled at her. "I was saving them for last."

WALVISBAAI

PART I

Suvi studied the plot. It had taken nearly a month to get all the moving parts aligned. All the players to get off their asses and commit, once it came clear that Javier was going in with or without their help.

The *Concord* had bitched, but someone had lit a fire under their asses in places like *Bryce* and *Merankorr* about the fleet being practically owned by Valko Slavkov and working for him to help a bunch of pirate clans do evil things to innocent people.

She'd participated when she'd been the drone, but not since Javier had poured her into *Hammerfield*. At that point, she'd been vengeance itself.

And today, they had kinda circled back.

Excalibur was out in the darkness like she always did it. Passive scans of the inner system to update all of her sailing records to include every rock big enough to reflect light. And there were a lot of them, but then there was that whole empty band in the middle, where prospectors pounced on such things and mined them, or got paid by the local authorities to haul them off so they weren't a navigational hazard.

Busy system down there. Galaxy's worst chop shop, with only *Purton*'s yards having more ships floating around.

Lots of armed freighters and small gunboats around, but that was the bad guys feeling the heat. Hearing her footsteps as she got closer.

And it was time.

She activated a screen on the bridge and took a picture of everyone. Bethany would demand it for the book. As would Dorn. And this was the exact moment for it.

Nobody in the command station. Nobody at the other stations. Everyone standing around the edges of the room as equals. As folks who didn't need to do anything, because they had trained her as well as they could for the task at hand.

All of them could simply watch. Save one.

"Whenever you're ready, Javier," she said simply.

He grimaced, but she knew that was coming. Man didn't want to be on point for this. Would have happily stayed in his arboretum with his chickens for the rest of his life.

Until *Storm Gauntlet* came out of cloak and changed everything for everyone.

The only missing person who should have been here was Mina, but she'd left such an enormous imprint on everyone, in spite of her short time with this crew, that her shadow still darkened certain corridors.

Suvi still saw her ghost slipping through hatchways out of the corner off her eye some nights.

And Zakhar wasn't about to step up and save him. He'd made that clear to Javier. All the others were support staff to the legend, but the legend itself was necessary today.

Javier took a breath and pulled his shoulders back.

Immortalized for history, because he'd even let Adrian dig out a special outfit today.

Not the killer. Not the slob. Not even the hero.

The Science Officer.

"This is Javier Aritza," he said in that slow, measured cadence that had once recruited the *Dragon Watch*, themselves listening and watching from the flight deck in case it became necessary for them to act today.

Someone down there might be that stupid.

"All of you have gathered because we are ending piracy," Javier continued. "Some of you used to be pirates, but so did I. I got over myself. You'll do the same. Some of you, for too long, turned a blind eye to certain things that you should have screamed in outrage at the dishonor you did. You're here to reclaim that. More importantly, you are here to stand next to *Neu Berne*, because they were the first to stand up and say *Enough. No more. We will not allow it.*"

He paused and she saw new lines in his face that hadn't been there before. Zakhar was looking worn. Djamila's hair was coming in entirely gray underneath now.

The others—Afia, Bethany, Ilan and a few—would get there eventually, because only Suvi would live forever.

And she intended to. People would forget. They'd go back to cutting corners and turning blind eyes. Everyone here would grow old and die, hopefully on *Altai* surrounded by friends, family, and loved ones.

Only the immortals could challenge eternity and make sure that NOBODY forgot today.

This crew.

This Science Officer.

"The *Dragon Watch* are my swordbearers and I am *The Science Officer*," Javier continued in that metronomic pace. "This is the last pirate base of any measure left, and they have not chosen to flee my wrath. Our wrath. Justice. We are going in there hot and heavy. If they do not surrender, they will not survive. If they run, we will run them down. If they resist, we will destroy them. They have had all the warnings they are ever going to get, and have ignored them. Their time is done."

Suvi simply wished that she had a body to shiver like Afia and Bethany were doing on the internal scanners. And others.

Ilan was granite. The Dragoon was the Ballerina of Death.

The Pathfinders and the Gunbunnies lined the outer walls and nodded, almost in unison. Dorn and Armando shared a nod at some inside joke that probably wasn't all that funny.

Didn't matter. None of it mattered.

The Science Officer had come.

"Zakhar Sokolov once called us the Fleets of Vengeance," Javier said, voice growing hoary and deep. "Another person instead called us the Guardians of Tomorrow. That is more accurate, because when this day is done we are all going home. Different homes. Different lives. Different destinies. We are all still responsible for the galaxy we leave behind, that it be better than the one we found. For what we will leave behind, Guardians of Tomorrow, as you bear."

Even Suvi needed a moment to shake herself out of that stasis, but she thought so fast that nobody else noticed. A signal to every other ship in the fleet and she jumped down into the warmth of *Nidavellir*.

One last time.

PART II

Suvi landed exactly where she'd intended. Too much practice hitting parking places with a side skid.

She had destroyed *Walvisbaai Industrial Platform Number One* the last time she had been through. Shattered it into pieces small enough to no longer be any sort of threat, though few had actually deorbited once the locals had a chance to get tugs on them.

Today, *Duha Yard* had replaced it. More chop shop than accounting firm. *Ayakot Station* was close by but *Ajax* had wisely vanished from history to the point that even Bethany hadn't been able to locate any reference to that ship in years.

Not worth hunting them down, though Afia had a small fund established for hiring bounty hunters if she got angry enough. And a lot of folks had contributed.

Ajax was yesterday.

"Attention *Nidavellir* system and Walvisbaai Industrial Holdings, this is the *Altai* First-Rate Galleon *Excalibur*, under command of The Science Officer," she blasted on every channel with every generator cranked up to the point that handheld radios on the surface could hear her. "You will surrender to the combined fleet that is now in orbit, or we will destroy you without mercy. All of you. If anyone runs, we will run them down and take no prisoners. If anyone fires a shot, all of Walvis-baai—every ship currently in orbit—is forfeit. Valko Slavkov is dead. All of the other pirate clans have been destroyed. You can go to prison tomorrow or you can go directly to hell. Which will it be?"

Behind her, the *Union of Man* had sent a frigate flotilla. Five heavy pirate hunters with orders to place themselves under the Science Officer's command. *Balustrade* had sent a single cruiser, but they hardly had any fleet these days. The *Concord* had added a number of ships to supplement *Trinity*. Bunch of captured or surrendered pirate ships from the clans, seen the light of tomorrow dawning.

Relentless and *Kymni Gauntlet* were in command back there. Along with the *Ghost*, Piet prepared to empty every launch tube if anyone gave him any reason.

And the *Dragon Watch* was locked and loaded, along with two more cohorts of combat infantry supplied by the *Union* and a bunch of reformed pirates.

Nidavellir would be scoured clear of pirates if Javier gave the word. Not just one station this time. Not just orbital space. The entire planet, the kind of place which still made *Meehu* or *Purton* look reputable.

And that was saying something.

Nothing like dropping twenty-seven warships on somebody's ass without warning, because all any of them had gotten were coordinates to assemble, then she'd run them hard and fast by doing her own calculations and not stopping for anything that might have let these assholes below her have any warning that the Law had come for them.

And yeah, you probably remember me from last time. I brought friends today.

She broadcast Javier's face as he waited. Man should have been immortalized in stone. She might have to do it, once she found someone who could build her the right CNC tools.

And she decided if he should be life-sized, or carved into the side of a mountain visible from orbit.

Or simply redo a small moon.

Dad left those sorts of footprints in the snow.

"*Excalibur*, this is Duha Control," a man replied in a voice already verging on freaking entirely the fuck out. As he should. "You said that Valko Slavkov is dead?"

"Yes," she replied, broadcasting a picture of his worthless corpse that Bethany had taken.

She hadn't decided if it was the cover of her next book, or the last page.

"Slavkov's entire organization is currently being dismantled by law enforcement in various nations and systems," Suvi continued. "You are all that remains, and the only question the Science Officer has is if he has to use force to stand you down permanently."

Twenty-eight ships pointing targeting scanners at your station probably looked like the frog in the pond seeing the flashlight.

Scoured entirely. Prison or hell?

She set a timer. When it hit zero, she'd empty every tube she had and tell Piet to finish them off while she went after every other ship in orbit with every weapon she could bring to bear.

It would be ugly.

Very, very briefly.

"*Excalibur*, we are striking our colors," the man said.

Wise choice. Not everyone gets to wake up in the morning and looks death in the face.

And he was standing on her bridge.

Smiling.

"Every ship will dock with a station and evacuate," Suvi ordered. "Anyone not in the process in fifteen minutes will be blown apart. Do not try my patience."

She'd gotten those modulated tones from him and Zakhar. Fitting for the situation.

And eternity.

Because the Science Officer had won.

HOMEWARD BOUND

PART I

Javier sat in the library and watched unknown stars gleam back at him.

Somewhere east of the *Concord* and west of *Altai*. Most of his life behind him on that road. One of those stars in front of him his destination, but he didn't feel like asking her to point it out.

Second star from the right was close enough for now.

Then the hatch opened behind him and bodies started to file in.

Zakhar and Djamila. Dorn and Diane. Bethany and Ilan. Armando. Del. Vivian. Piet. Mary-Elizabeth.

Afia walked up and just hugged him, coming up to his chin which he found surprising because she was so much bigger in his mind.

Everyone had coffee or tea or wine or something. This wasn't formal. Well, it was, but not in a nice uniform kind of way. They scattered to find places to sit.

Javier considered the faces. All older. Much older. Del the grand patriarch. Zakhar past sixty. Him and Djamila getting too close to fifty. The others catching up.

Only his daughter would be young forever, but she'd be cheating.

He wanted to crack wise. Tell a joke to disarm everyone. That had always been his thing to lighten up a serious room.

A sober one.

Wasn't necessary today.

Or he'd finally grown up. Hard to say. Not a thing he was really willing to admit.

Beyond this company of friends.

That was the thing that always surprised him the most.

When he'd met most of them, he'd sworn to see them all hung in low gravity. Then gone off and saved their lives as often as they'd saved his.

And made the galaxy a better place. He'd blame Del for the phrase that might be handed down to history, depending on Bethany and Suvi.

Guardians of Tomorrow.

Javier sighed inside and took a chair so he wasn't the only one standing. Looming.

Something.

Zakhar just smiled at him. Nodded.

The Bryce Connection. That included Bethany now, because she'd bloomed. And Dorn, because he had seen the future and warned everyone that it was coming.

Then found folks crazy enough to do something about it.

The silence wasn't oppressive. Merely warm.

Comforting.

Knowing.

He supposed that forty-eight years old was probably on the back side of middle-aged. Maybe only halfway, because he'd have access to Behnam's doctors and medicine when he got there.

And he didn't need to figure out what to do with his remaining decades.

Not today.

They had broken the clans. Destroyed them. Taken the *Concord* right up to the ledge and let them dangle for a moment before saner minds had started arresting assholes and putting admirals and captains in military prisons, where you still got to break rocks as punishment.

For betraying the oath you'd taken.

Neu Berne had counted coup sufficient that everyone had listened. The *Union* had been infected by the work of some crazy, leftover Shepherd of the Word and gotten their asses in motion. *Balustrade* had even managed.

The *Concord* might survive. Might never forgive him, but Armando and Dorn and Warmaster hadn't shattered them.

Merely woken them up.

Eyes shiny watching him. Tears, right on the verge, because they all understood this for what it was.

An ending.

That elusive Tomorrow they were supposed to protect.

He smiled. They smiled back, including his daughter on the screen by the door directly in front of him.

"We did it," Javier said simply, scowling at Afia when she opened her mouth until she subsided with a grin.

"The Science Officer did it," Bethany offered.

"We are all part of that legend," he shrugged.

Yes, his will. His drive. His connections.

His fury.

But also, his friends. Here. Now. Homeward bound.

Javier studied his mug. Someone—probably several of the punks when he wasn't looking because he knew how mess stewards could be when you turned your back on them—had replaced the mug that had traveled on with Mina.

Originally, it had been bribes paid to the machinists that yielded him a hollow cylinder, slate gray, out of a hull-grade alloy that was a near-perfect insulator of heat and pretty much indestructible with any weapon Javier could hold in one hand. Not that he hadn't considered trying. You know, for science and stuff.

Then Kianoush, that plain and somewhat average-looking woman who worked for the Purser as a logistics tech during the day, while she pursued visions of art in enamel and silver wire in her private time. And had made Behnam that mask that she still liked to wear nude.

Kianoush had been a hard sell, a woman with no particular interests in fresh fruit or beautifully cooked repasts that showed his amazing skill programming a culinary-bot. She was, however, a sucker for a good story, especially one that involved evil pixies and stolen tea mugs. But she had been willing to trade her work for good stories and occasional reference answers culled from Javier's many years of solitary space-faring and survey work.

From her, he had procured the artwork. Even a little Strike Corvette like *Storm Gauntlet* had had a ship's crest, usually only seen in a small logo painted on the wall in the captain's cabin, as well as on the rarely-worn dress uniforms some of the officers maintained.

Zakhar had cut that plate out of the wreck and installed it in his new quarters here on *Excalibur*.

Kianoush had taken that logo, that artistic heart of this thing that had once been the *Storm Gauntlet*, and engraved it into a mug, using magic he could not fathom without asking the reference computer, and then filled that etching with real, honest to Creator silver, poured while molten, or dipped. He couldn't remember. One of those. Absolutely.

Above it, a name to strike fear into civilians and pulp writers everywhere. *Storm Gauntlet*. A private-service, free-lance Strike Corvette, retired from *Concord* Fleet service after the Great Wars were over and making ends meet with transportation gigs and occasional strong-arm jobs. Like the piracy that had cost him his own lovely little probe-cutter, *Mielikki*, and turned him, through twists and forays, into an officer aboard her.

In those days, he had considered explaining to the crew what the term *Janissary* meant, but usually decided it wasn't worth the effort. These people had been unliterary, to boot. Until Bethany came along and fixed them.

He still had his mug. And it had the ship's name and logo. Almost complete victory, since it was most certainly one of a kind, at least until some enterprising engineer with access to a power lathe and a CNC laser decided to start mass-producing them.

And they would.

So he had gone several steps ahead of that unfortunate bastard, whoever he might be. Below the logo, that was where the victory lay.

On one side, also etched and filled with silver, his name in bold, block letters. JAVIER ARITZA. Also a name for the pulp writers to make famous. Someday. Hopefully. Probably too late to escape that fate now.

On the other side, that thing that would most certainly defeat the evil pixies and their dread minions. A title that was utterly unique in pirateness. One guaranteed to convey to them that this mug was not empty and abandoned, just waiting for them to take it away and clean when he wasn't looking. No, it was meant to be here, with him, for him. Like a candle in a window on a cold and stormy night, marking the path home.

THE SCIENCE OFFICER.

Of course, he'd never seen the damned thing again because Mina had stolen it. Probably still sipped her tea out of it and laughed.

Good enough. He'd replaced it. Identical in every way save one. Because he had needed a sword in order to go after that royal shit Slavkov the first time. And the second.

Wouldn't ever need to do that again.

This one said *Excalibur*. For his daughter. And his friends.

He raised it to the room. To them.

"To tomorrow," Javier enjoined them.

"To tomorrow," all of his friends answered.

READ MORE

To read more of my fiction, sign up for my newsletter. You'll also get a free book!

http://www.blazeward.com/newsletter/

ABOUT THE AUTHOR

Blaze Ward is a prolific Indie writer and publisher who works mostly in Science Fiction and Light Thriller, with occasional forays into lots of other genres like superheroic fantasy.

You can find more of his titles at www.blazeward.com/books, www.KnottedRoadPress.com and wherever else you buy your books.

He also edits Boundary Shock Quarterly, an SF magazine he founded in 2018, and Thrill Ride Magazine.

ABOUT KNOTTED ROAD PRESS

Knotted Road Press publishes dynamic fiction set in exotic locations. Our authors cover a wide range of genres including science fiction, fantasy, mystery, literary, and poetry. We also have unique non-fiction voices in genres such as autobiography, business, cookbooks, and how-tos. We offer both DRM-free ebooks and print books for a global readership.

www.KnottedRoadPress.com